Forerunner artifacts were the most valuable things in the known universe. Every one found was a possible clue to the grandeur and power of a people who had disappeared before the very Earth itself existed.

There was reason to believe that a valuable Forerunner power rested in the famous Ice Crown of the closed planet Clio.

The result of Psychocrat mind-blocking, Clio was a mass of conflicting nations, of barbarism and hidden wonders, and absolutely banned to the probers of the civilized galaxy. Nevertheless Offlas Keil and his niece Roane broke the quarantine—and made their secret landing.

And thereby primed a social atomic bomb that all the laws of the Service had been set up to prevent—with Roane as the potential detonator.

ICE CROWN

ICE CROWN

ANDRE NORTON

SF
ace books
A Division of Charter Communications Inc.
A GROSSET & DUNLAP COMPANY
51 Madison Avenue
New York, New York 10010

680975
Manufactured in the United States of America

1

Roane fought against closing her eyes, tensed her slight body until it ached. One could argue intelligently (she could hear Uncle Offlas now with that odious patience which always colored his voice when making any explanation to her) that such discomfort was all mental. If you fastened your mind on something else, the sensation of being entombed alive while in the express bolt would disappear. But she lay now in the padded interior of the speeding bullet and tried to endure.

Though she did fight her fear—the thought of smothering here—Roane clenched her fists, bit hard on her under lip. The pain of that helped. According to Uncle Offlas you could overcome *anything* if you willed it. Unfortunately, she fell far below his standards. Now that she had a chance to prove she was worth something to his plans, she must not spoil it.

Why, even the department head at Cram-brief had envied her this chance. And it was only because she was Offlas Keil's niece that she had it. The expedition to Clio would be a family affair—Project Director Keil, his son Sandar, and Roane. She tried to breathe evenly and slowly, to keep her eyes shut, forget where she was now, and think only of the goal before her.

Maybe once in a hundred, no, closer to a thousand times, did something like this happen. And she was so lucky to be a part of it. Only right now, even her brain felt tired. All that cramming! She— Well, it was like being an osbper sponge set in a pool and given the command to absorb. Only she could not swell the way

5

those did; she had to pack it all behind bone and flesh which was not able to expand. By rights her head ought to be so heavy with all that the briefing computers had hammered into it that she could not hold it upright.

Clio was one of the sealed planets. Yet because of the circumstances Uncle Offlas had definite orders to land there, to stay as long as it would take them to locate the treasure. Treasure! The very word gave one a shiver—though this treasure was nothing that anyone but a member of the Service would want.

Real treasure—precious, beautiful things—would not interest Offlas Keil at all. He might glance over it to classify it by historical period, but to him such would be toys. However, knowledge of the Forerunners—that was something else. And this treasure had been pinpointed by a hint there, a clue here, stretching over years of sifting, to a single general area on Clio.

Because Clio was a sealed world, the final stages of their search must be conducted in complete secrecy, as quickly as possible, using Service devices. And the Project demanded as small a task force as was necessary. Which had sent Roane to Cram-brief to learn as much of Clio as she might need to know.

She wondered what it would be like to live on a closed planet (not for the period of days they would set down there but for a lifetime). Of course, the whole theory which had established the closed planets was wrong; such manipulation of human beings broke the Four Laws. Clio had been settled two, maybe three hundred years ago when the Psychocrats dominated the Confederation, before the Overturn of 1404. It was the third such experimental planet rediscovered, though there were rumors that there had been more, no one knew how many. The blasting of the Forqual Center during the revolt of the Overturn had destroyed most records.

All those worlds had been chosen as sites for projects which were the particular interest of one of the Hierarchy of the Psychocrats. The original colonists, brain-cleared, given false implanted memories, were settled in communities which to their briefed minds seemed natural to their new worlds. They were then left to work out new types of civilization, or a lack of civilization—to be watched secretly at intervals.

When such inhabited test planets were now rediscovered, they were declared closed. For none of the authorities could be sure what the impact of the truth might do to their peoples. Less advanced they were, as well as mutated on at least one planet. But on Clio the inhabitants were entirely human, though they were living in an archaic way, much as Roane's ancestors had lived several hundred years before space flight.

What the Psychocrat who had established Clio had been aiming for was now not certain. But the Service thought he had set up something akin to the old Europa plan known on Terra. The large eastern continent had been divided into an irregular pattern of small kingdoms. The two western continents had been otherwise "seeded" with "natives" at a far more primitive level of culture—wandering tribes of hunters. And then they had all been left to their own devices.

On the eastern continent a series of wars for territorial expansion had ended with the establishment of two large nations, fronting each other uneasily across a border of small buffer states which still possessed their freedom, mainly because the two great powers were as yet unready to strike at each other. Intrigues, minor skirmishes, the rise and fall of dynasties were all a part of life on Clio. It was, to an onlooker from the stars, a giant game, though one in which lives were lost by a badly managed stroke of play.

In the west the tribesmen, too, fought each other; but since they remained on a more primitive level, the cost in blood had not yet been so great. However, Roane need not consider them. It was on the eastern land mass that her party would make their secret landing, in one of those small buffer states between the great powers.

"Reveny," she said aloud now, "the Kingdom of Reveny."

It was a strange word and she had had difficulty at first in pronouncing it. But no stranger than a lot of other-world names, some of them so utterly alien they could not be shaped or voiced by human vocal cords.

She had viewed the tri-dees of the site where they would do their prospecting, often enough to make the countryside familiar. But this was an old duty, part of her wandering life. Uncle Offlas had taken her along, sometimes like excess baggage, from world to world during his own wanderings as an expert on Forerunner archaeology.

Roane liked what she had been shown of Reveny. The district they must comb for their purposes was, luckily, sparsely settled, being mountainous and forested. Part was a hunting preserve for the royal family. The only settlement was one of verderers and keepers. The rest of the inhabitants were shepherds who moved their charges seasonally from range to range. If the off-worlders had luck and were cautious, as they must be, they would have no contact with any of these.

In the tri-dees it seemed a story tape come to life. There were actual castles with sky-pointing towers, colorful towns with crooked streets (so unlike the ordered dwelling blocks of her own people), and— But she must remember that it was very primitive. Wars were still fought across those fields. Roane shuddered, remembering a couple of tapes which had revolted both her mind and her queasy stomach.

The people of Reveny were, as far as could be determined, still under some type of conditioning process. Or else the initial training had been so complete as to repersonalize their descendants as well. She would undoubtedly find them as alien emotionally and mentally as they were akin to her bodily. That, if she had any meeting with them at all.

The sway of the bullet holding her slackened. She opened her eyes as it came to a stop. With a sigh of thanksgiving that that ordeal was behind her, Roane disembarked to look around.

"You're late—"

She turned eagerly, instinctively smoothing down the flare of her overtunic. Not that it would matter to Sandar whether she looked as rumpled as a wart skin, as she well knew. But it would be nice if he saw her, just once, as a girl and not an encumbrance.

"There was a delay at the Metro thrust," she said quickly and then felt provoked. Why was she always in the wrong with Sandar and his father? If there was any delay, any difficulty, it always involved her, never them.

She tried to put aside the need for apology as she looked at her cousin. He had not changed, not fallen from his normal superiority. Though why should he in a matter of only two months? There was no reason why he should have shrunk from the height he carried so well, grown irregular features in place of those almost-too-handsome ones, been denuded of the charm he was willing to exert for everyone but her. Sandar could wear the grimed coverall of a tubeman and still look like a tri-dee hero. In the Service tunic he was still Sandar the Great. She had heard him named that once by a girl she had met back on Varch. The fact that she was his cousin sometimes made her temporarily popular, just long enough for it to take other girls to learn how little influence she had with him.

"Come on!" He was already walking away and she had to trot to catch up. "We have just half an hour to reach the field before countdown."

He kept to that long stride and she had to hop-skip to match it. Resentment began to stir in her. When she was away from Sandar Roane always hoped they could be friends. But when they were face to face again she knew how stupid that hope was.

"My kit—" she cried.

"It came through. I stashed it in a holder."

"But we have to get it. Which way—" He was heading for the outside door.

Now he reached out and his fingers closed firmly, and none too gently, about her arm above the elbow.

"We haven't time, I told you. If you're late you'll have to take the consequences. And you won't need what's in it. There are full supplies on board ship."

"But—" Roane wanted to dig in her heels, pull back from his highhandedness. Only she knew he was perfectly capable of dragging her along by force. She saw the set of his mouth—Sandar was in a rage about something and he would make her the target of that anger if she gave him a chance.

Her shoulders sagged. Once more she was caught in the old pattern. Her two months at Cram-brief had given her a false confidence in herself. Just how false she now realized. She would have to leave her kit locked somewhere in this hateful building.

That she would not be bereft of necessities she knew. Uncle Offlas traveled with the highest degree of comfort any project allowed. But there were personal things —some which had been a part of her for a long time. It was hateful of Sandar, a bad start for the trip.

She stood quietly, still captive in his hold, as he hailed a transport flitter. Captive, yes; resigned, no. Somehow she was going to get the better of Sandar— somehow, someday. She stared down at her hands as the flitter spiraled up with them. They were small and brown; her skin was several shades darker than Sandar's. That both he and her uncle resented her mixed blood, she knew. Sometimes Sandar acted as if he did not even want to look at her.

The port was busy with four ships on the pads—one a stellar liner embarking a number of passengers. They swooped past its tall column to settle by a much smaller ship, which bore the insignia of Survey. Roane managed to avoid Sandar's hand and made for the ramp, trotting up it as she had so many times before.

She fed her ident into the port checker, saw the welcome light flash. A crewman stood a little beyond.

"Gentle Fem Hume." He consulted a ship map. "Third level, Cabin 6, ten minutes to countdown."

She made for the ladder hurriedly, wanting to reach the privacy of her own cabin with no more interference from Sandar. And she did, throwing herself on the bunk, although the warning bell had not yet sounded, snapping the protective take-off webbing into place.

The cabin was the standard one of a junior officer. There were cupboards in every possible section of wall space, plus a narrow slit of curtained door which must give on a cramped sliver of a stand-fresher. The bunk she lay on was comfortable enough, but the furnishings were all regulation. There was no sign of personal possessions about the dreary cell. If someone had been shifted for her, he had taken all his belongings with him.

Once more she wondered what it would be like to have a real, set-on-a-planet, immovable home where one dared accumulate things one fancied and enjoyed to look upon just because they were beautiful, or reminded one of some happy time, or were fun to own. If Uncle Offlas had ever had such desires, they were long since lost. And Sandar seemed not to care.

She hoped what he had said of complete equipment on board was true. Of course, on a dig one wore Service dress—a one-piece coverall of material suited to the climate, fashioned for hard use. And she had long known that any of the luxuries of feminine life, such as scents or the cosmetics that planet-rooted women dared to use, were not for her.

There was a warning clang overhead, the signal for last countdown. Roane snuggled deeper into the bunk's protective cocoon. Here they went again, for the—she was not sure she could even reckon now the number of times she had gone through the same procedure. Would there ever be an end to such wayfaring for her?

It was a voyage like any other. As soon as they were

in hyper Uncle Offlas sent for her to put her through a searching examination of what she had learned. He did not signify at the end any more than that she would do, providing she kept her mind strictly on her work. He then gave her a load of tapes and a reader and ordered her to make the best use of space time she could. She dared not protest, since she knew that sooner or later he would demand an accounting from her.

The voyage was as dull as most. On a liner, where there were many pastimes to amuse passengers, travel might be fun. But certainly Uncle Offlas thought that such intervals between jobs were for study only.

They made landfall at last—that is, their ship went into orbit well above Clio, and they packed themselves and their gear into an LB, the standard type of small lifesaving craft, which had been specially modified for a directed landing. It was twilight when their meticulously planned descent brought them to the surface of the planet.

All three of them hurried to unload the supplies and instruments, for the LB had a time setting to return it to the parent ship. And even that would then withdraw into a longer orbit. Though any sky watchers on Clio would not recognize a star ship, yet there might be talk of any strange appearance in their sky.

The first thing Roane was aware of as she man-handled out the boxes and containers was the wonderful freshness of the air. After the stale, recirculated atmosphere of the ship this was like breathing a subtle scent. She drew it deeply into her lungs.

They had no time really to look about until the last of the equipment was out. Uncle Offlas slammed the hatch and jumped back as the LB bounded up. Even during the short time of the unloading, twilight had deepened into night. Roane sat back on a box and brought out from the inner pocket of her coveralls a pair of night lenses. With these on she looked around.

They were in a glade surrounded by tall trees. Several bushes had been squashed by the LB, splintered and flattened, and the boxes they had tumbled out had torn and gouged up chunks of moss.

Uncle Offlas had a small map and was glancing from it to the right and left as if he hunted landmarks. Meanwhile Sandar forced open one of the padded containers and brought out a box which he balanced on his knees, bending close to read the dials on its top. He set two of these, then reached for another twin box to do the same.

"Good enough. Put it about twelve—no, perhaps twenty paces in that direction." Uncle Offlas pointed left. "I'll do the same with this." He picked up the second box.

Once those distorts were working they could set up camp. The distorts would prevent any unauthorized invasion of either man or beast native to this planet. Each member of their own party wore, clipped to the front of his belt, the broadcast which would nullify the effect for him.

By midnight they were settled in. Under Uncle Offlas's expert handling a working laser had cut a pit as deep in the ground as Sandar was tall. Over this arose, for more than an arm's length, a weather dome, which in turn was concealed by greenery which had been stass-sprayed not to wither for days. Their equipment, moved within, formed narrow partitions for three small cubbies and one larger one. And they dared to turn on a camp-sized beamer there while each prowled in turn around the clearing to inspect for any betraying light.

For a time they must work by night, sleep by day. Roane was tired enough to yawn her way to sleep as soon as she was free to curl up in her own cubby. Nearby were the detects and as soon as it became dusk again she would take one in hand and begin her first sweep of the area. Sandar would go in the opposite direction, while his father was in charge of assembling the com, setting out the other tools they would need as soon as a detect gave them a lead. It was apparent that Offlas seemed very sure they would find what they sought. In the past his confidence had never been so high. It was as if he had complete assurance they would make their find shortly.

Such belief was infectious. Roane almost expected to be able to report success on her first scouting trip. But she did not; neither did Sandar. And the third night they ranged farther afield, guided back to camp by distort signals. While it was impossible to get lost, Roane found that venturing alone into the wilderness made her slightly uneasy. She had never been completely by herself before. On board ship there was the cramped feeling, even in a private cabin, of other lives close by, just as the lifeless air one breathed had, as one well knew, been recycled many times. But here—with the night lenses to give her clear vision, she began to feel at last oddly free.

Midway through the fourth night she climbed a ridge, swinging the detect on its strap over her shoulder, using both hands to pull herself up. It had rained earlier and the grass tufts and the branches which slapped at her were moisture-laden. But the waterproofing of her clothing kept her body dry, and she relished the feel of the droplets on her face and hands, even though they plastered her short hair lankly to her skull.

Roane had passed by a road earlier, in fact had tumbled into it when a sleek clay surface made her slip. It had been an odd hollow, boring through greenery which grew on grassy banks taller than her head, and it was over-arched with a lacing of boughs which roofed it. Whether this had been done by purpose to make a tunnel hidden from sight or was merely the result of unchecked growth she did not know. But the surface was rutted and scored with hoofprints to tell her it was in good use. And she had hurried to climb out, using a broken branch to sweep away her own tracks there.

This ridge lay at right angles to that road and well above it. She did not get to her feet as she reached its crest, but squirmed along so that she would not be silhouetted against the sky. The moon was now well up and bright.

Thus her sight of what lay below was very plain. Roane substituted distance lenses for the night ones to study the scene carefully. For there was a village-sized collection of buildings.

Almost directly below was the major one. It consisted of two square towers about five stories high, connected by a building looking to be no more than one room wide but rising three stories. The towers and the roof of the smaller portion were all parapeted and there was a tall outer wall completely encircling the building. Two or three of the very narrow windows showed faint gleams of light, late as the hour was. The tower nearest her had a gate giving on a garden which ran to the very foot of the ridge.

The garden itself was cut by walks gleaming white-bright in the moonlight and there were beds of flowers formally arranged. But what kept Roane from withdrawing at once was that there were men busy in the garden. They worked in pairs, six in all, and the couples were setting up in the ground posts which supported large grotesque figures. Each one of these weird effigies bore on one forelimb an oval shield painted with a complicated sign, while the other forepaw, or claw, gripped the pole of a small banner.

These were being placed in line to face the lower story of the tower, and the work seemed to be no light task. The effigies were of animals or birds, or in one case a crowned and shrouded humanoid thing. But all were strange to Roane and she wondered if they had some allegorical significance.

Why they must be put in place of the middle of the night was the puzzle, and she watched until the last was braced in place. Then the men disappeared toward the buildings along a single cobbled street running to the main gate in the wall. Outside the fortress-like wall there were two lines of houses built of the same stone as the keep, but they were much smaller, the largest only two stories high. Their roofs were slabs of stone slanting sharply from the peaks, the ends of those turning up to be carved into heads of beasts.

It was a keep, a village, in miniature. And though it looked different from the tri-dee she had been shown, she knew it for Hitherhow—the principal royal hunting lodge of Reveny.

Did the setting up of the figures mean that the King was coming? If so, what would such activity in the forest mean to her own party? Of course the distorts would protect them. But if there were many hunters abroad, they would have to hide until the chase was over, and Uncle Offlas was not going to take kindly to that loss of time.

2

"What did they say in briefing?" Uncle Offlas was pacing up and down, chewing at his thumbnail, an old sign of deep thought. Now he rounded on Roane with that question. "Who might be coming—the King?"

"King Niklas is an old man, judging by planet years—would he be hunting?"

"I am asking *you*. You saw the tri-dees the snooper robots brought in."

"They weren't sure about anything. If it isn't the King—" Roane thought of the possibilities. "His children are all dead. He has one granddaughter—Princess Ludorica—"

Sandar laughed. "Now that's a mouth filler! How do they think up such names?"

"Be quiet! A princess—who else?" Uncle Offlas demanded.

"Why does it matter?" His son refused to be subdued.

"It matters a great deal, you fool! The rank of the hunter can govern the number of followers he brings along."

Sandar flushed. Uncle Offlas was really upset or he would never have been so short with his son. She hurried to tell the rest she knew.

"There's a Duke Reddick, a distant cousin of the King but a lot younger. That's all the snoops picked up."

"With all the preparations you saw"—Uncle Offlas fretted his lower lip with the nail he had been chewing on earlier—"it has to be one of the royal line. If it's the Princess we may be a fraction safer—she might be less keen on hunting. But I don't like such activity so close. It might be well to take day watches until we do know who comes. Time!" He balled his right hand into a fist and brought it down forcibly into the palm of the left. "We have to make the best time we can. The longer we remain planet-planted, the better chance of discovery—"

Sandar's head was up, he was sniffing the rising wind. "There'll be cover today; storm coming. But it won't be good to be out in it—"

His father had swung around in the same direction. The thin gray of dawn did seem to be more dusky than usual. And they could all see massing clouds.

"Several hours before that breaks. Roane," he said to her, "you take first watch, before the storm. Report in with this if it is needful." He handed her a wrist com. "And work your way in from the north; these foresters are trained trackers. Sandar, you set out the extra distorts. I didn't want to use up the charges so fast, but now there is a need. I'll put a repell as well as a distort into working order."

Roane sighed but not audibly. She did not relish crawling the long way back to the ridge. But in spite of being tired, and chancing discovery by storm, the thought of watching the pocket castle was exciting. And inwardly she was surprised that Uncle Offlas had set her to it. Except that Sandar knew more about setting distorts.

She slipped inside the camp and crammed some of the sustaining, if tasteless, E rations into her coverall. There was no reason to go hungry, and her stomach already felt empty.

Circling north brought her into new territory. She could waste no time in exploration, but she did all she could to wipe out traces of her passing, being careful to snap no branch and to smear out any boot track in the forest muck. This delayed her, so that the gray was lighter when she again reached the ridge. She had made one discovery during her travels, a second tower set in the woods, brush growing so high about it that it was almost masked. There was no door closing the opening in its side and the place had the appearance of long disuse. Perhaps it was an abandoned ruin. She would have liked to explore it and promised herself she would when she had the chance.

Now she watched both village and castle. There were lights in plenty at the windows. And she could see people moving about. The wooden figures were bright with color, and the flags they held snapped in the wind.

Roane was so intent on the scene that she was startled by a rising call, saw a man on the castle parapet wearing a brightly colored overtunic raise a horn to his lips to answer that. Riders were coming down into the village, led by a man who managed his reins with one hand while he blew a horn for a series of calls. Behind him rode another in the same fantastic clothing, the tunic overlaid on the breast in an intricate design.

There was a small troop of six then, riding in military formation, wearing metal helmets and carrying bared swords in formal salute. Behind them came two riders, followed by a longer train of armed men. One of the riders was a woman, her long skirt flapping

on either side of her mount as if it were slit. The skirt
was of a deep forest-green, and her tight jacket was of
the same shade, though it bore braiding of silver in
spirals across the breast.

From this height Roane could not see her face, for
she had the collar of a cloak turned up about her throat,
though the rest of its folds had been pushed well back
on her shoulders. And on her head was a broad-rimmed
hat ornamented with a cockade of long yellow feathers.

Her companion was in the same green from the boots
on his feet to the narrow-brimmed, high-crowned hat
on his head. Roane could see little of his face either,
though by his dress he must be of the high nobility.

The villagers had turned out to greet the company.
Men waved their caps, women curtsied. And the woman rider raised one hand in salute. All the mounts were
Astrian duocorns and thus the fact was brought home
to Roane that this was indeed a settlers' culture, established at the whim of a mind half the galaxy away,
with the resources of many planets to call upon. These
beasts were smaller and lighter than those Roane had
seen before. But there was no mistaking their curved
sets of horns as they tossed their heads, even danced a
little.

Roane watched the party enter the courtyard of the
keep, the woman and the green-clad man dismounting
before the main door. He bowed from the waist and
offered her his wrist, she touching her fingers to it formally. It was like watching a living story tape and Roane was enthralled. The brilliant colors, the people did
not seem real, rather story-inspired, and she could not
believe in them. It was one thing to have such reported
on snooper tape, another to see it in action. She slipped
away from her post reasonably sure of one thing,
that it was the Princess Ludorica who had just arrived.

Who the man might be, Roane could not guess; any
member of the Revenian nobility from Duke Reddick
down. She held to caution in her retreat, knowing she

must take the roundabout way back. And the time so spent brought the storm upon her.

Suddenly it was night-dark, so that if she had not had her night lenses she would have been lost. Wind caught the crowns of the trees with a fury which frightened her. Roane had been on many worlds; she had known storms of wind, of drenching rain, of whirling sand, wind-driven grit to scrape the skin raw. But then she had been in such cover as their camps afforded, sheltered from the full force of such gales.

Now, caught in the open, her nerve almost broke. She must find shelter. And for that there was only the ruined tower. With what strength she had left she headed for it.

Rain added to the hammer blows of the wind. Branches splintered and fell. Roane cowered away from one jagged club. The whip of lightning lashed across the dark, to be followed by a crack of deafening thunder. And the tree to which she now clung, thick and sturdy as it seemed, swayed under the pull of the gale.

She could not stay there, but dared she try to go on? There was another bolt of lightning, which found a target not too far away. Roane screamed, her voice swallowed by the thunder, and tried to run, beating at the bushes to force a path. Then she saw ahead the mouthlike doorway of the tower.

Once she gained that, she held tight, panting and gasping. Her clothing, meant to be waterproof, had kept her body dry. But her hair was plastered to her head; water dribbled across her face and into her half-open mouth. For a moment or two out there she had felt as if the force of the storm had torn away her breath.

Now she recovered enough to move on in, and then dared to use the beamer, set on its lowest power, to inspect what lay about her.

To her surprise there was furniture here. But as she went closer she could see that its presence was probably due only to the fact that it could not have been moved except by the greatest of effort.

There was a table hewn from a single thick slab of dark-red stone which was veined with thin lines of gold that glittered even in the weak light when she smeared away a deposit of dust. Inset in the top of this was a series of squares, alternating red and white, perhaps to form a playing board for some game.

Facing each other across this slab, which was mounted on round balls of legs, were two chairs lacking legs at all, the seats being square boxes with the high backs and wide arms. Both arms and backs were carved, the gray dust filling the hollows of the patterns until they could hardly be distinguished.

Against one wall was a massive chest, also carved. And beyond it was a stair set against the wall, the outer edge unguarded by any rail, fashioned of the same stone as the walls, not quite as red as that of the table, but a dull rust shade.

There were, in addition, two tall standards of rust-encrusted metal, the tops of which were level with Roane's shoulder. Each of these held a lamp, a bowl with a support for a wick.

A drift of leaves and soil spread inward from the doorless entrance. Roane went to the stair and began to climb, pointing the beamer to where the steps disappeared into a dark opening above.

It was when she came out on the second level that she discovered that the tower, which had appeared three stories high from without, was really only two. If there had ever been a third floor above, it either had been wood and rotted away or had been removed. She flashed the beamer up there to see only stone and mighty beams.

This second room had furnishings also: two more of the lamp standards, plus a chest, and on a step dais a wide bed frame of the same wood which formed the massive chairs below. It was in the form of an oblong box, full of an evil-smelling layer of what might have been rotted fabric, perhaps the remains of bed linen left to molder away.

There were windows, narrow slits, without any protection against the wind and rain which now drove spears of damp across the floor. Another bolt of lightning made the whole room brilliant. And then followed such a burst of thunder that Roane dropped the beamer and cowered against the chest, her eyes squeezed shut, hands over her ears.

It seemed to her the thunder filled the tower, which shook from the blast. Even when it had gone she was too weak with sheer terror to move. She had never known such natural fury before and it made her a prisoner.

How long that panic lasted—it could well have been more than one hour, even two—she never knew, but finally she began to think again. Uncle Offlas—Sandar—they were in the woods. Could the camp stand up to such a storm as this? What if the lightning hit—or a tree crashed down?

She fumbled with her wrist com, tried to tap a code call. But she listened in vain for any reply. The storm must be cutting off reception. If there was any longer a receiver—

Although the wind still moaned around the tower and now and then she heard a crash as if some branch or even tree fell, the very worst of the storm seemed spent. Roane brushed off the top of the chest, testing it gingerly lest it splinter under her weight, and then sat there, bringing out an E-ration tube and making a meal from its contents.

So heartened, she used the beamer once more and made a careful examination of the room. That the tower had ever been a dwelling place she doubted, in spite of the bed. Perhaps it had been intended for just the use she was now putting it to, a shelter for storm-stayed hunters.

The evil smell of the bed, which was growing stronger in the dank air, had kept her away from that portion of the room. But finally she ventured to approach it. The bed itself was like a box without a lid, the cavity holding the rotten stuffs. At the four corners stood carven posts, matched as well as tools could sculpture to the bark of trees, vines twined about in high relief, now much masked by thick spider webs which held dust and mummified insects to form a nasty draping.

But there was a small open space between the tall head (also much carven and possessing several niches in which were set miniatures of the bigger lamps) and the wall of the tower. The beamer there showed Roane something odd, a series of holes hollowed into the stone, as if they were a ladder by which one might mount to the rafters overhead. Turning the beamer on to full, she traced those as high as she could and found that they did lead to one of the great crossbeams. This had the suggestion of a secret way, which it would have been in truth had the walls been covered with any form of tapestry or hanging.

She was tempted to take that climb. But prudence argued that she had better be on her way again, ready to leave the tower as soon as the storm slackened a little more. And she knew she must go when the lightning, which she feared the most, ceased.

Only she was too late. Hovering at the door, watching the rain, debating whether or not she dared chance it, Roane saw a flash of color, heard the high nicker of a duocorn. Some hunters storm-stayed like herself? She jerked back, looked at the floor where the pattern of her tracks had been only a little blurred by her restless coming and going.

She jerked open the seal of her coverall and brought out a scarf mask. Using that as best she could, whisk-fashion, she retreated to the stair and the only hiding place she could think of—behind the head of the bed above.

Though she had snapped off the beamer at once, there was enough grayish light for her to grope aloft.

And she reached the upper story none too soon. She was no more than into the bedroom when she heard voices, the tramping of feet below. No more taking chances. She had already been far too reckless. Roane squeezed betweerr the head of the bed and the cold of the wall, her hands covering her nose against the putrid scent of the bed stuffs.

She could not see now—the wood before her had no cracks. But she could hear. The newcomers did not speak Basic, of course. But her briefing had given her a working knowledge of the Reveny tongue. And now she began to pick up words. They were coming up the stairs, how many she could not tell, though she tried hard to distinguish voices and number of footsteps. Now and again there was a metallic clang as if something had struck the wall, followed by exclamations she could not translate but thought were curses.

They moved out into the chamber and she could hear their speech plainly now.

"—ride on in this? Are you empty between the ears?"

"—not like it—" The second voice was hardly above a mumble.

"Back of my hand to him then! I tell you, this is as safe a place to keep her as the underway at Keveldso. Dump her in the bed there, snap this leash on her, and we can wait out the rain below. Think you she can turn herself into a snake maybe to get out one of those windows? And with us sitting nice and easy down here she is not going to come tripping down the stairs and do a flit. Nor is she going to slip this here leash neither. That is made of good sword steel and the collar's made to hold one of His Grace's direhounds. Try it, go ahead, try it, man." There came the sound of metal clinking. "We snap this right around her throat, so. Now she cannot get away withouten this key, and that goes right here on my belt latching. I weren't a hound help for nothing, not that I weren't glad to get away from those kennels neither!"

"He will not like—"

"Would he like it more if we was squashed into a jelly by some tree coming down on us? You saw what happened to Larkin. Made you sick, didn't it just? Maybe he has plans for this little bird, but those don't include having her smashed up—not just yet. He said to see she kept on breathing, and he said that firm, as you heard him."

"Yes—" But it seemed to Roane that agreement was made with reluctance. Once more she heard the clink of metal, then a laugh, and the first speaker continued:

"Nobody is going to break that. She's as well tethered as if she was half walled in this place. Come away and let her lie. Better do nothing to rouse her up; she is enough trouble limp. She was a fighting cor-cat before Larkin gave her that little love tap."

Tramp of feet, the sound of them on the stairway. Roane dared to breathe more deeply. The fetid odor of the bedding was worse, as the settling of the captive within its box had stirred up the nasty remains. How long would she have to hide? And could she stay where she was at all? That stench made her sick. She wished she had not eaten the E ration in spite of her hunger.

There was no sound in the room, though any slight one would be covered by the rising wind. The dying of the storm seemed to have been only a lull. It was getting worse again. From the words of the men she was sure that whoever they left here was unconscious. And she must have more air or she would be sick. She could slip along the wall, gain the open beyond the bed by one of the windows. It did not matter that rain was blowing in again; she must have the clean wind on her face.

But Roane moved with due caution, stopping every few inches to listen. And when she finally got from behind the headboard she froze to watch the head of the stair. There was a faint glow of light from below. They must have brought a lantern with them. But the room was dusky with thick shadows.

She took another step, heard the rattle of metal, tensed again, turning her head to look at the bed. A dark figure arose from the muck which filled it. And the smell aroused by that stirring brought a coughing, quickly muffled, as if the cougher was trying very hard to subdue those racking spasms.

Another flash of the revealing lightning burst. There was a girl in the bed, holding both hands over her mouth and nose, her shoulders shaking. And over those muffled hands her eyes were wide open, looking straight into Roane's.

3

Roane moved without any conscious volition, at least afterward she could remember none. When she was thinking again she found herself face down in the stinking morass of the bed, a struggling body pinned under her. One of her hands was across the girl's mouth, and Roane was using her own weight to try to subdue the other's struggles.

There was a sharp pain in Roane's gagging hand and she snatched it away instinctively. The girl had bitten her. But the shrieks she feared might follow did not come. Instead the other spoke in a low voice:

"Why try to smother me, you dolt?"

Roane jerked away, nursing her bitten hand. She fumbled her beamer out of its belt loop, set it on low, and turned it on. And with her hand about it for a shield, she held it full upon the other.

The pale face caught in that light was streaked with black smears; dark hair tumbled about it. Below the determined chin was a broad metal collar, and from that a chain stretched into the dark. The girl caught at the collar with both hands, worried at it, though she continued to stare straight at the light as if seeking Roane behind it.

"If you are not one with the offal below," she said in a whisper, "then who are you?"

"I came here to shelter from the storm," Roane said evasively, in a whisper even more constrained. "I heard them bringing you and I hid."

"Where?" The girl asked that eagerly as if the answer held some desperate meaning for her.

Roane switched the light so it touched the headboard as a pointer. "Behind that. There is space enough."

"But where you were does not tell me who you are," the girl returned sharply. "I am the Princess Ludorica!" And there was a note in her voice which canceled out the dirt streaks on her face, the clinging stench, the collar that confined her.

Roane looked at that collar, and in her a small spark of anger flared. By all the urging of her training she should leave her right now. She could use that niche ladder. By the strongest oaths known to her people she was pledged not to make any contacts. Revenian quarrels were no concern for off-worlders. The old laws on noninterference were strictly enforced. And yet—that collar—

"I am not of Reveny," she said, evading once again, striving to keep her answer as low as she could.

"Thus making this matter none of your affair?" the Princess snapped. "What are you then, a Vordainian spy? Or perhaps a smuggler from over-border? He who will not reveal his face nor speak his name cannot thereafter be troubled if we see him as a walking evil." She repeated the last as if she quoted some saying. "Can you be bought? My offer will be very high—"

Roane wondered at the calm control of the Princess. Instead of sitting in this odorous box with a chain and collar making her fast, she might have been at ease in her own palace, save that she held her voice to a whisper. And now Roane saw that what she had first though another smear of grime across the side of the girl's chin was the darkening of a large bruise. Now and then Ludorica did hesitate between one word and the next, as if she found speaking somewhat difficult.

"Who are those men below?" Roane had a question of her own. That they had so dared mishandle the heiress to Reveny's throne meant they were not common criminals. And the more she learned of what lay behind this, the better she could plan what to do. Though she already knew she could not turn her back on Ludorica.

"Since I had to play the swooning female, that they use me with less alertness, I did not see too much of them. They wear foresters' jerkins, I do not believe honestly. And how I came into their hands—" She shrugged and the chain tightened, the collar jerked, bringing a choking cough from her. "That I do not know. I went peacefully to sleep in my bed in Hitherhow. When I awoke I was lying in a bumping cart on a forest track with the rain pouring like to drown me. Doubtless that restored my wits. Then the storm struck us full, bringing down a tree. The cart took the brunt of that to the fore. I gather that he who drove it had no further interest in the matters of this world. They pulled me out and brought me here.

"I do not think you are a Vordainian," she said, changing the subject abruptly. "If you are a smuggler, you will be given full pardon, with a good purse added to it. Get me loose of this"—she pulled at the collar again—"and guide me to the post at Yatton." She still stared ahead as if she could see Roane clearly.

When the off-world girl did not answer, the Princess set her lips tightly for an instant and then added:

"It would seem you also have no reason to wish to be discovered by those below. Let this then be a case of your enemy is my enemy, so a truce between us for this one battle." Again she appeared to be quoting.

"Your speech is strange, you are not of Reveny, and you have not the inflection of Vordain, nor the tongue clicks of Leichstan. Unless you are some mercenary from the north— No matter, get me free and you can rest easy on the gratitude of Reveny for your future, and that is no small thing!" There was pride in her voice, and once more Roane could forget where they were and that she fronted a prisoner and not one seated on a throne.

After all, what could some aid matter? She had already interfered, by merely being here and letting the Princess know it. If she left now, always supposing that she could climb to freedom by the wall way, the Princess, in anger at being abandoned, might call her captors, or Roane, trapped above in some manner, could be discovered. But if she were able to get the Princess away, she could contrive to lose her in the woods. Let the Princess then believe that she was a smuggler, too deeply involved in some criminal activity to be more than wary.

The Princess seemed to think her a man, perhaps because she had glimpsed, by the lightning flash, Roane's coverall and cropped hair.

"All right." Roane gave grudging consent. "But that collar—" She leaned over to train the beamer first on the band around the Princess's throat, and then along the chains to where it had been fastened about one of the bedposts. There was a lock, but she could see no way of forcing it.

Which left the bedpost or the chain itself. Her hand went to a tool on her belt. To use that again went against all she had been trained and taught. It was odd, one part of her mind observed as she drew that rod out of its loop: the longer she stayed here, the more it seemed right and proper that she do as Ludorica wanted—as if the desire of the Princess awoke a companion response from her.

Roane hunched over, trying not to breathe in the fumes of the debris, held the rod out in the beamer's small gleam, thumbing the right setting. Then she touched the rod to the chain as far from the Princess as she could reach. There was a flash of light. Roane pushed the cutter back in her belt, gave the chain a quick jerk. It broke. She heard a small sound like a sigh from the Princess.

"You will have to wear the collar yet awhile," Roane whispered. "I dare not cut that so close to your neck."

"That I am free in so much is something to give thanks for. But there are still the men below. If you have a dagger—how do you—"

Ludorica had balled the chain up in one hand so it might make no noise as she moved. She reached the edge of the bed box, swung out to the floor, as Roane was doing on the opposite side. The Princess's white robe, or once-white robe, billowed around her. One of her braids of hair had come undone and the long locks, tufted with debris from the bed, hung about her shoulders. She clawed out the filthy rags with a small shudder of disgust as Roane joined her.

The off-world girl surveyed the Princess's clothing doubtfully. The only way out was up that toe-and-fingerhold stair, and surely the Princess could not climb it wearing all those folds of cloth. Bringing her charge (for now Roane accepted the responsibility which followed her never-clearly-faced choice) around to the back of the bed, she flashed the beamer on the holes and explained their hope. But facing it now, she found the future more dubious.

"Lend me your dagger!" Ludorica whispered. "Oh"—she made a sound close to laughter—"I do not mean to fight my way free below. But I cannot climb in this." She gave an impatient tug to the robe.

"I do not have a dagger—" Roane returned.

"No dagger? But how then do you protect yourself?" the Princess asked wonderingly.

What Roane did produce was a belt knife, and the Princess seized upon it eagerly, slashing her full skirt front and back, cutting strips to bind the pieces to her legs in a grotesque copy of Roane's coverall. Before she returned the knife to its owner she tested its point on the ball of her thumb.

"This is like to a forester's skinning tool, yet different still," she commented. "You have not spoken your name—nor shown me your face—"

She caught Roane off guard as her hand shot out, her fingers closing around the wrist which supported the beamer. The impetus of that attack worked. Before Roane could dodge, the other had focused that light to fully illuminate its owner.

Roane broke the other's grip, but too late. The Princess had had a good look at her, and being quick-witted as she was, she must have noted a lot. Roane was developing some awe of the other. A girl who had been dragged from her bed, brought to this place, chained up like a hound, assaulted by Roane herself, yet who managed to keep a level head, ask for aid, argue logically on her own behalf— Such was no common person, on Clio or off. And Roane wondered if under the same circumstances she would have done as well.

"You are not a man!" The beamer turned floorward between them, having done its work. "Yet your manner of dress—that I have not seen before. And your hair—so short. You are indeed strange. Perhaps the legends are true after all. If—if—" For the first time there was a tremor in the Princess's voice. "If you are one of the Guardians then answer me true—it is my right for I am of the Blood Royal, the next Queen Regnant of Reveny —if you are a Guardian, what has become of the Ice Crown?"

To Roane her plea was a mixture of command and petition, and it meant nothing. But a sound from below did. During their struggle on the bed and their escape from it, the storm had been dying; now they could hear the men moving below.

Roane caught at the Princess's hand as she switched off the beamer. If the men were coming for their captive, there was little they could do in their own defense. Back in camp were stunners; Roane longed for one now. But those had not been unpacked, since they had no need to fear any forest animal with the distorts on. And those of the team were well aware they were not to be turned against any native here unless in the very last recourse. She had the knife—which the Princess still held—and the tool she had used to break the chain, nothing else.

Hand-linked, they stood very still to listen. The room had grown lighter. Perhaps they would not need the beamer. Roane drew the Princess to the head of the bed and behind it. The sooner they proved whether or not the holes led to freedom, the better.

"Climb!" She shoved Ludorica ahead of her and hoped the Princess could do just that. As the other faced the wall, raised her hands to the niches, Roane crouched so she could watch the top of the stair. It was too bad that they could not bar that way—say, shift the chest across it. But one good look at that told her that such a feat was impossible.

It seemed that the Princess's breathing, the faint scratching of her fingers and toes (for she was barefoot), were very loud. Roane strained to catch any answering sound from below.

The Princess was now well above the level of the headboard, straining to reach the shadowy crisscross of the upper beams. Roane started after her. It was, she decided, about equal to climbing a steep slope, save that she took each lift with the fear of at any moment being caught. Her breath rasped harshly in her own ears and she tried to control that fear, thinking not of what might happen but of what she must do in the next moment and the next.

"There is a place of flooring here," the Princess called down in a whisper, "and, I think, a door. This must be an overreach—"

What the other might mean, Roane had no idea, but she was heartened to know that her companion seemed to recognize something well known to her. Then

Roane's hand, reaching for the next niche, scraped a solid surface and she pulled herself out on a platform laid across the junction of two beams.

"There is a door to the roof. I have drawn its bolt," the Princess told her. "But it may take us both to lift it. It must be a very long time since this was last opened."

They crouched shoulder to shoulder on their knees, their four hands flat over their heads against a wooden surface. The dry dust they so raised sifted into Roane's face and hair, but she closed her eyes to it and said—

"Now!"

At first it seemed that that barrier had been firmly cemented by time. Then there was a giving which led to a greater exercise of strength. A crack of light grew wider as they strained. And, as if some further fastening gave way, the door lifted with a rush. Fresh, rain-wet air blew in upon them.

Roane drew herself up and out, turning to lend a hand to the Princess, who was making an effort to follow. They were on the roof of the tower in the full open. Around them ran a waist-high parapet. And it was day, though the rain clouds hung heavy above. Roane dropped the door into place. That they had bettered their case much was doubtful. Unless they could stay here in hiding until the men below left—which she thought was a very slim chance.

But the Princess was crawling on hands and knees around the parapet, stopping now and then to run her hands over its surface, almost as if she were in search of something she was sure she would eventually find. Even as Roane watched she paused and her fingertips outlined a space first on the parapet and then on the surface under it.

"We are favored by fortune," she said. "There is indeed an overreach here."

Roane went to look over the parapet. Some distance away the edge of the cliff backing the tower jutted out.

The girl tried to measure the distance between that and the tower. But it was too far to hope for a crossing—lacking a jump belt of her own civilization. Yet the Princess was now brushing at the roof, sweeping away the debris left by years of wind sowing.

"Ah—here!"

She had crawled some distance back from the parapet, and now she dug away at what seemed to Roane an ordinary crack between those slabs of stone which made up the roof. "Your knife—give it to me! This must be loosed."

Again Roane believed that Ludorica knew what she was about. She passed over the blade, nor did she voice the protest she felt when the Princess rammed its point into the crack.

Small rolls of black were gouged out, the Princess smearing them away with her hand. Now Roane could see that the break was much wider than it had first looked, so that a few minutes' work cleared a recess wide enough for Ludorica to get her fingers into. She motioned impatiently to Roane—

"Move back—over there. This may take some time; the packing is very old. But these were meant for escape means during the first Nimp invasions and I have never seen one yet which would not answer. Though I must find the lock stone."

She moved her hand back and forth, manifestly working her fingers within the crack. Then, even as the trapdoor had given, there was a thin grating sound and the stone block moved, sliding as a drawer toward the parapet. A whole section of that, as wide as the moving slab, sank out and forward as if on invisible hinges.

"Help me—" the Princess panted.

Roane scrambled to the opposite side of the slab, pushed at it. It slid on and on, passing out over the now horizontally leveled section of parapet to form a narrow bridge which did not quite touch that rocky spur beyond but came close to closing the gap.

The Princess sat back on her heels, panting with

effort, her dirty face flushed. "We must be quick; these do not hold long—"

Roane did not try to take that narrow path on her feet but crawled on hands and knees, and was careful to keep her eyes to the tongue of stone which she must traverse. There was a giddy sensation in her head. She had never been fond of heights, though she had fought that fear through the wandering years of her life. This was the worst test she had yet faced.

She reached the end of the slab. There was still open space between its end and the ledge. She jumped, landing heavily on the stone. Then she stood ready, holding out her hands, to aid the Princess.

It was lucky that she did, for just as Roane took firm grip of the wrists the other girl held out to her, the stone tongue trembled, moved, backed toward the tower. She was just in time to jerk Ludorica to safety. The slab rolled into place, the parapet arose, and their bridge was gone.

"Now—for Yatton—" The Princess was trying to order the remnants of her robe. She took a step and then gave a sharp exclamation, holding up a bare foot to brush at its sole.

Roane thought of her own plans—to aid the Princess and then fade away into the woods, leaving the other to go where she chose. Now she discovered that she could not desert her companion. The rain was chill and the Princess was barefoot. How long would it be before those men in the tower found their captive gone? And then—how long before they ran her down again?

"Where is this Yatton of yours?" Roane demanded impatiently. The only alternative would be to take the Princess back to camp, and she could foresee only outright disaster in that. Either way she was in deeper trouble with every passing moment.

"Two leagues—nearer three." The Princess raised her other foot to brush at it. "To speak the truth, I do not believe I can walk that without shoes. It would seem my feet are too tender for such wayfaring."

"We cannot be too far now from Hitherhow."

The Princess, having brushed her feet, was now busied in coiling the collar chain about her slender shoulders in a strange and ugly necklace. "I do not return to Hitherhow—not until I am sure—"

"Sure of what?"

"Of how I could be lifted from my bed there so easily with no guard's hand raised to prevent it." She eyed Roane bleakly, and then her eyes focused on the off-world girl far more searchingly.

"You—you are surely not one of us. But a Guardian would not have needed to climb that wall stair, cross a safety bridge. A Guardian, by all the old tales, needs merely to desire a thing and it becomes so. I do not know what you are, and you will not tell me who—"

"I am Roane Hume." Roane had not meant to say that. It was again an odd compulsion to tell the truth which moved in her before she was aware. "I am not of Reveny, but I think I have proved I mean you no harm."

"Roane Hume," the Princess repeated. "Your name, too, is strange. But this is a time of many things which are not as they once were." She had continued to eye Roane closely, but now she smiled and held out her hand.

And when she did so Roane experienced a melting inside her. It was as if no one had ever really smiled at her before, asking her aid, not demanding it impatiently. And her own well-tanned hand caught those whiter, if dirty, fingers and squeezed them for an instant before she remembered again that she, least of all on this world, had any right to commit herself in friendship, or even in a fleeting companionship.

"You pay no homage. In this you are like a Guardian," commented the other. "Is it that where you come from there is no difference between those of the Blood Royal and others?"

"Something of that sort," admitted Roane cautiously.

"I do not believe that one of Reveny could live easily in such a strangely ordered place," the Princess began and then laughed, put her fingers to her lips as if she would catch back those frank words. "I mean no disrespect to your customs, Roane Hume. It is only that, bred in one pattern, I find a different one bewildering."

"We have no time to discuss it." Roane fought back her own desire to ask questions, to know more of Ludorica. "If you cannot return to Hitherhow, and it is impossible to reach Yatton, then where will you go?" *She* must be on her way, but still she could not abandon the Princess.

"You have come from somewhere." The Princess seized upon the very solution Roane dreaded. She had no idea what Uncle Offlas might do if she turned up at the camp with this bedraggled fugitive. That the end would be drastic, she could guess. But there did seem to be nothing else left to do.

"I will take you there then." Her voice sounded harsh and cold in her own ears. She tried to think of some other way. There was one feeble hope. She might discover a hiding place in the woods, leave Ludorica there, get supplies, clothing, footwear for her, and eventually start her off to her own people. A project in which there were as many chances for failure as she had fingers and toes. But there was nothing else—

Now she turned to study what she could see of the tower and the woods. That they would be tracked she had no doubt. Therefore she must leave as devious a trail as possible. At the same time she must give the Princess as good a chance of escape as she could.

"We must head that way—" She gestured north, away from the camp. The detour would buy them time.

They climbed down from the ledge and the Princess must go slowly. Finally Roane took her supply bag, dumped its contents into the front of her coverall, slit it with the knife, and bound the halves about her companion's feet. That done, they were able to march at a better pace.

The rain continued to fall steadily, if not with the force of the storm, and the Princess was shivering. Roane had a new worry. Immunized as she was through the arts of her own civilization, she was aware that those without such medical protection must be highly susceptible to exposure. What if Ludorica became ill, what if— Their future was far too full of such ifs. Roane should lead her directly to camp. Only the stern conditioning of Uncle Offlas kept her intent on leaving a confused trail which might ward off disaster.

But, she realized at last, Ludorica could not stand much more. Though the Princess made no complaint, she lagged behind. Twice Roane returned, having missed her, to find her charge leaning against a tree, holding to the bole as if she were lost without support. And finally she must half carry her along.

It was then they came to one of the stony hills Roane recognized as a landmark. On its side was a raw new gash. And there was the smell of burnt, smoldering wood. Lightning must have struck and, in so striking, started a landslide.

Where that had passed now gaped a hole. The slide must have uncovered a cave, or at least a deep crevice. Here was shelter and Roane brought the Princess to it.

4

They were not too far from the camp, Roane knew. She could leave the Princess here, go for the supplies she needed and return. And she refused to think of all the difficulties which might face her during the performance of that plan. One step at a time was best.

Once they pushed into the raw opening in the cliff wall the rain no longer reached them. And though the opening itself was narrow, it widened out, stretching into the dark as if they had entered a place of considerable space. Lowering the Princess to the floor, Roane unlooped her beamer, turned it to full.

This was no natural cave. She was startled by the evidence the light made plain. It was the anteroom to a tunnel, one that she had enough knowledge of archaeology to know had not been formed by nature. In fact the walls were so smooth that she went to lay a hand on the nearest, finding that her fingertips slipped across it as they might on a sleek metal surface—though it still had the outward look of native stone.

Swiftly she triggered the control on her detect, heard the answering tick which told her she was right in her guess. Not only was this a nonnatural cut into the cliff side, but it bore a reading for ancient remains. By chance she had stumbled on the very site they had been prospecting for! Roane brought up her wrist, ready to try again to relay her news via com. But before she pressed the broadcast pin she remembered.

Bring Uncle Offlas and Sandar here—let them find the Princess— They would never allow any inhabitant of Clio to go free with the news of this discovery. If their cover was so broken, they would not only be under the ban of the Service; they could be planeted for all time wherever the authorities sent them. Uncle Offlas, Sandar, their careers blasted, blacklisted in the only field they knew— Their only alternative would be to silence the girl now sitting hunched on the stone, coughing and rubbing her hands across her flushed face. That silencing would not mean death, as it might have once. (Roane had heard the horror tales of the early days of space expansion.) But it might mean memory blocking, or even transportation off world into a limbo for Ludorica. Either way the innocent would suffer. All Roane could do was buy time and hope for some miracle to occur. Her head ached with her inability to see her way clear. She did not know what there was about the Princess that so enchained her sympathies. Perhaps she was being affected by a faint shadow of the original conditioning which had repatterned the settlers here when this unhappy test world had first been conceived.

As she stood there, caught in the net of the dilemma, a hand gripped her wrist, tightening above the com which she must use if she were to be true to her people and her training.

"What is this place? It is no cave!"

She had believed the Princess too sunk in exhaustion to be fully aware of her surroundings. But Ludorica was now on her feet, staring into Roane's face, not accusingly, but as if she could not wholly believe she saw what her eyes reported.

"You have done it!" The Princess swayed as if it were hard to stand on her bruised feet. "You have brought us to Och's Hide! The Crown—give me back the Crown!"

"Please, I do not know what you are talking about— what crown? And Och's Hide—" Roane protested. Was it possible that a Forerunner find had already been made in Reveny, that they were too late? But the Service snoopers had picked up not the slightest hint of any such happening, one which would have caused stir enough to leave a deep imprint on public memory.

For a long moment the Princess stared into the eyes of the off-world girl, as if by the very force of her will she would get the truth from Roane, past any ambiguous or false answer. But whether she might have decided that her companion was lying Roane was not to know, for there was a dull roar from the mouth of the opening.

Roane whirled, the Princess clutching at her for support. Recklessly she turned the beamer on the opening to the outer world. But that door was no longer there. Instead the harsh glare of the beam showed a curtain of rocks and earth, with bits of splintered bough and torn leaf caught in it.

Crying out, Roane pushed aside the Princess, ran to tear at the fall which had corked the entrance. She was able to scrape out some of the rain-slicked clay, pull at the branches in it. But underneath was a boulder she could not move. Though perhaps she could use the power of her tool to undercut it.

"Are—are we trapped?"

Roane had gone to her knees, was holding the beamer steady on the boulder. In one way her own problem was solved. For both their lives now depended upon help from outside—from the camp. Only the men there had the equipment to handle this easily.

"Yes. I do not have power enough to undercut this. I shall have to call for help." Should she warn the Princess of the results of that? Or continue to wait, always hoping that something might happen to make a hard choice easier?

"This could be Och's Hide. If we must wait for help, need we remain crouching here? For if it is the Hide and I can find the Crown—" She drew a deep breath. "For me, for Reveny, this could be the greatest day in a hundred years!"

"What crown do you seek?" Roane thought of the many forms that Forerunner discoveries had taken in the past. There *had* been a few times when such had consisted of objects which could come under the age-old designation of treasure—gems, weird art forms of precious metal, and the like. Though what were more important by far, and what they had come to seek here, were machines, records, and the clue to such a find had been enough to make them risk search on Clio.

"Our crown—the Ice Crown of Reveny." The Princess answered almost absently. She no longer watched Roane but gazed into the shadowed passage. Then she did turn, and her face was stricken with a shadow of fear and her hands went to her mouth, covering her lips. When she spoke again it was in a very low and shaken voice.

"That is a great secret, Roane Hume, one that only

41

two people know—my grandfather the King, and I. And I have sworn by that which is most sacred to our people not to speak of it. Now I am forsworn."

"But I am not of Reveny, and I shall swear as you wish to say nothing." Roane, made uncomfortable by the bleak look on the other's face, was quick to answer.

"If this is Och's Hide, then the harm is small, covered and forgotten in a greater good. But I *must* know! Come, use your light and let us look—"

If they stumbled on Forerunner remains and the Princess saw them— But what did that matter now? Roane had to do what she should have done long ago.

"Let me first call for help to free us." She fingered the com, moving its button in the camp call. Waited— and saw the answering code flash on the dial, demanding— But she interrupted with her own terse signal, of where she was and what she might have stumbled upon. Though she made no mention of the Princess.

The answering flash was a jubilant series of dashes, promising all speed. She had forethought enough to add then a warning of people in the forest, thinking of the searchers which might be combing there.

She half expected some question from Ludorica, but the Princess said nothing, only turned the beamer on the passage.

"Can you not tell me more of what you seek?" Roane asked as they started on.

"Knowing a part, there is no reason now for you not to hear it all. The Ice Crown is the crown of Reveny, given by the Guardians at the far beginning. Just as the Flame Crown is for the rulers of Leichstan, the Gold Circlet worn in Thrisk—but surely all this is known to you. My grandfather, King Niklas, came to the throne while he was yet a boy and his stepmother-under-second-rights, Queen Olava, was regent in his name—though she was no true kin, not even of the Blood Royal, having been taken in a marriage on the left hand by my great-grandfather when he was well into his dotage. She was of the line of Jarrfar. They once held this hill country and tried twice to make a kingdom of their own. However, having no crown power from the Guardians, they of course failed.

"But it was in their blood to rule and they did not lose that desire, even when their lands dwindled and they held only a stead keep and two villages. Olava had great beauty, and it became the plan of her people that they might achieve by an ambitious marriage what they had not been able to do by force of arms. So they gathered their resources and brought her to court, humbly presenting her as a handmaiden.

"The King had long been a widower. Oh, he had had his ladies during those years, but they were only passing fancies, and he chose shrewdly such as would be easily satisfied with small favors and not beg for greater. But though Olava seemed of a like sort in the beginning, she was not! And—well, it is said she had had occasion, before she came to court, to visit a certain wise woman who dabbled in things better left alone. But then such is always whispered of a woman who rises rapidly in the favor of a high-born man. As time passed she became first a wife of the left hand and minor law, and then the Queen—though she was not allowed to touch the Crown lawfully, for all her pleading and intrigues. My great-grandfather might be besotted with her, but he was royal born, and it is very true (though some today think this is also a legend) that the crowns choose who will wear them. And once they have so chosen, that king or queen cannot surrender them during his lifetime. It is a protection the Guardians set upon them. Though sometimes it has led to death for the proposed wearer, he being killed that another might present himself to the crown.

"So Olava had to bide her time until death reached for the King, hoping that before his son might confront the Crown for its choosing, her own candidate might take it. And he was her son—though the King would never let him drink from the kin-cup and thus acknowledge him as a true blood son before the Court, since he was not fully of the Blood.

"When the King died, they went to fetch the Ice Crown for the choosing. Though Olava tried to prevent my grandfather from standing before it, the choosing went as it has always done and he was proclaimed king. However, he was but a child and there were great lords enough favoring Olava to say that the old King had named her regent with them as a council to advise her.

"A common enough tale, one which has been told before. But what had not happened before is that when my grandfather came of an age to put on the Crown and thus assume all power, the Crown, brought from safe-keeping for the ceremony, disappeared immediately thereafter before it could be returned.

"For Olava dared what never had been dared before. She took the Crown, meaning thus to defeat my grandfather. And the power of the Crown blasted her as it always does those handling it unlawfully. But before she died, my grandfather finding her privately, she laughed and said that it had gone to Och's Hide and that only chance might now find it. Her clan, she said, would guard the way to it, and only when it accepted one of them would it appear again.

"Since then there has been this hidden darkness in Reveny. We dared not let any know of the loss. And since it has not yet been needed to hail a new king, the secret has been kept. My father died during a hunt in these very hills, but what he sought was no animal of the chase, but Och's Hide. Two of my uncles also died young. The third disappeared. And now—King Niklas is very old, and it has fallen on me to take up the search. For if I cannot stand before Reveny with the Ice Crown when death claims him—then our line comes to an end. And Reveny itself will be overrun by Leichstan or Vordain, where true wearers of crowns rule. A land without a crown is a land without name or being. So the Guardians decreed in the far beginning."

"Has it ever happened that a country did lose its crown?" asked Roane.

The Princess shivered, but with more than just the chill of the passage through which they walked now.

"Once, in Arothner. The crown—it was the Shell Crown, for Arothner was of the sea—was destroyed in a tidal wave. And what followed was horrible. The people —a madness fell upon them. They turned upon their own lords, upon each other, so that all the nations on their boundaries set up armies to keep them in their own torn land. And thereafter it has been accursed and no one goes there for fear the same mind-blasting force might strike them. What was once a great nation with many ships, and the trading city of Arth as its capital, is now only barren waste, and if any still live there, they are no longer men—

"At least the Ice Crown has not been destroyed, for then the same fate would have fallen on Reveny. And to that hope we hold. But it must be found!"

"It would seem that there are those who also know the secret and do not want this crown discovered—if your father and the others died and this has happened to you."

"Yes." The Princess's lips tightened. "I guess and think I guess rightly, though I have no proof, that it is Reddick's doing. Though I never thought he would go so far as to have me taken out of Hitherhow when it was well known I was within those walls. There must be some desperate need to bring him so into open action. It may be this passage he would protect. Roane, does it seem warmer here to you?"

Ludorica slowed, put out her hand as if to touch the wall, but did not quite complete that gesture.

She was right! The chill which had closed about them in the fore part of the passage was gone. This was like walking under a gentle sun, just comfortingly warm. Roane touched the wall. There was warmth

45

there, more so than in the air about them. And also something else, a faint vibration.

Excitement surged in her. A Forerunner installation still alive? It had happened on other worlds—Limbo, Arzor. If that were possible then this would be one of the *big* finds, and anything—even breaking cover on a closed planet—would be forgiven the discoverers! This could be the answer to her problem.

"What is it?" Ludorica, watching her closely, must have read the elation on her face.

"I do not know—not yet—" Roane returned quickly and then asked:

"Who is Reddick, and why would he want to hold the Crown?"

"Though the King would not claim Olava's son, he ennobled the boy and gave him command of Hither-how in his lifetime, a right which must be renewed in each generation. Reddick is his grandson. But so might he have the secret of Och's Hide. If I can only find the Crown, Duke Reddick has no chance. Then he cannot lay hand to it before the King's death, or as long as I live—"

"As long as you live," Roane echoed her meaningfully.

"You mean—but of course! That is why—he had a double purpose." The Princess nodded. "Stop me from searching, or else make sure if I did chance upon it— Which also means—" Her face now mirrored now only determination and cold anger but also fear.

"Roane, I have not seen King Niklas for five days. It was he who told me I must make haste to find the Crown, gave into my hands all he had denied me for years, the clues he had tried to sift and follow, all that my father and uncles had when they went seeking. Perhaps he is more ill than he would have me know, or else has since grown worse. And Reddick knows this. If the King were himself, the Duke would never have dared to have me stolen from Hitherhow."

"Do you not have someone to depend on?"

"None sharing the Crown secret. But if I can now find that and reach Yatton or the border, I can cross over into Leichstan with the Crown and gain a breathing space in which to rally the loyal lords. My mother was a princess of Leichstan, though she died at my birthing and he who sits the throne there is but a distant cousin. Yet I can claim blood kin, and all must aid one who wears a crown!"

She flicked the beamer ahead. "Come! If it lies here —do you not see? I must have it, and soon!" Now she began to run.

But the beam had picked up something else, a change in the wall to their right. Roane pressed to that side and then halted at a slab of transparent material. Inside—an installation! It could be nothing else. Rows of machines, with here and there a flashing point of colored light. She pressed her face to the glass, trying to see more of what lay there. But the light was too intermittent—she had only glimpses as one flash was echoed by another. Green, blue, red, orange, a multitude of colors and combinations. Yet those did not reflect into the passage where she stood.

"Come on!" The Princess was ahead, paying no attention to what held Roane fascinated. "Why do you stop?"

"The lights—this must be an installation. But what—"

Ludorica came back reluctantly. "What lights?" she demanded, flashing the beamer directly onto the panel, thus revealing two machines of pillar shape inside, spinning off flecks of color.

"What lights?" The Princess pulled at Roane's arm. "Why do you stand staring at bare wall and talking of lights? Are you mind-twisted?" She dropped her hold, drew back a little.

"What do you see there, then?" Roane asked.

"Wall—just as there, and there, and there—" With a stabbing finger the Princess pointed ahead, to the side, behind them. "Nothing but wall."

Roane was shaken. But she *did* see a strange installation behind a transparent panel! She could not be mistaken or imagine that! There could be only one reason why the Princess did not see it too—conditioning!

And such conditioning could mean something else. Roane's thoughts took a leap into dark surmise. Perhaps what they had uncovered was not Forerunner remains, but rather something left by the Psychocrats who had decreed Clio's fate. While such a find might not have as much impact as the discovery of a genuine Forerunner installation, it could be important in another way. The Service knew little of the techniques of conditioning on the various closed worlds. To discover part of such an experiment might excite those in fields beyond that which Uncle Offlas represented. So she might have a bargaining point after all, some claim for consideration for the Princess.

"It is just bare wall!" Ludorica proclaimed again, still backing away from Roane, now eyeing the off-worlder as if she expected some dangerous outburst.

"A trick of the light." Roane thought that a feeble answer, but she knew that if the Princess was conditioned she would resist even the thought of what might lie there.

"Trick of the light?" repeated the Princess doubtfully. "Oh, perhaps Olava set her own safeguards against seekers. I have heard of such tricks but they only work with some people." She now regarded Roane pityingly and put out her hand. "Let me guide you past. I cannot be so bemused, you know. None of the Blood Royal can be caught in a fore-set mind-maze."

Ironic, Roane thought with wry amusement, a case of the blind leading the sighted. But if the Princess was willing to accept that explanation, she should be thankful. She did not look again at the panel.

Shortly thereafter the nature of the passage changed. The wider, smoothed walls gave way abruptly to a narrower way with rough rock on either side—as if those who had cut this path had used a natural break in the cliff for their purposes and this was the original cave unmarked by their improvements.

As the beamer caught the narrowing of those rough walls the Princess slackened pace, looked puzzled.

"Why should it change so?" she asked, more as if she questioned in her own mind than expected an answer from her companion.

"Do you still think this is Och's Hide?"

"What else could it be? There would be no other reason to cut a passage through rock. Yet—"

"Wait!" Roane lifted her free hand, held it before that crevice. "There is air—a current of it. Maybe there is another way out ahead."

They found the narrow passage a rough one. Twice walls closed in, so that they had to scrape through, and Roane had no idea how far they might be from the entrance. What if those from camp cleared the blockage there and did not find her? But at least they would have her report and so go exploring. Of course, the men might run into difficulties raised by some hunting the Princess and thus be delayed.

As they emerged into a wider space Roane spoke:

"I do not know about you, but I am hungry."

"Do not speak of food!" retorted Ludorica. "When one has nothing, it is better not to dwell on that lack. Let us get out of here—"

"But I have provisions of a sort," Roane countered. There was no use in trying to conceal such things as tubes of E ration when so much else in the way of cover had been broken, and she was painfully hungry.

"Where? You carry no provision bag—" The Princess once more turned the beamer on Roane, who had already unsealed her coverall and brought out one of the tubes. There were only two left, and with their rescue still uncertain, it was better that they now divide one between them.

The Princess stared at the tube. "You carry food so? But there is not enough in that to make even a quarter of a meal if you hunger as I do."

"This is a special kind of food, made for travelers," Roane explained. "A small portion, say half of this tube, is equal to a full meal. It does not taste as the real food you know, that is true. But it is as good for the body, and it will give us strength. If you hesitate, I shall eat first." She measured off half the length of the tube, squeezed the contents bit by bit into her mouth without touching the edge to her lips.

Her companion watched her with deep interest. And when Roane had done and passed her the tube, Ludorica put it to her mouth in turn. She made a slight face as she tasted the paste, swallowed.

"It has little flavor, as you warned. Truly I do not think I would relish many meals taken so. But when one hungers there need be little choice of dish; any food will do." She finished the tube quickly and gave it, empty, back to Roane.

From long training the off-worlder wadded it into a ball, which she hid under a loose stone. The Princess had set the beamer upright as one might a candle, and its light, reflected from the roof over their heads, showed them that the space in which they now stood was a true cave.

But it showed something else, too. Roane gave a start as she caught sight of it, snatching up the beamer to turn it full upon what lay there. That had been a man once. But she had seen ancient burials enough not to be squeamish. These bones lay half buried under a fall of rock which concealed the skeleton above the waist.

She heard an exclamation from the Princess as the light caught a spark of fire to one side of the crushed bones. Roane stooped to pick up a band of metal in which were set small gem stones. It was a fine piece of work, the stones making small flowers among raised leaves of the metal.

A moment later the circlet was snatched from her hand, the Princess turning it about in her own fingers.

"The arm ring of Olava! This is Och's Hide! And the

Crown—the Crown!" She turned around, searching the
walls of the cave as Roane swept the beamer. But
the side wall opening which had once existed where
the skeleton lay crushed was filled in past their exploration. There was now no opening at all that Roane
could see.

5

"If it was ever here," Roane pointed out, "then it must
now be buried under that fallen rock." Privately she
thought the bracelet a very small clue.

"But it can be dug free!" Ludorica crowded as close
to the mound as she could and still avoid the skeleton.
"You say those you know will come to free us from the
outer cave. They surely can aid here to find the Crown!
Let me but rest my hands on it and Reveny has naught
to fear, for then as long as I live no one else can claim
it—"

"As long as *you* live. What then, if, once you have
found the Crown, your enemies find you? How long
will you continue to live?"

The Princess looked back at Roane, her eyes wide
with what might be shock.

"But no common man can raise his hand against the
wearer of the Crown; such are under the protection of
the Guardians. Any such death must come *before* the
Crown has rested on the chosen's head."

"But the Crown now would belong to your grandfather, would it not? So long as he remains alive you
will be in danger."

"True. But if what I fear is also true, and that is in

a manner proved by the fact that Reddick moved against me so openly, then the King is very near to death. The Crown will know that; it has many strange powers. All the crowns do. They are the hearts of the countries possessing them and their lives are those of the nations—as was proved at Arothner. No, when your people come they must dig for the Crown. It still exits and I must find it!"

And that influence she was able to exert at times, which Roane recognized but somehow could not resist, brought Roane to half agreement now. Yet enough of her fought that compulsion so that she was able to persuade the Princess to return to the other end of the passage to meet their rescuers.

That Uncle Offlas would come she had no doubt, but how long he would take was another matter. Especially if he had to avoid searchers in the woods. And she said as much in warning to the Princess.

"But you can send a message—though why tapping on that ugly arm circlet carries a message—" Momentarily she was diverted. "I do not know who you truly are. But that you are not of Reveny, nor of any kingdom I know, I will swear to. Had you not brought me out of that tower, I would not—" Again she paused. "But I stand here and not in the hands of Reddick's men, so I have a measure of trust in you. Send another message to those you say will come to unseal us; tell them to use my name to the garrison at Yatton. There is there Colonel Nelis Imfry. He was of the palace wards before he took service with the March Guards. Summoned in my name, he will come. You may tell your people, if those clicks really talk, to say to him—"

"No." Roane shook her head. "They will not go to Yatton nor any other place for your guard, no matter what message I send."

Perhaps she was wrong in being so definite about that. It might arouse Ludorica's suspicions even further. But she must make plain before the camp party arrived that they would not give the Princess any help in solving her complicated problems of dynastic inheritance.

"My people are sworn"—she tried to put the situation into words the Princess would understand—"by oaths, very tightly binding, to have naught to do with the affairs of others. I have already broken this oath by what I have done since we met. For this I shall have to pay. But you will find deaf ears if you ask for any aid from those who come."

They were passing the wall panel which the Princess could not see but which so fascinated Roane. The latter kept her eyes resolutely turned from temptation. And at that moment the com on her wrist flashed. She did not need the beamer light to read the sparked code.

Sandar! But no mention of Uncle Offlas. Only a sharp demand that she turn the call beam higher so that he would have a guide.

"They are here now!" She began to run along the smooth flooring, not caring whether the Princess followed or not.

Back in the entrance cave she again faced that plug of stone and clay, cautiously, since she did not know the force of the tool they would use to clear it. And she threw out an arm to hold the Princess to an equally safe distance.

The latter had given no vocal protest when Roane had denied her help. But she was smiling with anticipation. There was such an aura of confidence about her that Roane was uneasy. Perhaps she should have given her the whole truth in warning—not only that Ludorica could expect no aid, but that those who came might take her into another captivity, that her quest for the Crown might well come to an end here and now. Roane half opened her lips, was about to say what she must, when there was a shifting of earth about the plug. The stone which was its anchor disappeared.

Roane caught her breath. They were using *that* tool! Then indeed they were ready for desperate measures; such were unboxed only at times of extreme need.

She glanced at the Princess. What effect had that sudden disappearance of a very large and heavy rock had on her companion? But she could detect no sign of surprise, only a deepening of that confidence which was going to be so rudely shattered soon.

Fresh air bearing the damp of the rain blew in. Then Sandar, stooping a little, came through. He was alone, and in his hand—Roane gasped but she had no time to move, to warn. He had already pressed the button of the stunner. Beside her the Princess wilted to the rock floor. For the first time in her life Roane faced her cousin with open anger.

"Why did you do that? You did not even know what—"

His mouth had the same twist as Uncle Offlas's could wear upon occasion. But this time it did not daunt her as it might have in days only shortly past.

"You know the rules. I saw a stranger—" he said harshly. "Now—" He looked down at the detect he carried, as if Ludorica were no more than the rock he had blasted out of existence. Then his face lost a little of its grim cast. "But you are right! There is a find here—"

Roane was on her knees by the Princess, lifting her limp body to lie against her shoulder. Ludorica would sleep it off, of course, but she must not remain here. The dampness of that inflow of air was already reaching her. Roane did not know how disease might develop on Clio, but she was certain that the inhabitants could not endure long exposure without suffering for it.

"Leave her—she'll keep!" Sandar came to her side. "What's inside?"

"An installation. You can see it through a plate in the wall down there." She made no move to guide him.

Nor did he wait for her, but switched on his own beamer and trotted away in the direction she pointed, while she was left with the problem of the unconscious

Princess. Uncle Offlas and Sandar would be solidly united against any plan of freeing Ludorica; Roane had known that. But she determined that the Princess would have shelter and care even if she herself had to face such pressure of their wills as had always before frightened her.

She was still holding the girl against her for warmth, interposing her body between that of the Princess and the damp inflow of air, when Sandar returned.

"I don't know what it is. It may be Forerunner. But at least it is not of present-day Clio," he reported.

"Maybe something of the Psychocrats, to do with the settlers' conditioning."

"How do you—" he began and then shrugged. "Who knows before we take a closer look at what is in there? Now—there are men searching the woods. I had Eight-fingered Dargon's own luck trying to dodge them. Father has had to extend the distorts to cover this area. Who are they after—her? If so, we give her a brainwash and dump her where they can pick her up. Then our troubles are over."

"No."

"No, what?" He stared at her, Roane thought (with wild laughter stirring far within her), as if she had suddenly grown horns or turned blue before his eyes.

"No brainwash, no dumping. This is the Princess Ludorica."

"I don't care if she's the Star Maiden of Raganork! You know the rules as well as I do. You've broken them already by being with her at all. How much else have you spilled?" He was twirling the setting on his stunner. Roane went cold with more than the wind.

She drew the small cutting tool from her belt. "You try brainwashing, Sandar, and I'll burn that stunner out of your hand. Drop it—now—or see how you like a seared finger! I mean exactly what I say!"

He eyed her with even greater astonishment. But he must have read the determination in her eyes. There had not been many times in the past when Roane had been faced by some major demand upon her will and courage, but twice that had occurred in Sandar's company and he must remember now her reaction.

"You know what you are doing?" His voice was very cold. He still held the stunner, but she noted, with a small sense of triumph, that his finger was now carefully away from the firing button.

"I know. Toss that over to me!" Her tool did not waver. She might have used close to its full charge when she cut the Princess's chain, but there was enough left to give Sandar a burn and at that moment she would not hesitate to do just that. The captivity, her own feeling of inferiority and helplessness, to which the domination of the Keils, father and son, had sentenced her for so long was like the Princess's metal collar and chain.

That restless desire for freedom which had been born at Cram-brief was coming to a flowering here on Clio. Certainly she might know far less than her uncle and Sandar, be now under their orders, but she was also a person in her own right, not a robot they had programed.

Not that all this flowed coherently through her mind now. But she was determined to stand up to Sandar. His callous solution to the problem of Ludorica had acted on Roane like the cut of a whip—not to lash her into a slave line, but rather to awaken her resistance.

Sandar did not try to reason with her. Not that he ever had. He had given orders, she had meekly obeyed —until he and his father had had her wrapped in a cocoon of acceptance. But larvae develop in cocoons and in time they break free.

He tossed away his stunner. Roane steadied the Princess against her, held the cutter steady until she could reach out and close her fingers about that weapon.

"Are there any searchers near here now?"

"As long as the distorts are on they will keep their distance without knowing why—you ought to know that!

But that will hold only for a short time. We shall have to move quickly."

"Good enough." Roane tucked the cutter back in the belt loop, kept the stunner in her hand. "Now we'll go. You carry her."

"It won't do any good," he said. "You know that. Father has discretionary powers. He'll make the final decision and there will be no repeal. Also, you're finished with our team. I trust you understand that!"

Roane would consider that future when she had time. The here and now were more important—getting the Princess to shelter and seeing she stayed out of the hands of her enemies.

"You'll carry her," she repeated.

Carry her he did. Enough of Roane's training remained, even as she enjoyed the heady sensation of ordering Sandar around, to prompt her to use the last of the tool's powers to bring down another fall of earth as a mask for the hole. She hoped that would keep its secret. For what lay within and the fact that she had discovered it were all she had left to bargain with.

Though the distorts were on, Sandar took no chances, setting a fast pace, even though he had the inert weight of the Princess draped over his shoulder. Roane walked behind, intent on concealing their back trail.

So they reached camp. At least Uncle Offlas was not there, and Roane ordered Sandar to put the Princess in her own private cubby. She set to work then, stripping off the soaked, mud-caked rags Ludorica wore, tugging loose the strips of cloth making her improvised leggings. And she had the Princess rolled into a heated sleeping bag when the chief of their party did tramp in.

He came straight to the cubby and looked at the Princess with no readable expression on his set face.

"Who is she?"

"The Princess Ludorica, heir to the throne of Reveny."

"And the story?"

He had a recorder ready, Roane noted bleakly. She was going to be condemned out of her own mouth. But 'here was nothing else she could have done. To her, Sandar's suggestion was unthinkable.

In the clear, terse manner of making a report which had been drilled into her, Roane began her story—the storm, her refuge in the tower—their flight, the cave—what she had found there—the Princess's tale of the Ice Crown, and all the rest.

Uncle Offlas listened without comment, though Sandar stirred now and then as if he wished to voice some derisive interruption. Yet he did not. And having concluded, Roane waited for the storm to break, knowing that verbal lightning could be as disastrous as the real.

"As for this girl," he said first, "we can attend to her when it is needful. But this find of yours—you saw it, Sandar?"

"Yes. What I could make out through the panel. It may not be Forerunner, but Psychocrat. It could have something to do with the experiment on Clio."

"Either way, it is apparently a find of importance. We can report that, along with this." He looked at the Princess as if she were not a human being at all, but some object which must be disposed of. "However, we have a matter of two days before the com can relay properly to the right orbit pickup, and by that time we should have much more information."

"What about the Princess?" his son demanded. "They are going to keep hunting her, and we can't run the distorts on high for long. If we do as I wanted and brainwash her—then leave her where they can find her—"

Roane knew better than to voice another "No" right now. She had no weapon to back it up. That confidence which had supported her began to ebb. She might be able, for some moments of wrath, to stand up to Sandar. She had no defense against Uncle Offlas.

"For the moment they are hunting to the north. And I would like to know more about this crown she believes hidden in there. Once her memory is erased we can learn nothing. We haven't the equipment for being selective in such matters. We can wait—for a while. Now, I want to look at that installation.

"As for you"—he spoke to Roane—"you must realize what you have done. You are not a blind fool, just a fool. And I would suggest you think upon that folly. Consider the future which you have just thrown away."

This was much milder than the blast Roane had expected. Though a moment later, after the men had left the camp shelter, she realized that considering a bleak future was a punishment in itself. The least she could hope for was to be planet-bound on some world the Service selected, forbidden ever again to use any skill she had learned. They might even demand that she be brain-censored also. She shivered and put her face in her hands, though she could not shut the dire pictures out of her mind.

Why *had* she done all this? Looking back now, she was certain she could have remained hidden in the tower, perhaps even made that climb into safe hiding above, without having dealings with the Princess. Such evasion had been a part of Roane's training from the start. What flaw in herself had forced her out of the ways of prudence?

Again, she could have left the Princess once they were free of the tower. She might have done this—or that— But in every choice, she had made the one to condemn herself to Uncle Offlas's justice and she knew what she could expect from that.

She could not use her find as any bargaining point. Uncle Offlas would claim it had been made by chance alone. The only new information she had was that the Princess was conditioned not to see the panel—and any more Ludorica could supply about the Ice Crown.

Since they did not have the techniques here to drag information out of Ludorica against her will, perhaps she could be forewarned to bargain— But for that she must be conscious, and how long—

"What did they say about me?"

Roane was startled. The Princess could *not* be conscious—she had gone down at Sandar's stunner blast. But her eyes were open and watching Roane.

The off-world girl had no idea how this miracle had come about—unless a difference in planetary inheritance was responsible. She had never known one to recover so quickly from a stun beam. But she must take advantage of it before the others returned, give the Princess warning.

"Listen!" Though there was no one in the shelter and she made sure the recorder was safely off, Roane leaned very close before she spoke. "They want to take away your memory, so you cannot remember us. And then—then they may give you to those hunting you."

She had expected some expression of disbelief from the Princess. But though the other's eyes narrowed a little, she showed no surprise. Instead she asked:

"And you believe that they can do this thing—take take away my memory?"

"I have seen it done to others."

"I believe you believe it, yes. But whether it can be done to one who has the right to a crown—" Ludorica frowned. "If I could get the Crown—I must get the Crown!"

But Roane had a question of her own. "How long have you been awake? It is important for me to know."

"A memory which is useful, eh? Very well, this I remember clearly—a young man wearing clothes such as yours. Why is it with you, Roane, that men and women dress alike? Even our peasant girls delight in their bright skirts and would think your wear very ugly and drab. Yes, a young man. Then all is blackness as in a sleep without dreams. Until I lay here—wherever here may be—and you were taking from me those disgraceful rags to make me clean and warm. But I thought it well to learn what I could before those others knew I was awake.

"So they wish to take away my memory and give me

to those who would like me best in the far deeper sleep of death. Why would they do this to a stranger who has worked them no harm?"

"They fear your knowing of their presence here."

"And what act of thievery, or worse, do they plan that they fear any knowledge of their presence may spoil?" There was a new sharpness in the Princess's voice. "It is the Crown! You seek the Crown! But it is the truth that I told you—for one not of the Blood to take it means a wasting death. Which one of our neighbors sent you to destroy Reveny so? And are you so careless or dedicated that you will kill yourself to achieve your ends?"

It was no use. Roane could not explain without telling all. But with a conditioned mind—would Ludorica accept her explanation any quicker than she would believe in the installation she had not been able to see?

"We came here to search for a treasure, but I will swear to you by any power you wish to name that that was not your crown! Until you told me of it, I did not know of its existence. Nor would it mean anything to me. What we seek is not of your time. Oh, I do not know if I can make you understand. Before Reveny was a nation, before your people came—at a time so distant we have never been able to reckon it—there were others. They may not even have been like us in form and they were gone before our form of life came to be.

"But in some places they left things behind them, hidden things. And from these our wise men try to learn something of them. They had greater knowledge than we possess. They were able to do things which we can hardly believe are possible. Yet we know that they did them.

"And every such find we can discover adds to our small store of knowledge, makes it more likely that some day we can learn more of their secrets. My uncle and my cousin, the young man you saw, are both trained to hunt down such treasures. And I have been schooled to help them, since I am of their family and supposed so to keep their secrets." She was trying hard to set this within a framework of planetary custom. "By revealing myself to you I have broken a very strict law, and I shall have to pay for that. But you are not at fault—"

"So you believe this is wrong, the taking of my memory?"

"Yes. And yet—"

"Yet you also have a way of life to uphold, even as we of the Blood," the Princess interrupted. "Yes, that I can understand. But I tell you, Roane, I do not propose to let them take my memory and give me to Reddick. Nor do I mean to lose the Crown when my hand may be only inches from it. I am treating you as one treats an honorable enemy. If it be war between us, let us say so, and from this moment the rules of war will hold."

"I do not want war. But my uncle, my cousin—"

"Yes. And what will happen to you, Roane? Will they also take away your memory as a punishment for aiding me?"

"They might, yes. Or they can send me to a place where I shall have to abide for the rest of my days."

"A prison? And you will let them do this to you?"

"You do not understand. They have powers you cannot conceive of. And there are others behind them more powerful still. They will do with me in the end just as they choose."

The Princess sat up. "I do not understand you. You are strong of body, quick of mind. This you have proved. Yet you will let them take you—you sit here and *wait* for them to take you!"

"*You* do not understand!" Roane thought of the devices they could use to hunt her down. Uncle Offlas might even call in Service aid. The Princess might be conditioned in one way, but, Roane saw now, she herself was conditioned in another, unable to break free without aid—

"Stay if you will," Ludorica said. "But I do not remain here to have them play with my mind."

"Where will you go?"

"To Yatton, if I can escape Reddick's net. He is a stubborn man and will not lightly let me out of his hands. And you—will you remain here waiting for prison?" There was a faint scorn in that.

But Ludorica could not know. To run was hopeless, ending in defeat. If Roane could persuade the Princess to bargain with Uncle Offlas— Only the time for bargaining might already be passed. Roane shook her head. Slowly she arose.

"If I help you to Yatton—" At least she might protect her from Reddick's men. If she could keep the Princess safe, there might be a little hope for a later bargain.

"If you help me to Yatton, I think there will be no more talk of memory stealing, nor prison, for either of us!"

6

"Food first." Roane went to the stores, triggered the heat caps on those containers she thought held the most sustaining nourishment, brought back her selection.

There was clothing, too. Ludorica's collection of rags was useless. Roane could give her an extra coverall—it would, with its strange make and fabric, be one more thing to explain to any native, but there was no help for that. She had compromised her standing with the Service past repair. But there was no reason why the Princess should be surrendered to an alien "justice" which to her would be the rankest injustice.

As she hunted for clothing and boots she rubbed her forehead with her scratched fingers—not because of any ache there but because she could not wholly understand how she had been drawn into this tangle. Roane had wanted nothing but shelter from a frightening storm, and all this had come from that perfectly natural desire. Somehow it was as if all her training, all she had been drilled in as "right" or "wrong," had been overturned once she met the Princess.

With a sigh, she spread out the coverall, ready for Ludorica, who was sampling cautiously the contents of a container.

"But this is good!" commended the Princess. "It is much better than what you carried with you in the cave. How is it that you have it hot? For you did not take it from any stove—I saw you!"

"It is another of our ways," Roane told her wearily. She was very tired, wanting nothing more than to lie down in the warm and comfortable bed bag, to sleep. But instead she mouthed two sustain tablets, which would ease her fatigue. Then she ate her share of the meal.

The Princess finished first and was now fingering the coverall. She and Roane were much of a size and Roane did not think it would be an ill fit. She showed her how to work the inseal by merely running a finger tip along it, and the Princess gave an exclamation of surprise and pleasure.

"But what ease you have in dressing! Though there is a beauty to buckles and lacing. And"—she surveyed her slender figure, muffled now in the alien dress—"I do not think I would like to wear this for long. Wait until we reach Yatton, Roane. Then I shall exchange gifts with you—and I think"—she eyed the other critically—"you will look well in our dress. Though it is a pity about your hair. Perhaps it will grow in time. Ah, I know! You can wear a Charn bonnet, that will be proper. Wine yellow for your dress, and a bonnet with tyra ribbon for cording—"

Roane laughed. She felt as if she had slipped from the real world into fantasy. How could she, Roane Hume, be sitting in a Service camp listening to the Princess of Reveny describe a dress of high Clio fashion meant for her to wear? Perhaps it was best to treat this venture as a dream, to drift along with the tide of events rather than trying to fight them. But for a wistful minute or two she wished it could be true, that once she *could* see herself as the Princess visualized her.

"Best hold a dress in your hands before you don it," she commented. "I know we are a long way from Yatton—*if* we ever make it."

Roane took what precautions she could against being traced. She unbuckled her work belt and laid it straight on the floor to study its cargo of tools. The beamer—yes, with fresh charges. Not the detect, nor her wrist com either; they were linked to devices in the camp. The cutter—no. Though she had betrayed the Service in some ways, she would draw the line with that. It could be lost—and, found by another, arouse too much speculation. A small medic kit and—

"Have you aught here to free me from this?"

Roane looked up at the clink of metal. The Princess was pulling at the collar, its chain dangling down over her shoulder.

"Come closer to the light and let me see."

The Princess stooped so that Roane could inspect the small lock hole, which had not been visible in the tower. The off-world girl brought a larger kit. She tried two of the tools it held, inserting their tips into the hole, prying with them. With a click, the collar sprang open.

"Ah." Ludorica jerked it off to rub her throat where red marks showed. Roane reached for the medic kit, squeezed out a fingerload of soothing paste, and applied it carefully.

"Ahh—" The Princess sighed again. "That takes away the soreness. Another of your many marvels. With your food in me, your clothing on my back, and now your paste of herbs, I feel as if I could front Reddick and be victor. Though I know well that is a belief I should not put to the proof."

Roane continued to choose supplies. Not a flamer, of course—but a stunner was another matter. In the first place, its inner workings would be instantly destroyed if handled by anyone who did not know its use. Service personnel had to be furnished with some form of protective weapon for other worlds, and this refinement was the ultimate result of much research. It could not kill, though on the highest voltage it could cause brain damage—as Sandar had proposed to use it.

She had refurnished her belt—beamer, stunner, the medic kit, a bag of rations, but nothing which would link her to the camp or the camp to her. When she was done and ready to go, she saw that the Princess had gathered up the collar and chain, winding the latter around the former for easier carrying.

"Why take that?"

"Why? Because it was put on me. There are those I shall show it to when I tell my tale, and they will be the hotter against Reddick. Women are not treated so in Reveny. Even more will it be resented that a Princess of the Blood was chained like an animal. I do not know how deep or wide Reddick has made his move against the throne, but that he has done this to me is a warning. There may be those who follow him without knowing what manner of lord he is. And to those such a symbol as this"—she shook the collar and the links clashed against one another—"will lead to second thoughts. Let me but reach Nelis—"

Roane took a last look at the camp. It was no different from the ones she had known on half a dozen worlds. Yet now she had the feeling that once she walked away she was turning her back on everything which had always been. So, as she glanced from this to that, all had a slightly unfamiliar cast, as if they were already strange and she was one apart.

At least yesterday's rain had stopped, though there were still effects of the storm to be seen as they moved from the bubble half buried in the muddy earth. Out in the open Roane was wary, not only of Reddick's men, but of Uncle Offlas and Sandar. She quickened pace. And the Princess, her feet now protected by boots, matched her stride for stride.

That Yatton lay to the north was all Ludorica could tell Roane. The Princess was not used to traveling except by well-defined roads, and all that lay here were foresters' tracks. Nor had she any idea how far away from their goal they might now be.

"Sending Nelis there three months ago was perhaps another move of Reddick's," she commented. "All I know is that he is loyal only to the true line. Ahh—though these boots are better to tramp in than bare feet, I wish for a duocorn. My good, fleet Zarpher—or even Batlas, though I have named her slug-crawler in the past!"

She paused, one palm against a tree trunk for support. Her face was drawn and there were dark shadows, almost matching her bruises, beneath her eyes.

It had been well into afternoon when they had left the camp, though the cloudy sky made it dusk in the thicker parts of the woods. Although they had borne north as steadily as they could, there had been many detours forced by the rough country, so they could not have covered too much distance. The only hopeful note was that they had seen no searchers.

Roane, to her surprise, discovered that the Princess had an acuteness of sight and hearing besting hers, often pointing out some trace of bird or animal Roane missed. She smiled at Roane's comments, saying that Hitherhow had been her favorite place when she was a child and that she had often gone with the foresters.

"But that was when Duke Reddick was still a palace squire in Thrisk. And would that he had remained! He was sent to Thrisk in exchange for the second son of the Duke of Zeiter. I think all hoped he would make a marriage of merit. What did happen"—she shook her head—"not even I know. Though the King was told. And after, he sent Reddick for two years to Tulstead. Which is a place to make a man think twice before he wishes to settle therein. Reddick came back much altered—for the better, my grandfather thought. Though he might have known that the blood of Olava was not to be so purified. Anyway, the Duke's actions thereafter were such that he could not be denied his rights to Hither-how. That beautiful place! To be so tainted! But let me get the Crown—"

"And what of your grandfather?"

"We are blood kin," Ludorica answered slowly. "He is an old man and to him I am merely a means of preserving our House. He wanted a prince; he must take me. So for the years since my Uncle Wulver's disappearance, I have not been a person—myself—but a tool in his hand. That he is right makes it no more easy for me. If he dies I shall be a little sorry, for in his way he is a good man, and has always done his best for Reveny. But it will not be true heart-sorrow. I have none close enough to me to strike that deep." She spoke as if stating a fact she had long faced.

"And with the Crown you rule Reveny?"

"I do! Then Reddick shall learn what it means to reach for what is not his. I have already made plans— since I do not know how far he has flung his net, nor in what places it lies to entangle me. I shall get Nelis and his men to escort me, and ride to Leichstan, cross-ing the border where one may slip over with no eyes upon one. Then we shall go to Gastonhow where the High Court summers. As blood kin I can treat with King Gostar—" She hesitated and the chain of the col-lar rang as she turned it.

"He has sons, two still unmarried. One such would be an acceptable prince consort for Reveny, and such a marriage would pacify that border at least. So he will be ready to listen to me. Then—with a chance to gather loyal forces—I shall find the Crown and ride to Urkermark City. If I enter with the Crown and with border peace secured, Reddick will have no one left to guard his back. The ambassador at Gastonhow is

Imbert Rehling, who was cup-brother to my father in their youth. He will arrange it all once I get to him. Yatton, the border, Gastonhow—it is all a straight move."

It might seem a straight move to the Princess, but Roane thought she could see a good many places where trouble lay. However, that was none of her concern. She would get Ludorica to Yatton, if she could. What happened thereafter would be the result of the Princess's actions, while Roane returned to camp to take what would be waiting for her there. All she would have to offer in her defense was that the future Queen of Reveny would be in her debt—always supposing Ludorica did become Queen.

"And how do you get the Crown?"

"We know now where it lies. Once I have support behind me I can find it. But those to go there with me to loose it from the rocks must be carefully chosen. This is a story which must not spread. Nelis I can count on to the death and beyond. He will know others that I can trust."

Roane wondered if she was as confident as she sounded. But the off-world girl was not prepared to question it. She was too intent now on the fact that night was coming. The night lenses—she had forgotten those. How could she have been so stupid? The effect of the sustain tablets she had taken was wearing off, too. And it was very apparent that, for all her push and courage, the Princess was in an even worse state. They would have to rest, eat, and perhaps spend a portion of the night in whatever shelter they could find.

That in the end proved to be in the lee of the trunks of two trees brought down in the storm, their broken limbs still flying rags of withering leaves. The girls tramped the smaller branches and leaves into an untidy nest and hunkered in together. Roane brought out E rations and they ate. By the time they had finished it was dark.

The Princess slipped into an exhausted sleep, lying in a tight curl, her head pillowed on a tree limb. But they would have to keep watch! Roane battled her own deep fatigue as the long minutes slipped by.

Sharp pain in her shoulder—Sandar was prodding her with a Gamelean longsword. He wanted her to get up—march—show him a crown of ice. If he took that into his hands he would be a ruler— He drew back the sword, to turn the point on her again—

Roane opened her eyes.

"Up!" The command came out of deep dusk, was enforced by a prod in her ribs. Not Sandar—

One of Reddick's men! Roane's sleep-rooted daze cleared a little. She moved her hand toward her head, only to meet with a sharp blow on her wrist, delivered by the man standing over her.

"Keep your hands in sight—try nothing. And on your feet!" His orders were terse, and she could see he held a weapon ready to enforce them.

So they had been captured in their sleep. But Roane was still too tired to know more than a remote dismay.

"What do you do, Sergeant?" That demand came from the Princess.

"My duty. You are on Royal land without a warrant. You shall so answer to the Captain."

"That is right, Sergeant," the Princess replied briskly. "But you will act with more courtesy, or *you* shall answer to the Captain, and that answering will not be pleasant. Touch us not again!"

Perhaps the imperiousness of that command had its effect, for he withdrew a pace or two. There was pale sunlight about them. And in the full light stood three men. They wore a uniform of boots, tight breeches, and tunics which were latched from throat to waist with metal, the skirts cut to flare out over the hips to mid-thigh. These coats were of a rust brown, and each bore on the right breast a complicated symbol worked in purple and green, the same colors appearing in a small tight crest of feathers jutting from the bands of their high-crowned, narrow-brimmed head-gear.

Each wore a sword slung in a shoulder baldric, and their leader had drawn his weapon in threat. But in addition they had other weapons Roane recognized as being the most lethal on Clio, hand arms which fired a solid projectile.

"You are of the Jontar Cavalry," Ludorica said. She faced the Sergeant and he stared at her, plainly puzzled. "Your Colonel is Nelis Imfry. Him I would see and speedily."

"You will see the Captain." The Sergeant might have been momentarily disconcerted by her attitude but he had regained his composure. "March."

March they did, through a tangle of brush into a road which was a trail of beaten earth. And there waited four duocorns, another man holding their reins. Roane found herself uncomfortably mounted behind one of the men, the Princess behind another. This was not, the off-world girl decided, an easy way to travel. But it did bring them to another tower, or rather a set of towers, not too unlike the one in which Roane's adventure had begun. Only these were in use, and they formed the pillars of a gate with a threatening port-cullis, through which the forest track went to join a much better road.

The Sergeant had spurred ahead, and by the time the rest arrived, there was an officer awaiting them. The insignia on his collar was in the same purple and green and his cockade of feathers had an extra metal embellishment.

He looked curiously at Roane, but when his glance went to the Princess his eyes widened and his astonishment was plain. He moved swiftly to the side of that mount and held out his hand to aid her down.

"Your Highness!" Then he turned upon the Sergeant. "Off with you to the Colonel; tell him we have found the Princess!"

The Sergeant took a second look and climbed back

into the saddle. Under his spurs the duocorn leaped under the gate arch, thudded out into the road beyond.

Roane was aided from her own perch far more gently than she had been bestowed there. And she followed the Princess up to the second floor of the left-hand tower, where chairs were hurriedly brought, the second having been summoned by a hand wave from the Princess for Roane's accommodation.

"Your Highness, we have been out hunting for you. When the word came by courier bird last night that you had disappeared from Hitherhow, the Colonel dispatched three companies in search—led the first one himself. But how—" He had glanced several times at her coverall, and at Roane, as if he wanted explanations he dared not ask for openly.

"I was taken from Hitherhow," Ludorica answered, "from my very bed. By the grace of the Guardians, and the good will of the Lady Roane Hume here, I escaped whatever fate was intended for me. For the rest—it is not to be discussed openly. But you I have seen before. You accompanied Colonel Imfry to Urkermark on the occasion of the last birthday review of His Majesty. You are Captain Buris Mykop, and you come from the stead of Benedu."

"Your Highness, but only once did I have the pleasure of being presented to you—and you remember!"

She smiled. "Does anyone forget those who serve them faithfully? It is not strange to do so. Rather it would be unfitting and strange if one did not."

She leaned forward suddenly and tossed the collar wound with the chain onto the top of a nearby table.

"You see there, Captain, a small keepsake of my adventure. That collar was fitted to my throat for a space, the chain was well anchored to hold me at another's pleasure."

The Captain looked from the Princess to the chain. He put out one hand to touch the collar. When he turned, his face was grimly expressionless.

"And who did this, Your Highness?"

"I do not know—yet. But doubtless all shall be made clear in time. It suffices for now that that did *not* hold me as was meant. And for that, thank my Lady Roane." She nodded to her companion, and the Captain gazed at the off-world girl as if he would impress the sight of her on his memory for all time.

"What day is this? We have been turning night into day for our traveling. I can no longer reckon clearly."

"It is the fourth day of Lackameande, Your Highness."

"And it was on the second that I rode to Hitherhow," she said. "There has been no word of weight out of Urkermark?"

"None, Your Highness. By all accounts the King rests comfortably with no change in his condition."

Ludorica relaxed a little. But that she did not altogether rely on that report was proven when she asked:

"The Leichstan border is within two leagues of here, is it not? This is the Westergate?"

"That is true, Your Highness."

"And what—" But what she might have asked was lost in sounds below. A moment later another man came into the room with a rush which halted when he saw Ludorica. He was tall and young, but there were already lines of responsibility on his face.

Beside Sandar's finely cut features his would seem blunted, plain, of a coarser mold. Yet Roane found she was staring at him as the Captain had earlier done with her; she wanted to fix his face in her mind. Though why, she could not have told.

His hair was close to the shade of his tunic, a rusty red-brown, but his eyebrows were as black as the Princess's, and one had an upward tilt which gave him a slightly cynical look.

The way he eyed Ludorica now made Roane a little uncomfortable, as if to be witness was taking an unfair advantage. Then that expression was gone as he crossed the room, took the hand Ludorica held out to him, and raised it to his lips, bowing before her with a grace Roane would not have credited him with had she not seen it for herself.

"Good greeting, my Princess!"

"Good indeed, kinsman." It seemed to Roane that the Princess stressed that last word deliberately. It might have been a private code, or a warning. "I hear you have been searching for me."

"Did you believe we would not?" He spoke with a drawl, and he smiled as if inviting her to share some small joke. "But as always, my Princess, you have managed to prove yourself a worthy daughter of kings and have not needed our efforts after all. Captain," he said to his subordinate, "we might well all enjoy a glass of lasquer, and—have you yet lunched, my Princess?"

"Lunched?" She laughed. "Kinsman, we have not yet breakfasted. Though we did sup—by my Lady Roane's good will." She nodded to Roane. "Roane, this is my good kinsman and dear friend, Colonel Nelis Imfry, of whom I have already told you."

The Colonel bowed, perhaps not quite as low as he had to Ludorica, but with that same amazing grace. Somehow Roane found her tongue—though as she was not quite sure of the formal terms of address in Reveny she fell back on those of her own civilization.

"I am honored, Colonel—"

"The delight is mine, my lady."

"It is by her hands alone I am found again, kinsman. And now—Captain Mykop says there is no ill news."

The Captain himself had disappeared.

"You expected some?" the Colonel asked.

"Because of my adventure, yes. Nelis, he would not have dared such a move had he not had some private news which led him to believe the King was near his end."

"But I will wager nothing can be proved against your charming cousin," the Colonel returned, the adjective in that speech made an epithet by his tone.

"Naturally not. But, Nelis, there is something else—a secret. You must hear it, and perhaps also others, those you can well trust. May we speak openly here?"

"Yes. Let them bring refreshment. Then you can talk. It cannot be so immediate that you must go fasting to tell me, can it?"

But the Princess did not echo his smile. "It may be, Nelis, it may just be."

He frowned. But just then the Captain entered, behind him a soldier with a laden tray, the burden of which he set out on the table while the Colonel poured yellow liquid from the bottle the Captain had produced.

"You also, Nelis, and Captain Mykop." Ludorica motioned to the waiting goblets.

"I give you a toast," said the Princess when they each held one of those, "and that is the King's good health!"

Roane let the slightly tart, refreshing liquid fill her mouth. She read meaning into what might be a conventional toast. Ludorica indeed had need for the continued health of her grandfather, unless she could gain her long-lost crown.

7

Roane glanced from the Princess to the Colonel and back again, wondering what lay between the two, who seemed to have forgotten her existence. Though the Princess made an obvious point of addressing him with warmth, yet he in return appeared to set some barrier of formality between them. They faced each other now across the table where the remains of the best meal Roane had yet had on Clio still lay.

Ludorica had told her story in terse language—of the loss of the Crown, of where she now believed that it lay. And when she finished, the Colonel made no comment, but instead looked to Roane.

"And how does the Lady Roane come into the matter, beyond the fact that she has been of great service to Reveny in her actions toward Your Highness?"

Since the Princess made no answer, Roane spoke for herself. Again she must say more than she wished to. Always she plunged deeper and deeper into disaster for an off-worlder.

She told the edited story she had given Ludorica—of the hunt for ancient remains which had brought her people here. But when she had done the Colonel looked far from satisfied.

"You do not, Lady, say from whence you come, you and these other treasure seekers—?"

Roane hesitated a long moment. "Colonel, have you never served under orders given to you in confidence, which you cannot disclose to others? Or, if you have not done this, are not such cases known to you?"

"That is true. Though I have not, until this hour, dealt with aught which is not common knowledge."

"Then accept that I must be silent. But I swear to you that those I serve mean nothing ill to Reveny. In fact before we came here, we were pledged to do nothing to bring us to the knowledge of your countrymen, nor to influence affairs here. In this I have erred, and I shall have to pay for that."

"They can make her lose her memory—or put her in prison—" broke in the Princess.

"She told you that?" The Colonel's eyes were cold now.

"Yes," Roane returned baldly. It was plain he doubted her. "They can do this—whether you believe it or not!" Her chin went up a fraction of an inch as she met disbelief with defiance. "And now," she said to the

Princess, "I promised to bring you to your friends. This I have done. So I shall go—"

"Not so!" The Colonel's words came sharp and swift. And Ludorica put out her hand, caught Roane's wrist where it rested on the table, as if to hold her prisoner.

"Whether you wish it or not," the Colonel continued, "you have chosen your path, my lady, and you must continue to follow it until the Princess is out of danger. Your Highness, let this lady remain with you. It is fitting that you have a companion when you cross the border. And it would seem fortune favors you with one who dares not betray secrets lest she betray herself even more."

Roane flushed. Did he jeer at her now, or issue a challenge to prove she was as she said? She was a little afraid, for she did not doubt he meant what he said—evidence that he was prudent, for the wise thing for him was to keep her close. That she had not foreseen this simple end to the action puzzled her. It was all a part of that muzzy thinking which she had done ever since she met Ludorica. Almost as if she were conditioned—

Conditioned! What if the Service techs had been wrong and their off-world guards did not hold? Or at least not entirely, so that subtly she had been taken over by the force which existed to make Clio a closed world? A new spark of fear was born in her. She was she, Roane Hume, who could perfectly remember a life beyond the stars. She was not a subject of a ruler on this forgotten, living museum of a world! And that thought she must hold to.

"You are set on this plan then, Your Highness—to go to Leichstan for aid?" The Colonel, having delivered his order, seemed to have forgotten Roane again.

"There is the Crown. I do not think that, even if Reddick knows where it lies, he quite dares to reach for it while I live. But with my death, he believes—or I would in his place—that the Crown will acknowledge him. For unrecorded though his descent may be, there is a trace of the Blood in him. He may have taken me only to make sure I was under his control when the word he expects comes. But that he ever meant I live on past that hour—" She pointed to the chain and collar. "That is good evidence he did not. And Leichstan can prove a refuge until we are sure of what we do face now."

She seemed to accept very calmly the fact that she was the target of her cousin's intrigues. But perhaps such intrigues were so common on Clio that they were a part of daily experience. Maybe one held one's position here through a series of struggles in a deadly game.

"Reddick must still be at Hitherhow. We can take him there!" The Colonel's brown hand twitched as if the fingers wished to hold some weapon.

"Not knowing how far his plans extend or what support he can summon? That would be folly. But if I go to Leichstan I can claim aid, and I have put myself beyond Reddick's reach, given us time to find the Crown and learn the true state of the King."

"Leichstan is ambitious," the Colonel returned slowly.

"So is Vordain to the north. If we must ally ourselves—which? I wish this no more than you do, kinsman. But if one must choose between alliance and alliance, Leichstan through friendship is better than Vordain by force."

The Colonel looked down at the cup he held as he turned it around and around. He might be reading some message in its depths.

"There is a price for such alliances," he observed in a very level voice.

"That I know also," the Princess returned. "But to everything on this earth there is a price, kinsman. And to me Reveny comes first, its safety and future. I am what I am by reason of birth, of much training. Were there another of my House to carry sword in battle, perhaps I could turn my thoughts from what must be done. But there is not. And I believe that this lack is also of Reddick's doing. Before the Crown falls into his grasping hands I will do much. And the way lies through Leichstan—though I must go there without any of the trumpeting of a royal progress. You have wardered the border long enough to know its secrets. Nelis, there must be some hidden way across, and not far from here—"

"Smugglers' ways are rough going."

The Princess laughed. "None can be worse than that I have lately used. Though this"—she looked down at the coverall—"is very durable clothing for such work, I think it would be better if I entered Leichstan wearing something less noticeable. I know that I cannot expect an army post to produce clothing for a lady, but can such be obtained for us both?"

Nelis Imfry smiled, as if the Princess's request had a somewhat lighter note.

"We do not have much provision for ladies, that is certain. If you are willing I can send to Fittsdale for peasant clothing."

"Well enough. That they be fit for riding is all that is necessary. And you have an escort for us who knows these smugglers' ways?"

Now the Colonel laughed. "Indeed I do, Your Highness. We have held these hills so long that we know the four sides of every rock. And since the smugglers in question are bound for Leichstan and not for our side of the border, we have no ill will to fear."

But when he had left, Roane made one last attempt to break free from this current carrying her farther and farther into danger.

"I must go back!"

Ludorica shook her head, a smile on her lips.

"But, my dear Roane, indeed you must not! If what you said is true, that they will treat you ill for what you have done on my behalf, then all the greater reason not to. Also, suppose you are taken by Reddick's men—do not think that he will not use harsh means to learn all you can tell him. The mere fact that you are found in a Royal forest after my escape will make you suspect. You wear such clothing as is strange, carry mysterious tools and weapons— Yes, you would make a puzzle Reddick would work hard to solve, and the solving would not be to your comfort. We ride for Leichstan. And when the Crown is in my hands, then shall we in turn treat with your people. Never go to a bargaining, Roane, unless you have that on your side which is a mighty aid."

The Captain came to show them to his quarters in the third story of the tower, and there Ludorica announced they had better get what rest they could, since no one could guess how long the journey across the border might last. That she was as close a prisoner as if she now wore the collar and chain, Roane knew. There would be no slipping away from this place, unless she used her stunner freely. And then the chaos she would leave behind— She shook her head. She could do nothing but hope for the future.

She slept, and it was twilight when the Princess aroused her with a gentle shaking. On the floor sat a very large tub, into which Ludorica now poured steaming water.

"As a bath," the Princess remarked, "this is a primitive affair. But we are undoubtedly lucky in this time and place to have one at all."

She shed her clothing and stepped carefully into the tub, kneeling to splash its meager contents over her, rubbing with a bunch of rough fibers which left foaming streaks on her smooth skin.

"If you will pour the rest now—" Ludorica indicated another jug and Roane obeyed. The Princess arose and made good use of the towel her companion handed her.

"Now—if we empty this into that other—"

The Princess anchored the towel more firmly about her as they dumped the water into an outsize bucket and refilled the basin for Roane. Though this was far different from the more efficient freshers she had always known, she found it good. The soapy substance oozing from the matted fibers of the scrubber had a fresh, herbal odor she liked.

Ludorica sorted a pile of clothing, holding up one garment and then another to measure against her body. She laughed.

"Nelis has the name of being one who does not notice women too closely. But this is proof his cold reputation is not deserved. These are a good fit. We shall go reasonably well clad. Now—the brown for you, and I will take the blue."

Roane dressed in the unfamiliar clothes. They were clean, if creased, and to them, too, a good herb scent clung. There were no mirrors, but she thought the Princess right. These fitted well. The skirt was full, ankle length, and its folds felt odd against her legs so long used to coveralls. In contrast the bodice was tight, laced from belt to just under her throat with silken red strings. Embroidery of the same shade of red bordered those lacings. The dress itself was a pleasant yellow-brown. There was also a hooded cloak lined with red, and a close-fitting cap with a turned-back border, embroidered all over with small, very skillfully fashioned red feathers.

The Princess wore dark blue, her trimming a vivid green but otherwise differing none from Roane's. There was no cap for her. Instead she combed and braided her long hair, allowing the braids to lie free on her shoulders.

"Very good." She looked from Roane down along her own person, then back to Roane. "We eat now and then we ride. At least it is a clear night. Nelis thinks it will remain so, and he knows this country well enough to speak with authority."

They descended to the lower room, where the table was once more set with food, rounds of cold meat, bread, and fruit. The man who rose to greet them was not in uniform but wore a dusty gray suit, with a close-fitting cap which allowed only his face free, for it had a lower frill lapped about his neck, fastening under the chin.

"Nelis!" Ludorica seated herself in the chair he drew out for her. "You?"

He laughed. "Did I not tell you that I knew these hills well? Do you think I would let you ride them alone, Your Highness?" Then he became serious. "You will have your escort of picked men, men from my own stead. They own me overlord as well as field commander."

"But if Reddick learns you are gone, he may suspect—"

"We have worked out a scheme for that. Remember, you are lost out of Hitherhow. I am searching for you with a flying column and am thus hard to reach, very hard. As far as this company is concerned—though we can answer for their loyalty—they will march within the hour to patrol west of Granpabar, which is territory I do not think the Duke dares invade as yet—seeing as how the lord there has good reason to dislike him."

"Trust you, Nelis—" The Princess laughed, too.

"I hope you can, Your Highness," he cut in, still sober. "I hope you can! I understand your reasoning, and it was ever the way of your House to play boldly at need. But there are many ways this play can go wrong. Do not be too confident—"

"Which urging I have had from you many times in the past! No, there is something now which gives me confidence, Nelis. Reddick could not have foreseen the arrival of Roane to spoil his plan. So far every throw of the wish sticks has turned up in my favor. Oh"—she held up her hand when he would have spoken—"I cannot count on such fair fortune's continuing. But while it is with me, let us make the most of it, just as we shall now make the most of this most excellent food."

They were not, Roane discovered to her silent relief, expected to ride duocorns alone. She had never guided such a mount in her life, and to begin riding lessons now—there was no time.

To keep their cover of peasant women, who did not usually ride alone, she and the Princess must ride pillion, the Princess with the Colonel, Roane behind one of the other men. All wore the drab civilian dress. And under the cloak she still had her belt, which she determined to cling to. Possession of that gave her the feeling that she was still Roane Hume, not a stranger to herself also.

By dawn, after threading a maze of dusky valleys and scrambling up hillsides where they must dismount to walk their animals, they reached a pass through which the wind blew cruelly cold. Roane was glad of the cloak. Twice they had halted to let the third man of the party scout ahead. But there had been no alarms. And now the Colonel pointed down the slope before them.

"Leichstan, but Gastonhow lies a good eight leagues on. We shall have to rest and change mounts before we reach there."

"We cannot go to any inn," the Princess protested.

"Neither can we go far on worn-out duocorns," Imfry returned. "With those clothes you are of Reveny right enough, but many border families have kin on either side. There may well be a wedding to which we have been bid—"

"Not so! A wedding would have been far-cried. These people will know what chances even from hamlet to hamlet. It had better be a birthing, perhaps in a head homestead. We can pick straw for a babe garland as we go."

"It never ceases to amaze me, Your Highness, how you know all customs—"

"But it should not, kinsman. Of what use is any ruler to her people unless she understands their ways? Oh, I know that there is in some countries the odd belief that there is no common meeting point between king and subject. But that is not so with my House and never has been."

"A point which has kept your line safely enthroned."

"Until now! And then that dark shadow comes not

from my own people but from kin. And kin quarrels are always the most bitter."

But it seemed that the Princess's plan was not to be put into practice, for their scout returned with the news that a party was traveling the main road to the nearest inn and that he had recognized one face among the travelers.

"Kaspard Fancher!" the Princess repeated.

"I fear"—the Colonel had dropped his voice a little—"that our period of favoring fortune is over. Fancher is—"

"I know well what he is," Ludorica interrupted. "Which means that Reddick has given me credit for trying to reach King Gostar. But he also knows that I am not altogether stupid, however much he wishes that so. Very well. Fancher may be riding with all the support the Duke can raise for him, but Reddick is not yet King of Reveny, nor even close to the throne. I am the Princess, and Imbert Rehling was my father's good friend. He will smooth my path to Gostar, and Reddick cannot prevent that."

"If we reach Rehling—"

"The Court is at Gastonhow, so all ambassadors will follow. It is early in the season for such a move, but King Gostar cherishes this young second queen of his. The rumor has it that she may present him soon with a princeling—so he has brought her to drink the waters of the Faithwell."

"Superstition!"

"Perhaps—but then again perhaps not. There was a Guardian at the Faithwell; that has been attested to beyond any doubt. And also there have been many cases of women in difficult childbirth being soothed by its waters. Why, Gastonhow was built by Queen Marget because she feared to lose her fourth child, having three others die as she still lay in bed from the bearing of them. She stayed there during the major part of her time of carrying and thereafter bore five sons and three daughters with no ills."

"History! What does it matter now about Queen Marget? If the court is at Gastonhow and Fancher goes here, we must be very sure of our ground. Best send a messenger—"

"But why should we not just push on the faster to Gastonhow ourselves?"

"Not until I am sure what awaits us there."

"Sure of what? That Fancher is here to make what trouble he can? We know that. Lord Imbert will prevent him from seeing the King, and he cannot work mischief with Imbert himself. But—perhaps— Perhaps you are right, Nelis. It is better not to spoil our plans now for the want of a little caution. And I shall give the messenger that which will get him speedy speech with Lord Imbert." The Princess pulled at one of her long braids, breaking loose five hairs, which she counted carefully before she knotted them together. "Now a resuah leaf—"

"Games?" asked the Colonel.

"Games—with a purpose. But a game Lord Imbert will remember, for I shared it with him. It was when he came to me after my father was newly dead. He had taken me to his Lady Ansla—she who was High Lady of Kross in her own right—for the King would have me away from the Court as he ailed. Lord Imbert liked the old tales. He has ordered many of them collected from the Tork singers and copied out that they may not be forgotten. And one was of the Lost Lady of Innace. The geas which was laid on that lady was broken by leaf and hair. Yes, he will remember and listen to your man."

The Princess had been searching through the vegetation around and now made a swift pounce, catching up, earth-covered root and all, a plant with long narrow leaves. The largest of these leaves she twisted free, wrapping her knotted hair about it.

After their messenger departed, mounted on the duo-corn Imfry judged their best, they headed on at a much-curtailed pace. Here, close to the heights where they had crossed the border, the country was wooded, so that they had to turn into one of those overhung, branch-roofed lanes. And this brought them to a bridge which was more ornate and even wider than the road they had come, as if the latter had once been a more important thoroughfare than it now was. On the opposite side of that arch was a small single-story tower, built in the form of a triangle firmly wedded to the bridge. Even the two very narrow windows in it were wedge-shaped.

"Have you any way money?" Ludorica asked the Colonel. "I see this is a vow bridge."

"An old one. The vow must have long since been fulfilled."

"How can we know that? Have you money for the alms slit?"

He brought a small bag from the front of his tunic, passed it back to the Princess.

"Be sparing with that, Your Highness. I had no time to gather a fortune before we left."

She loosened the drawstring, felt within the bag, and pulled out a round of metal.

"A plume will suffice. We travel with clean hands and no malice at heart."

As they came to the three-cornered building, the Princess leaned from her pillion and tossed the coin into the open window near to hand.

"For the good of him who built the way, for the good of those who walk the way, for the good of the journey, and the good, surely, of its final ending," she intoned as if speaking some formula.

"His name"—she moved her forefinger through the air, tracing the curves and angles of some weather-worn carving on the wall—"was Niklas and he was lord of— The stead seal is too badly worn to read. But it is a good omen that we ride by one Niklas's favor!"

The road ahead was not concealed by drooping tree branches, but rather edged with hedge walls. It was wider, also, and the dust of its surface was slotted with wheel ruts and hoofprints, as if the road which joined from upriver brought more traffic.

No longer could the duocorns be kept to a steady trot. When their riders stopped urging them, they fell into an amble. The morning they had met in the pass was now well advanced. They had broken their fast in the hills but Roane was hungry again. And it seemed to her stiff body that they had been riding or walking for half a lifetime. Those with whom she traveled seemed to need little rest.

Suddenly Imfry reined in his mount, held up his hand. One of the duocorns blew and then was silent. Far off Roane heard it now—the sound of a horn, clear and carrying.

8

Roane stood at the window. Between her fingers she held caressingly the soft folds of the heavy curtain. She loved the feel of that, the strange luxury of the room behind her—it was like coming out of the cold to the warmth of a welcoming fire. As yet it was early morning, and no one seemed to stir in the great house. But there was life in the street before its tall courtyard gates.

A boy had come out of a shop, sprinkling down the cobbles before the door from a holed can which he sloshed back and forth without care, nearly sending its spray on the wide skirts of a passing woman. Those skirts were gray, with scarlet flowers bordering them, to match in vivid color the bodice of her dress. She walked with a free, swinging step, one hand raised to balance a basket on her head, its contents hidden by a covering of leaves.

She was only the first of a small procession of such wayfarers, their gray and scarlet almost a uniform, each with a basket aloft. The boy with the sprinkler cried out something and they turned smiling faces to him. It was all like watching a live tri-dee.

Roane remembered her impression of the house as they had come to it the night before. It was large, three stories high at least, all of stone, the windows on the lowest level being very narrow. There was no growing thing to break the drabness of the courtyard pavement, and the only spot of color was the symbol on the house face—she could see an edge of it from here—facing the gate, representing the might of Reveny.

She had not met the ambassador on whom Ludorica relied so much. In fact she had not even seen the Princess since they had entered a side door and been shown almost furtively through dark hallways by a single servant. Though she could not complain about the room in which she stood, nor the willing serving maid she had sent early away. Only—Roane felt uneasy as well as somehow charmed by her surroundings.

All of it had a dreamlike quality. Though in the beginning it had been more of a nightmare when that horn blast had sent them into quick hiding. There had been a troop of horsemen, and the identity of two of the riders had disturbed the Princess and the Colonel, though neither had explained why to Roane. Instead of pressing on themselves after that other party had passed, they had waited until nightfall. Then they had ridden hard, across fields many times, to reach a crossroads. There they were overtaken by a carriage, curtained at the windows, with four of the large draft duocorns to draw it.

Their messenger rode on the box beside the driver, and the letter he delivered to the Princess banished the shadow from her face. She waved it triumphantly before the Colonel.

"Did I not say so? Lord Imbert gives us good welcome—and certainly softer travel. Ah, I feel as old as the hills with every bone in my body aching to tell me so!"

The interior of the carriage was dark, but no one raised its curtains. Roane found it hardly more comfortable than riding, in spite of Ludorica's words. The swaying of the body on a sling of straps—which took the place of any springs—made her queasy. But her companions settled back against the cushions as if this were the height of comfort, and the Princess went to sleep, her head against Roane's shoulder.

Twice they stopped for fresh animals, and the second time a basket of cold but good food was handed in. Only Roane, hungry as she might have been under other circumstances, could but nibble and wish herself back in normal life.

They had come to Gastonhow in the middle of the night. And she had fallen half-dazed into the great curtained bed behind her. But for all her fatigue she had awakened early, as if she had been alerted by some inner alarm.

Now she turned from the window to view the room again, seeing much more than the limited lamplight had shown her.

The bed, which dominated the room, was extremely large, almost a quarter the size of a camp bubble. Having most of her life fitted into very narrow spaces, in camp, on board ship, she was not used to such freedom. It stood on a two-step dais and had four posts carved with flowers and leaves to support a canopy with curtains that Roane had not suffered the maid to draw about her, tent-fashion, the night before. Both the curtains and the cover on the bed were fancifully patterned by needlework.

All the colors were bright, almost too strident for her taste. The walls were boldly painted with designs in the same shades. There was a table with a wide mirror, a backless stool set before it, to her left. On her right stood a tall cupboard with double doors. And there were chairs, stools, and a smaller table or two scattered around.

She moved before the mirror to gaze at her reflection. The white folds of just such a night robe as the captive Princess had worn hung about her slim body. Against that her weathered hands and face looked very dark and brown. Her short hair had grown enough since she had left Cram-brief to form a fluff on her forehead and behind her ears. And that too was odd against her deep tan, for the locks were a pale yellow-brown which sometimes held a hint of red when the sun touched them.

By the standards of her own civilization Roane had no beauty and had early learned to accept that. And, since her roving life had taken her into the wilderness of unknown worlds, she practiced none of the cosmetic arts used by the women of the inner planets. Beside the Princess she was certainly very insignificant. How much so, she had not realized until now.

There was an array of pots and bottles on the table. Roane sat down eyeing them, wondering who had supplied these, what they held. Then, emboldened, she investigated. The first was a small yellow pot, very smooth to her fingers, lidded by a stopper fashioned as a half-opened flower. It contained a paste with a sweet smell. She ran a fingertip tentatively over it but had no idea what might be its use. As her explorations continued she made many guesses. There were smaller pots of red which perhaps colored lips or cheeks, though she had not seen anyone wearing the elaborate designs painted on forehead, cheek, or chin which were in high favor on some worlds. There was one narrow box of black stuff flanked by a tiny brush—and more beautifully shaped bottles and flagons, each of which held a sweet scent.

"My lady?"

Roane started and nearly dropped a delicate transparent bottle. Over her shoulder in the mirror she saw the maid carrying a tray on which rested a covered bowl and a cup.

Roane gave the morning greeting of Reveny. "Sun and a fair wind rising—"

"With thanks to you, Lady. Will you morn-sup now?"

There were berries in the bowl, intermixed with what seemed cooked grain, sweet contrasting with tart. The mug contained a thick, hot drink she could not identify. She was sipping at that when the door opened again and she faced the Princess.

Now Roane saw her in clothing becoming her station —the full-skirted dress of a deep green, with wide lace flecked with threads of silver turned back in cuffs, a collar of the same dew-and-cobweb material lying on her shoulders. The hair which had swung in braids during their journeying was now piled and pinned into an imposing structure on her head. There was about her such an air of consequence that Roane arose to pay her tribute.

"Roane." Ludorica did not move with a stately gait but sped across the room to catch the off-world girl's hands in hers. "We are safe here. And my good Lord Imbert has gone to speak to the King. Fortune has favored us. And once we see King Gostar—" She laughed. "Oh, Roane, you will enjoy it here! There will doubt-less be a ball—did I not say he had sons to be settled, and what better way can a gallant display than at a ball? And we will ride in the Brogwall in an open carriage as is the fashion and—and—and—"

The Princess could be any girl from one of the inner planets thirsting for pleasure. But Roane found she could not match the other's high spirits. And Ludorica must have quickly sensed her lack of response, for she lost some of her sparkle as she asked:

"What is it, Roane? Truly we are safe here, perhaps more so than in Reveny, until the full of Reddick's schemes be known. And you—you do not have to fear losing your memory or being shut in a prison. This is a day for a light heart, not a sober face. Or perhaps yours merely looks sober because you are still wearing a night robe. White is *not* a color which becomes you! But that is speedily remedied."

She pulled upon a bell rope and the maid returned, to scurry about under a rain of orders so quickly delivered, Roane was not sure of their number or kind.

It was later, when she sat once again looking into the mirror, that the dream seemed even stronger. There were drugs, forbidden drugs, which could do this to one, produce an alternate life for their user, so entrancing a life that he or she clung to the fantasy, fought return to reality. She had not used those and yet she was enmeshed—surely that reflection was not of any Roane Hume she knew.

The soft fabric of her gown was a shade of yellow, but woven in such a way that each fold as she moved was overcast by a hint of rose. Lace, not as wide or as ornate as that which bedecked the Princess, but still finer than any other she had ever seen, ruffled about her brown wrists, rose a little behind her head to make a fragile frame for her thin neck. Not for her the piling of hair, but rather a lace cap curving to a point over her forehead, from which folded back two wired wings, as if an alien bird had settled there.

And her face—they could not take away the browning that years of exposure had painted on her, but they had made knowing use of the contents of many pots and bottles. So that brown was enhanced, and she was vividly alive as she had never seen herself before. Viewing herself so, she gained the courage natural to her sex, the armor a woman dons by knowing she looks her best.

Ludorica clapped her hands and laughed. "My Lady Roane, but this is how you were always meant to look! Not to go in that ugly dress like a man. Why do you desire to look so plain when it is the true duty of any woman to look the best she can, no matter how the Guardians may have designed her face at birth?

Come now, you must learn to walk properly in skirts, my dear-like-a-man-that-was!"

Exiling her doubts to the back of her mind, Roane followed the Princess. They came out into a wide hall, one side of which was hung with panels of needlework between other strips painted in the same bright colors which had lightened the bedroom. The other wall had windows, four of them set out in bays. And those windows were checkerboarded with clear and colored glass, the colored being wrought in complicated patterns. Overhead the ceiling was molded in balls and leaves in high relief, those also painted. And at the far end was a large fireplace, while at intervals down the length of the hall were braziers of metal on tripod legs, from several of which curled scented smoke.

There was no one in that hall, neither servant nor master. But when they went through the door at the far end and came to a staircase a man did appear, to stand at the foot of the stair awaiting them.

He uncovered his head (for he had been wearing a soft flat hat of colorful stuff with a big ornament of gold) as the Princess descended, and bowed. His clothing was richly trimmed with metallic embroidery and he fitted well with his surroundings.

"Your Highness—"

He was middle-aged and had allowed his facial hair to grow, a custom new to Roane, who knew only spacers, who went with smooth cheeks and sometimes even totally denuded heads so that space helmets would fit the better. But the lower part of his face was masked by wiry gray hair.

"My dear lord." The Princess held out her hand. "You must meet my good companion, the Lady Roane Hume. Roane, this is Lord Imbert, who gives us shelter in our troubles."

He bent his head to kiss the Princess's hand. Then he turned a searching glance on Roane, one she found disturbing though she met him eye to eye.

"I am honored, my lord." Gathering up the full folds

of her skirt with either hand, she essayed what she hoped was a passable curtsy. She was not too graceful. And those eyes watching her had in them that which daunted her confidence.

"We have much to be grateful to you for, my lady, we of Reveny." Unlike his stern and rather colorless outward appearance, his voice was warm and rich. Roane's first estimate of him changed. When he spoke it was as if another person awoke behind the mask he presented to the world. "We have our Princess safe, and all who serve her now are very welcome."

He bowed again with a smile. But when she watched him without listening to his voice, Roane felt a chill in his manner. Words could provide screens for thoughts. Though the Princess valued Lord Imbert Rehling so highly, Roane did not feel for him that trust the Colonel inspired in her.

"You are very kind." Her words sounded feeble. The stately language of Reveny was so foreign to the clipped Basic of her own people that Roane found it difficult to use it readily.

"We are going to view your garden, my lord." Ludorica smiled at him with a sparkle in her eyes. "What I have seen from the window of my bedchamber promises well—"

"Your Highness"—his voice took on a deeper timbre —"such a faring would not be wise at this time."

"A walk in the garden not wise? But why?"

"Your Highness, as you know, Fancher is in the city. And the Soothspeaker Shambry as well. You yourself saw them both traveling hither."

"But this is Gastonhow and the Embassy of Reveny under the mastership of my best of friends, Lord Imbert Rehling himself," she countered. "What have we to fear from Fancher, a man without any lord here in Leichstan? As for the Soothspeaker, yes, we saw him. But what has he to do with us, or Reveny?"

"It would seem something," Lord Imbert began and then glanced at Roane, as if he willed her withdrawal.

Perhaps that was the fashion of the court, but she did not pretend to be more than she was, a stranger caught up by chance in their ways. She stood where she was and the Princess said impatiently:

"Do you speak openly—the Lady Roane knows all."

He shrugged and continued. "Very well, Your Highness. The Soothspeaker has foretold King Niklas's death to the exact hour."

She sobered instantly. "How much value can we put to his words? No, I will not ask you that, my lord. We all have our own opinions of such gifts or talents. And Shambry has foretold with remarkable success on several occasions. Though I have heard—less loudly—that he has also had his failures. To foresay the King's death, however—he must be very sure to do that. But why comes he out of Reveny into Leichstan? Unless—"

Ludorica looked down at her own hands as if she held there something very precious the others could not see. "Unless he would be out of Reveny before his foreseeing can be proved. What excuse does he give for coming?"

"That he has matters of great moment for King Gostar which will affect the future of his House, and that he was bidden by his gift to come."

"By his gift! Then he is very sure—"

"Just so," cut in Lord Imbert. "And it is against all custom for him to be so persistent. He has lately been at Ichor, and the Lady of Ichor—"

"Was once Reddick's very dear friend. But surely here, well guarded in your house, my lord, I need not fear any web to entangle my feet. Why, you yourself said to Nelis that he could leave us here and go with a free mind. Why, if you had these reservations, did you say that?"

"For the simple reason, Your Highness, that this news had not yet come to my ears when the Colonel rode forth. And it is best also that he return to his command, for if your journey has not yet been discovered, his return will help to keep it secret."

"A secret? I did not think that here—" She hesitated and then continued. "But let me see King Gostar and all will move as we wish."

"There, too, you must practice patience, Your Highness. The Queen is not in good health and King Gostar is much concerned about her. He is never at the best an easy man to deal with. Rather is he sometimes prey to odd whims and sudden changes of mind, so that no one can predict what he will do. For the past three months, since he learned the Queen is carrying a child, he has not even been to the secret sanctuary of the Flame Crown for guidance.

"He will receive no delegations from the council and has refused his ministers audiences. Even to reach him with a message may take some time."

"And time we may have in scant supply!"

"I understand, Your Highness. But I am being frank with you. We shall have to approach the King with care. An incautious move on our part may arouse him to refusal before we even state the case. He has done such many times, more times even than his people have general knowledge of. Now—you will note, Your Highness, that you have seen few servants in this wing of the house. That, too, is on purpose. The fewer who know that you are here, until I have some understanding with the King, the better. For we have not only to fear his changeable tempers, but also interference, perhaps directly from Fancher, indirectly from Shambry—or so I suspect.

"The Queen is much taken with foreseeing and there is good reason to believe that once she knows Shambry is here she will have him summoned to read for her. Once gaining her attention, he could defeat us with ease. For he is a subtle man with more to him than the usual Soothspeaker. He already tells the day and hour of His Majesty's death with confidence. What if he adds to that some direful word concerning yourself? Could you then get a fair hearing for your plea? Ill luck is too real a thing to most kings and lords."

"What hour and day—no, I do not want to know lest I begin to believe it too. So I can do nothing but wait?"

"Hard as it seems, Your Highness, that is so. And not only wait with good grace, but also stay within these walls and let none have a chance to see you. You thought yourself safe at Hitherhow, and what happened? I have guards here, but how can I swear that all of them, and of my servants, are true to the old loyalty and that none of them secretly supports Reddick?"

"It is hard to believe," Ludorica said slowly. "I feel, as one trying to cross the Bog of Snelmark, that any step may be the wrong one. But suppose the King—" She turned a little away. "Very well—tell me, how long does this smooth-tongued Soothspeaker give him yet?"

"Four days—until high noon."

"Four days! And he would not dare to make such a prophecy if he were not sure it would be proved true. Four days, and if I am not back to Urkermark by then with the Crown— I must consider this carefully, Lord Imbert."

"Do so, Your Highness. In the meantime, for your own sake, keep within these walls and out of sight. What I can do to reach King Gostar, and there are several ways that can be tried, that I shall do."

He left them with another bow and the Princess turned to Roane. "It would seem that we cannot enjoy the garden except through a window. But that we can do in the gallery. Come aloft again."

They returned to the long upper chamber and Ludorica brought Roane to the middle bay so they could look out. There were few flowers below, rather hedges and shrubs trimmed and clipped into fanciful shapes, many resembling the statues which had been set out at Hitherhow before the Princess's arrival.

"It is very well kept," commented Ludorica. "One has the feeling that were even a single leaf misplaced such would be instantly noted. Lord Imbert has a liking for such formality. There is a large garden such as this about his stead keep in Reveny. The Lady Ansla never cared much for it. She had her own place and the sweetest-smelling flowers grew there. Also a pond with an erand nesting, and the bird used to stand so still in the water one would believe her a statue—"

"The Lady Ansla—she is here?"

"She is gone." The Princess did not look away from the window. "It was the frost fever. I did not even get to put the fareforth candle in her hand—though she had been so good to me. When I came she was already closed away. I think that when I was small she was the only one who cared for me, Ludorica, and not because I was the Princess."

Though they could not go out into that stiff garden, nor even out of the section of rooms which had been made over to them, they found enough to occupy their time. Ludorica amused herself and Roane (to the latter's mild astonishment) by coaching her temporary lady-in-waiting in the duties of her position and furnishing her with the current gossip of the Court of Reveny—though due to the King's age and illness Court life had shrunk to a few shadowy functions and those only observed through necessity. Roane absorbed it even as she had the learning at Cram-brief, but found it more interesting. The Princess's description of the nobles and courtiers, their backgrounds and motives, were so detailed that the off-world girl thought she would know each when she met him—*if* she ever met him.

Deep in Roane herself something began to grow. She would smooth the soft flow of her skirts, glance now and then into a mirror, finger some cushion glowing with beautiful needlework or an ornament. All this was far different from the treasures of her own civilization, yet surrounded by such she was not ill at ease nor unhappy, but rather relaxed. If she was dreaming, she wished less and less to awake. At least, as she reflected with dry humor, if she ever got back to her own people she could supply enough data on this Psychocrat experiment from the point of view of those caught in it to amaze the Service.

On their second night at Gastonhow she was sitting in front of the mirror about to unpin the birdlike bonnet when Ludorica slipped into the room, a long, fur-lined cloak over her arm, her eyes alight with excitement.

"Imbert has done it! I am to go to King Gostar secretly. But not alone, Roane—Lord Imbert thinks you should be with me, that you can bear witness about the tower and your testimony will carry force. Hurry—there is a coach waiting. Where is a cloak?"

She opened the wardrobe and rummaged among its contents. Roane hurried to the bed, to her private hiding place. She felt under the wide pillow and drew out her belt with its off-world equipment. Even temporarily she was not going to be separated from that.

9

The coach awaiting them in the dark courtyard was like the one which had fetched them to Gastonhow. As then, heavy curtains hung in place across the windows, and in the light of a single lantern the interior looked very dark. Lord Imbert himself stood to hand them in, and he murmured something in a very low voice to the Princess before putting out his hand to Roane as she tried to manage the folds of her skirts on the small step.

There was no Colonel to share their ride this time, but the cushions were softer than those of the equipage which had brought them to Gastonhow. The door closed and they were in the total dark, for there was no riding lantern.

"No light!" Apparently the Princess found this strange, but then she added, "I suppose Imbert wishes us to be as inconspicuous as possible."

"Where do we go?" Roane pulled her cloak about her. The evening was chill and there was a cold which seemed part of the coach itself, as if the vehicle had not been recently in use.

"To Gastonhigh. It is a stead used by the royal family—by Immer Lake. I suppose the Queen wishes more quiet."

A swing of the coach sent Roane against the Princess and she heard Ludorica laugh.

"My dear Roane, feel along the wall and you shall find a hold strap. It is best to make use of those when the pace is swift."

Roane groped for the anchor, running her hand over the side she could not see, though now and then came a faint glimmer of light around the edge of the curtain, as if they drove by some well-lighted site. She found the loop and took firm hold on it, but she wished they could raise the curtains, just so she did not have the impression that they were imprisoned in a jiggling, swaying cage. And once more her stomach rebelled against this form of travel.

"My mother was King Gostar's cousin," the Princess said. "I wish I knew on what terms they were. It might strengthen my appeal if they had parted in friendship when she went to Reveny to wed. If he had kind memories of her—"

"Is there any reason why he would not?" Roane asked.

"There are feuds not only among the stead lords, but also in the royal Houses. Am I not so caught with Reddick? And the House of Hillaroy, which is King Gostar's, have been noted for their quick tempers and many strange actions, even as Imbert has warned us about Gostar. It would seem that since the Guardians cut communication with men there have been many changes in the course of history. Only when we hold the crowns can we be sure of surviving such changes. I must get the Crown! At least Nelis will do what he can to further the search."

"You sent the Colonel to hunt the Crown?" Roane tensed. What would that mean for Uncle Offlas and Sandar? If a large party of Revenian troops showed up to prospect along the cliffs and so meet the men from the camp— She could see such trouble as had never disgraced a Service operation before. Why, they might even have to lift off!

"He knows the country, and him I can trust. If he moves in boldly, Reddick cannot face him, since I do not believe that until the King is dead the Duke will dare to come into the open."

"But the Crown—I thought you wanted to keep others from knowing it was hidden."

"No one shall. For Nelis will wait for me to take it up. None can touch the Crown save me. Nelis is only to find the way to it."

But what of her own people? Roane thought of them and clung to her strap anchor as the coach rocked on. They must now be traveling at the fastest pace this vehicle was capable of maintaining.

"King Gostar must be impatient," she commented. "It would seem that he wants us in a hurry, or is this the usual speed of a royal coach?"

The pace grew even faster. In spite of that anchor loop she was shaken back and forth, and she gulped and swallowed with grim determination not to yield to the queasiness of her much-abused interior.

"This—is—too—fast—" The Princess's words came in little gasps as if shaken out of her. "What can they be—"

There came still another burst of speed and the swing of the coach was such that Roane was sure she could not stand it long before disgracing herself by being thoroughly sick. She held her free hand over her mouth and fought for control.

"What—" The Princess's voice rose a note. "Roane!" And now her cry was a danger alert. "Feel alone the edge of the window if you can. Are you able to raise the curtain?"

Roane tried, but found it difficult. Finally her groping hand did touch what she judged was the edge of the curtain. But that did not yield to her tug. It was rather as if it had been nailed or otherwise sealed in place.

"It is the same on this side! The curtains are fastened down. Now, Roane, can you lean forward, find the latch of the door?"

It seemed perilous to try that. Roane feared that if she loosed her finger-cramping grip of the anchor strap, she might be thrown against the narrow seat facing her. But she stretched and, between more and worse jolts which sent her back and forth, ran her other hand over the inner surface of what she was sure was the door. There was no latch, nothing but a smooth surface. And her fear of a trap added to her sickness until she longed to scream for them to stop. Then came another spell of really violent rocking.

"I—cannot—find— It—is all—smooth!" she gasped.

"Nor—can—I—on—this—side—"

"But why—" Roane began when Ludorica answered her.

"Why? Because we are prisoners. But of whom? Lord Imbert? No—unless he feels he must manage me for some reason he has not told me. But I can guess, Roane, that we are not now bound for Gastonhigh."

"Where—" Roane was thrown back by a particularly heavy jolt and cried out at a sharp pain in her side.

"What is it?"

"My—but how stupid! I have a light." The belt she had brought with her, how had she come to forget it? That lapse of memory was another symptom of the fuzzy thinking which had bothered her for days. It was almost as if she did not want to, or could not, remember the familiar things which had been a part of her off-world life. With one hand she worked the beamer out of its loop and turned it on low.

"The doors!"

But she did not need that direction; she had already turned the light on the one through which they had entered. And her exploration by touch had told the truth. There was no sign of a latch. When she moved the beam up to the windows they could see the strips of wood which sealed the curtains down.

"We are prisoners until we arrive and they—whoever they may be—are willing to let us out. But our future hangs on who is behind this—"

"Reddick?"

"Not with Imbert aiding—unless there had come a message purporting to be from the King. Or a substitution of coaches, or— We could offer as many reasons as we have fingers and perhaps still skip the real one. It suffices that we are prisoners, and the reason is less important now than the fact. What other tools or weapons have you that may get us out of here?" As usual she went directly to the most important matter.

"I have this beamer, and a medic kit, and a weapon." Roane thought of the stunner. "It does not wound, only puts to sleep the one caught in its ray—"

"Such a weapon as your cousin used on me in the cave? But how clever of you to have brought that, Roane! We need only wait until they let us out and then you can put them to sleep and—"

"I shall do what I can," Roane said slowly. What she did not want to admit was that disturbance which came upon her when she had to make a choice between off-world and Clio matters, and which she now felt. She had used the beamer without really thinking, but to handle the stunner so was a differt matter— Never before had she experienced anything like this. Or had she? Conditioning! She had gone through conditioning on numerous occasions—mainly to prepare body and mind to resist some planetary stress hostile to her species. But once that was done she had never been consciously aware of its effects upon her. Now it was as if her mind, when turned in certain directions, worked more slowly, and she shrank from off-world weapons—weapons fashioned to repel aliens from their use.

To prove this point to herself, she held out the beamer to the Princess. "If you will hold this—".

Then Roane laid her hand upon the butt of the stunner, although she did not draw it. And she had to force herself to move. Her fingers shrank from touching the smooth metal. By the Tongue of Truth, what had happened to her? The cover which kept such a weapon inviolate on another world was operating against *her!* She was frightened as she had never been before in her life. Ludorica must have read that emotion in her expression, for she asked quickly:

"What is it? What is the matter?"

"It is nothing," Roane said quickly. The Princess was entirely too sharp-eyed, and she must not let her suspect—the more so when she did not know the truth herself. "The rocking—it makes me sick."

Ludorica grimaced. "I have traveled often by coach, though it is better to ride mounted, but never at such a wild pace. I, too, would like to—"

What she might have said was never uttered, for the gallop began to abate and the swing became less violent. They slowed and came to a halt.

"Be ready," the Princess ordered. She still held the beamer, training it on the door to shine full in the face of whoever opened it. Roane forced herself to ready the stunner.

But nothing happened. They listened closely and could hear, very muffled by the walls, a faint jangling. Only the door did not open.

"I think we are changing duocorns!" the Princess said. "A fresh team, which means a longer journey. Already we are far past the distance to Gastonhigh."

She must have been right, for only moments later

there was a shudder through the coach and they were on the move again, first easily and then back to the rocking run which shook them so. Roane stowed away both stunner and beamer, not wanting to exhaust the charge in the latter. She was battered, sore, as if she had been beaten and bumped. But mercifully that second pounding did not last long. Once more they slowed to what was hardly more than a walking pace. The coach body tilted at an angle which suggested that they climbed. The Princess spoke again:

"We return to Reveny."

"How can you tell?"

"This is hill country and the only hills close to Gastonhow are those of the border. Now there are only two possibilities as to who will meet us—some representative of the King, or Reddick!"

"But you think the latter."

"Imbert must have been tricked. Yes, it will be best for us to expect the worst. I was foolish indeed—"

Either the dark which had held them for so long was lightening a little or else their eyes had adjusted. Roane could now make out the outline of her companion braced beside her on the seat.

"Fancher and the Soothspeaker—and how many others, some planted certainly in Imbert's own household as he suspected. But even he could not have thought how deep their plans ran. Nelis—we can depend upon Nelis. Perhaps we shall have a chance after all. It rests now on where they take us."

The Princess was quiet and Roane believed she must be weighing one chance against another. She had respect for Ludorica's courage, endurance, and wits. But even those three in combination could not bring her safely out of some kinds of disaster.

It was time, surely it was time, for Roane to begin to think of herself. She had the stunner, against which on Clio there was no defense, and with it she could break free from any party ready to greet their arrival.

Then, back to camp—if camp still existed and Uncle Offlas had not gone off-world.

The toiling of the coach became even more labored, and then its climbing slant leveled and it stopped. Again no one came to the door. There was a wait, during which they became fully aware of all their aches and bruises. When they started on, it was plain that they were now going downhill—luckily at a very slow pace or they would have been flung forward against the other seat. The slope of the road they followed must be steep. It did level out later, so that they rode in more comfort, and the light seeping in around the curtains grew stronger.

"It is full day. And we must cross the border soon. If we pass a gatehouse—" Then Ludorica shook her head. "No, they would not risk such passage unless they have good reason to believe this carriage will not be inspected. Yet this must be the main highway. A coach could not travel a lesser road. They must have a good plan—" She stopped so short that Roane turned to look at her.

The furred hood of the Princess's cloak had fallen back, her head was a little forward, and she was staring at the coach wall directly ahead. Roane followed the direction of that survey.

From some crack there puffed a thread of white vapor. Roane caught the taint of a new odor against the musty closeness of the atmosphere.

"They—they drug us! That is upus smoke!"

Ludorica dropped her hold on the anchor strap, threw herself at the wall, holding a fold of her cape over the inflow of white. But it was little use—there were two more spirals at opposite sides. They could not hope to stop them all. Roane's own move was not to try to hold out the menace but to force her belt into as small a package as she could.

Squirming about, she got up the heavy folds of her skirt and fastened the belt under it, though her fingers worked slower and slower and her head spun so that she had to fight to finish that job. Her last view of the Princess was of Ludorica sliding down the wall of the coach, away from the vent she had tried to cover, to lie upon the seat. And a moment or two later Roane followed her into the same unconsciousness.

She was warm, too warm. This was like lying under the desert sun of Cappadella. Roane stirred, brought up a hand to shield her face, her eyes, from the bite of the sun. But she did not lie on sand. Fabric of some kind drew and wrinkled under her as she moved. She opened her eyes.

Above her was dark wood, while across her face a bar of sunshine nearly blinded her. She turned her head fretfully. Her mouth was dry; her lips stuck together, and she parted them with difficulty. She wanted water, more than she ever had in her life, even in the desert country the sun reminded her of.

In the rays of the sun, on a small bench not too far away, stood a flagon. The shape of it promised what she needed so badly. Roane pulled herself up. Movement was a trial of strength, for she needed all the force of her will to make her body obey. She braced herself on stiff arms, her attention all for the flagon which might hold water.

Swinging her feet to the floor was an exhausting effort. She did not even dare to try to stand, but instead fell to her hands and knees and crawled toward that bench. She raised her dead-weight hands and somehow forced the fingers to close upon the sides of the flagon, pulling it toward her, tipping it so that its contents did splash, not only into her gaping mouth, but across her chin and down the front of her dress. The moisture in her mouth brought her farther out of the daze. She sat on the floor, the flagon still between her hands, and looked about.

The room was small with a single window, across which was a screen of bars. The walls were stone. The bed from which she had crawled lacked any ornament and beside it, on another bed, lay Ludorica.

The Princess's cloak trailed half off her, her face was flushed, and she breathed with a puffing sound, clear to hear now that Roane had time to note it. Even as the off-world girl watched, she stirred, flinging out her arm as if to ward off some danger in a none-too-pleasant dream. And she murmured words Roane could not distinguish.

The small beds and the bench on which the flagon had stood were the only furnishings. There was a door opposite the beds. It had metal banding across it and a lock plate as large as Roane's palm. She had no doubts that if she managed to reach it she would find it securely fastened. There was no question that they were prisoners. But of whom and where?

Carefully she put the flagon back on the bench and struggled to her feet. Her head swam and she closed her eyes, fighting vertigo. From the bench she lurched in the direction of the window, bringing up against that opening. But at least she kept her feet.

What she saw below was a courtyard with a wall around it, a solid gate fastened by a bar. Beyond that wall showed the green tops of trees, and yet farther away were rises of heights not unlike those about Hitherhow. Hope glimmered in her. If they were in that country she could find her way back to camp.

"Hot—thirsty—" The murmur from the bed brought Roane around, holding to the wall for support as she moved.

The Princess struggled up. She was pulling at the lacing of her bodice as if to loosen it. The delicate lace of her collar was crumpled and her fine dress smeared with dust and badly creased.

Roane preserved her balance as best she could, made for the bench, and then to the bedside with the flagon. She held it with both hands for the Princess to drink.

Ludorica drank, sucking with the same desperate

need Roane had known. And when she signified she had had enough, there was very little left.

Now the Princess surveyed the room. Her eyes fixed upon the window and she wriggled off the bed, wavered to the wall, and inched her way to that opening, catching the bars with her hands. Roane joined her.

"Do you know where we are?"

Ludorica did not look around as she answered.

"As to where we are exactly I cannot say. But that peak"—she loosed her right hand to point—"I know. It is within a half league of Hitherhow. And I think we must be on some minor stead—perhaps Famslaw—so it is Reddick after all."

"You mean this is his land?"

"Land of close kin. But how—" Then she gave a little gasp. "Look there!"

At one side of the courtyard very close to the wall was a coach with a brilliant device painted on its door. It had carefully curtained windows, and although there were no harnessed duocorns and no coachman, Roane was certain it was the one which had brought them here.

"The coach—" she began.

"Of course! But that symbol—on its door—"

Roane could not understand the importance of that but the Princess was continuing:

"That is Lord Imbert's own! No coach with that on it would be stopped at the border. That was how they got us across."

"Wait—" Roane's memory stirred. She thought back to the dusky courtyard at Gastonhow, when Lord Imbert had handed them into what was to become a prison. She had seen the door in the lantern light; there had been no design then—or else it had been covered in some manner. "That was not on the door before."

"What does it matter? It served its purpose."

From somewhere over their heads there was a sharp call, which was answered by a horn note. And that fanfare was answered in turn by activity. Men appeared in the courtyard. They wore green or gray and fell into two lines at attention while two of their number ran to draw the gate bar.

"How dare he?" demanded Ludorica.

"What is it?"

The Princess turned a flushed face to Roane. Her eyes were wide and there was about her such an aura of barely leashed anger that Roane was glad it was not she who had aroused that emotion in her companion.

"That is the royal call! No one but those of the Blood dare use it. It is my call—*mine*—by birth alone. I am heiress to Reveny—there is no other!"

The gates opened and once more the call sounded close and loud, as the trumpeter himself rode through. Over his tunic he wore a loose-sleeved coat stiff with metallic lacing, one half red, one yellow. Behind him came a second rider wearing a yellow uniform tunic, his hat hiding his face. But the breath came out of the Princess in a furious hiss.

"Reddick! And he rides behind the heir's own herald! Treachery, black treachery!" Her hands closed and wrung upon the bars as if she would pluck them out of their stone setting and hurl them spear-fashion at her cousin.

10

Roane pressed against the iron-barred door, her ear laid to its surface, but she heard only the pounding of her own heart. She longed for one of the snoop devices of stellar civilization. Even time she could not measure, but she thought it had been a long interval since they had come for the Princess, leaving her here alone.

Ludorica had gone willingly, apparently only too eager to face her kinsman-jailer, as if that royal trumpet had carried her in flaming anger over the border of caution. Roane had been startled by that response, since she had looked upon the Princess as able to keep a cool head.

Only this was no quarrel of hers. Since Ludorica had left, Roane was able to see the whole situation in proper proportion. She had only one duty, to get out of this strongbox and back to camp. And the Princess had given her that mountain as a guide.

However, there was escape from this room, the keep itself, to negotiate first. Without any tools but a stunner and a beamer, how could she do it? For a second time she knelt on the floor to examine the lock. This type was archaically simple, of course. She could force it if she had proper tools. But there was nothing useful in her precious belt, nothing in this masquerade on her back (the clothes she had enjoyed so much when she put them on, now crumpled and soiled, made her impatient for her coverall). Her cloak and the Princess's lay on the bed. Roane went back to run her hands over fur and fabric—and so discovered that Ludorica's hood had a stiff support to hold the fur in place.

Roane picked at the seam, finally, with her teeth, breaking the threads at one end. She pushed and pulled until she held a length of wire. With this in hand she returned to the door.

The sun which had awakened her was gone from this side of the keep, and the hills were throwing long, dusky shadows out to clutch at the walls. Her jailers had brought her a plate of bread and dried meat when they had taken away the Princess, and she had eaten all of that. They had not been near her since.

Roane crouched, listening. Sounds at last. But not from beyond the door—rather in the courtyard. She ran to the window. Duocorns saddled and ready. Four men—seven mounts. Lanterns were lit to banish the dusk.

Out of a portal immediately below her issued a party of three. One was Reddick, by his uniform, and he came with one hand around the Princess's wrist, though she moved without a struggle toward the waiting mounts. The other man was dressed in dark colors and had a cloak collar up about his throat, a peaked hood pulled over his head.

He held his hands at breast level stiffly before him and between them something glinted in the lantern light. When they came to the duocorns, he swung around to face the Princess. What he held so carefully he raised to eye level before her. And at the same time Roane caught faintly his voice intoning words she could not distinguish.

Reddick boosted the Princess into the saddle, where she sat quietly. But the reins of her duocorn he kept in his own hand. And as the gate bar was withdrawn and they rode out he continued to lead the Princess's mount. Then the gate closed behind them.

Roane could only guess at the meaning of what she had seen. It was apparent that they had the Princess under some kind of control. She had seen too many like scenes in the past. But how they had achieved that (save that it must have something to do with the object the man held) she did not know. At any rate, their going left Roane on her own, to make her break for freedom.

Waiting was always hard. She kicked and pulled at her hampering skirts as she paced back and forth. These would be a hazard to her. Perhaps somewhere in this pile of stone she could find more suitable clothing.

She had no lamp and as soon as the dusk was thick enough, she knelt again at the door to begin her delicate manipulation with the wire. A job such as this needed patience. She had to keep her mind and hands under control as she worked. But at last there was a click and she edged the barrier open a little at a time,

relieved to see there was no show of light on the other
side. She slipped through and shut the heavy door
carefully behind her. This was a narrow hall with two
other doors. Beyond was a stairhead. Even as she stood
listening, able now to hear muted noises made by other
inhabitants, the click of approaching footsteps rang an
alarm in her mind.

Roane crossed to the doorway nearly facing that
from which she had come. To her great relief, that
yielded under her push so she could step within. A
flash of the beamer showed her a room like that she
had quitted. She turned to watch the hallway through
a narrow crack.

The newcomer had reached the head of the stair, a
man wearing the uniform of those who had ridden with
Reddick. He carried in one hand a small tray on which
rested a dish and another water flagon. A lantern swung
in his other hand.

As he came to the door of her late prison, he put
down the lantern, fumbled at his belt for a thong on
which were strung several large keys. Roane aimed
the stunner at his head and pressed the button. He
crumpled to his knees without a cry, then slid forward
on the floor.

Kicking angrily at her skirts, she ran to him. He was
not too large to handle and she dragged him into the
room. The flagon had fallen on the floor, most of its
contents leaking into a pool, but she drank what was
left and scooped up from the dish a round of coarse
bread and meat, chewing as she went out, set the
dishes inside, locked the door.

Then she sped back to the other room, where she
had seen a promising heap of clothes, untidy on a
chest. To get rid of these skirts and be able to move
with ease again! The fit was bad; the owner of her
new wardrobe was a much larger and heavier person.
But she drew the jerkin tight about her with her precious belt inside, rolled up the sleeves, stuffed material
torn from an underskirt in the toes of the boots to make

them fit. There was one of those hood caps which let only her face show, and she pinned its laps under her chin. Her discarded clothing she thrust within the chest.

The lantern still stood beside the other door and she was vexed that she had forgotten it. Perhaps it would be wise to take it along. With stunner at the ready and the lantern in her other hand, Roane sped to the stairs and looked down. There was another hall below with dim lighting. And she could hear the sound of voices and smell cooking, though that odor was none too appetizing. Her good fortune had held so far. She could only gamble it would continue.

For all her efforts her boots sounded on the steps and she was alert to any movement below. If she had to leave by the huge barred gate— But surely there were easier ways than that! She would even dare the wall if she had to.

The lower hall led to an open archway. To her right there was a door, firmly closed, which she hoped opened on the courtyard. Roane blew out the lantern, set it on the floor, and went to that closed portal. With infinite care she slid the locking bar out of its hooks, fearing at any moment that some one of those in the room ahead beyond the arch would notice her.

Five men sat at a table eating, while another moved back and forth bringing fresh supplies of food and drink. Roane balanced the bar against her for a moment, then set it carefully against the wall and tugged at the door.

The fresh air of night met her, dispelling much of the fugginess of the hall. It took only a minute to slip through and close the door behind her. Now— She lingered in the shadow to survey the courtyard. That coach was still pulled close to the wall at her left. Beyond were stables—she could both smell them and hear the stamp of duocorns.

Though she studied the top of the wall and the tower behind her, she could not spot any watchman. But she dared not count that such a one did not exist. Her attention kept going back to the coach. If it were as close to the wall as it seemed, could she use it as a ladder to reach the top? But to get down the other side— She would need a rope. Harness—such as was still draped over the carriage shafts? She darted over to those.

To climb into the driver's seat was easy enough. Roane hunkered on that, watching for any sentry on the walls. The bulk of the tower showed several faintly glowing windows, but the evening gloom was thick enough to hide the carriage roof.

Once more she slid to the ground and fingered the harness. The buckles were easy enough to loosen and reclasp, and by careful work (she made herself go slowly, to test the strength of what she did and for fear of noise) she had at last a length tougher than rope, which she thought would support her weight. With this coiled about her shoulder she again sought the seat of the carriage.

There was still a space to climb and the smooth wall offered no holds. For a moment Roane was baffled, and then she investigated the uses of her present perch. There was the cushioned seat, which could be upended to lean out against the wall. But, could she balance on the upper end of that?

The wall above—but of course! There was a stand-ard-pole there, one of a pair, the other on the far side of the gate. No banner flew now, but it would provide anchorage if she could just throw—

Roane stood on the denuded seat of the carriage by the unsteady bridge of the cushion. She whirled the weighted end of the strap rope around her head and sent it flying. Up and out it went, to clang against the wall with a sound which, to Roane, was like a thun-derclap. But it did dangle there, and it had encircled the pole above.

She must move fast, reach that dangling end before the cushion bridge could turn under her feet. She poised and leaped, one end of the strap in her left hand, her right reaching for the other.

She had been correct in fearing the instablility of the bridge; it gave way. But not before she had grasped the other end of the strap to which she clung. Fortunately, the cushion sank only a little, not so much that she was left hanging with her full weight on her outstretched arms. Bringing both ends of the strap together, Roane climbed, struggling over the edge, hardly believing she managed it without disaster.

To slide down the far side was much easier. And when a flick of her wrist brought the strap down to her, Roane coiled it around her body. She could still make out in the dusk the peak the Princess had said was a landmark. There was a road running in that direction, not one of the tree-and-brush-hidden lanes, but a clear cut through the forest. Her best move would be to keep to that, ready to take to cover if she met any other traveler.

The route was not too deeply rutted and the footing was secure enough. She set out with a ground-covering pace she had learned long ago. Now that she was out of that prison, she must plan ahead. To get back to camp, if the camp was still there, was, of course, the first step. If Uncle Offlas could learn what would happen—that the seekers of the Crown would be close to their find—

Roane's thoughts veered. The Princess—where had she gone with Reddick and for what purpose? Surely Ludorica had been under some compulsion, though she had walked to her mount and had ridden out docilely enough.

Ludorica had her problems, but Roane had hers also. These were no longer the same. Again Roane was puzzled. Why had it been so important all the time she was with the Princess that Ludorica be helped in any manner Roane could devise? And now—why did she feel as if released from some tie?

Had all the imprudent and ill-considered (from the

point of view of the Service) actions of the last few days come from the fact that she had been the Princess's companion? And why, when that companionship had been broken had the strange influence of Reveny's heiress gone? Was it something in her own temperament which made her more receptive to suggestion?

Roané had had enough training in forms of communication, briefing, and controls, as practiced by both men and machines, to know that such an influence might exist and that it could be part of the mystery of Clio. In some very old civilizations, even in the dim past of her own before it had left its native planet to pioneer a thousand other worlds, there had been ages when kings were also priests credited with divine powers by descent.

Suppose those who had set up the experiment on Clio had made use of such memories, giving the families they had selected to rule a mystique which bound their subjects to them? But then how could Reddick or other rebels find any followers, or dare themselves to go against such influences?

Those who had made Clio a testing ground for their theories would not want a stagnant society. Perhaps the influences would not affect those of equal rank, or would only hold for periods of time—say when a monarch was in dire danger. Or—she could supply a multitude of plausible answers.

But could she in turn use such suggestions to counter the accusations made against her by Uncle Offlas and the Service? Admittedly they would be glad to learn all they could about Clio. And if there was such an influence, a psycho-tech could verify that. But she would have to reach camp—and hope that native activity around it had not led Uncle Offlas to order withdrawal.

Roané now regretted most of all not bringing her com. Why had she not? Why, her thinking *must* have been influenced! To have been so afraid of being traced by her own people!

She shook her head. With every passing moment she was more and more unable to understand her own actions. The answer was, of course, that they must avoid the Clio natives in order to escape this influence set up to prove theories for men long dead.

The road she followed took a turn and then another. But never did it veer too far from her landmark, and Roane kept to it. It did not seem to be traveled by night; at least she heard no sounds such as might be made by men, only those of wild life, a crashing in the brush as if something ran from her. A full moon was rising and its silver light lay along the road.

Roane reached a place where there was a turn away from her landmark as the road angled sharply north, crossing a stream. But the running water could now be her guide. Perhaps at some seasons it was a full river, but at present it had shrunk so that sweeps of gravel and sand edged it on both sides. And she used the nearer bank for her new path. Twice she disturbed animals which had come to drink, one a quite large but seemingly timid beast which let out a mournful hooting cry as it plunged away. She kept her stunner ready in the event she met something more belligerent.

Shortly thereafter the moonlight revealed deep prints in the soil, hoof slots. Duocorns, she was certain, a number of them. And there was a broken branch or two here and there to suggest passage had been forced by a mounted party. They were heading in the same direction she had taken. And though she had little training in woodcraft, Roane suspected the prints were fresh.

The party with Ludorica? If so, all the more reason for Roane to reach camp with her warning. They could be kept away from the actual site by the distorts. But too much use of those not only would exhaust their charges, but might awaken dim wonder in men who had been more than once subconsciously thrown off trail.

She need fear only one thing really—seeing the Princess again. Because in her own mind Roane had come to accept her idea that Ludorica could demand her aid as a fact. Also Uncle Offlas and Sandar must be warned of the same danger, though they had not succumbed to it when the Princess had been in their hands earlier. But then she had been under the effects of the stunner.

In the moonlight the night was very white and black —shadows had sharp edges. Suddenly Roane paused and put her hand to her head. The first small touch of discomfort. She knew it for what it was—the first warning of a distort. Then she realized what she might have to face. She was not wearing her counter beam—the distort would have the same effect on her as it did on those it was designed to discourage. She could only hope that she might use the warn-off as a guide and force herself on into what she was most reluctant to approach.

Not far away the trail of the riders turned, leaving traces in the brush of their passing which suggested a quick retreat. That, too, had been caused by the distort. But Roane kept on course, though not much farther. The attack came without warning. Out of the night snaked a loop to encircle her chest-high, jerk tight before she knew what was happening to her. She had no time to use her weapon, for her arms were pinned to her sides, and then a body crashed against her, bearing her to the ground.

The weight was withdrawn but she was held in a grip which all her struggles could not break. She was pulled to her feet, turned to face a party of three, though a fourth must stand behind her holding her.

In the moonlight she recognized the leader of her captors and as she gasped breath back into her lungs, she managed to get out his name:

"Colonel Imfry!"

"Who are you?" He came closer, peered into her face. She saw his expression of surprise.

"Lady Roane! But what—where is the Princess? Free her instantly!" Question and command followed fast on one another. The grasp on her shoulders loosened, and with a twitch the rope circlet fell to her feet.

"Where is the Princess?" the Colonel asked again as he put out a hand to steady her.

"She rode out of the tower with Reddick."

"What tower—where—" She thought his grasp tightened as if he would shake the truth out of her.

"Let me get my breath." Roane determined not to be again swept in involvement.

"Of course." His grip loosened. "I pray pardon, Lady. But with Her Highness in Reddick's hold—"

She made her story as terse as she could. Though she was not able to name the prison from which she had escaped, save to give the Princess's name of Famslaw, the rest she reported up to the time she had seen the Princess ride away.

"They used a mind-globe on her," the Colonel interrupted. "And that coach with Rehling's symbol— I am sure he played a double game for all her belief in him. There is only one place they could be heading for now—to find the Crown. And you, Lady, know where that is. You can take us there. There is something strange— We have been wandering for two days unable to come near the landmarks the Princess gave me. But we must reach there now, or Reddick will use the Princess to claim the throne and then do with her as he wishes—"

"No!" Roane jerked out of his light hold.

"No? What do you mean?" He was startled, looking at her now as if she were a person and not merely a way to aid Ludorica.

"No, I will not go with you!" She had the stunner still. With it she sprayed him and the two men behind him as she pivoted to bring it also on the one a pace or two behind her.

They staggered, but they did not go down. However, she believed the blast enough to keep them unsteady until she could get away. She plunged straight ahead, into the full force of the distort, wavering herself under that mind-dazing blast, but enough the mistress of her body to keep staggering on in a direction she did not believe any of them would follow. And she did not waste time looking behind to see.

Brush whipped about her. She flung up her arm to shield her face from the sting of lashing branches. Always she was buffeted by those distort rays meant to bewilder. She tried to blank those as best she could, to reach the safe zone beyond the barrier. Let Ludorica and her henchmen find their own way out of their troubles; she was not again going to be drawn into their games.

11

The waves of the distort *were* less effective—she must be close to the edge of the protection zone. Roane plunged on, not trying to pick any path, merely attempting to get free of the influence. Then—she was in the clear!

Before her was the glade of the camp. She expected some challenge and threw back her hood so they could see her if they had picked up her image on tri-dee com. But there was no sign of life. Nobody here—but then where?

Roane half expected that the entrance might have been set on a new code, not answering to her thumb identification. But it opened as readily as if she had left it only moments earlier. So they had not yet exiled her.

There was no one within any of the small cubicles. But in the one that had housed their work tools were significantly empty racks and niches. They were at work somewhere, and she thought it could only be in the cave.

Roane went to the com. She could call from here— warn them. But even as that thought crossed her mind, she saw that the planet-side hookup had been detached. In its place was the off-world call ready for use. Either they had already arranged for lift-off, or else they expected that they must do so at a moment's notice.

She snapped down the replay level. Immediately the tape replied in code.

"So that is how it is," she said aloud. They had reported, and had received orders that they must make any investigations in three planet days' reckoning, be ready then for lift-off. As to when that deadline had been set, she had no idea.

There was one thing she could do now. It might not in any way mitigate her eventual punishment, but it would prevent Uncle Offlas from censoring anything she said.

Roane found a clear report tape and fitted it into the case which, once sealed and numbered, must be produced and could only be opened on the Service ship. She sat by the table, took up the mike, but thought out carefully what she would say before she thumbed it to *Go*. A simple story of what had happened was best. Thus she dictated the course of events which had been followed from her first meeting with the Princess.

She added as concisely as she could the conclusions she had drawn concerning the Crown, the conditioning, all she had herself experienced. This might well be disallowed by the authorities, but the experts would have access to it. When she had done Roane pressed her thumb to the sign slot with relief. There was nothing Uncle Offlas could do to alter that.

Now she was so very tired that her bones ached. The fight against the distort had left her so exhausted she could hardly get to her feet. But she dared not sleep now, give way to the ache in her back, the weakness in her legs! She had to warn Uncle Offlas and Sandar. They might stumble upon some party prospecting for the Crown.

Colonel Imfry—the stunner blast had been low; he and his men would not be incapacitated for long. But with the distorts holding they could not trail her.

Roane pulled at the unfamiliar clothing she wore, dragged it off piece by piece. She pawed through her now very meager wardrobe. One more suit—or would that be the right choice? If she went to the cave perhaps the Clio clothing would be less noticeable. But— her mind must be more clear—

Somehow she got to the small fresher, forcing her tired mind to focus on dialing. This ought to jolt her awake. Moisture gathered on her body as a haze rose about her. She buried her face in it eagerly, drew breaths of it into her lungs. It was like coming out of a dire murk into clear, fresh water. But she must be careful; not enough and her fatigue would return, too much and it would induce euphoria, which could lead her into some overconfident, disastrous move. This was a device to be used only when some danger demanded stimulation of mind and body, and then sparingly.

The fog cleared, she climbed out and rubbed down her damp body, no longer aware of aches and pains. With a bed robe wrapped around her, she went back to the control room.

No warn light on the off-world com. She was alert enough now to read the other dials. At one she paused, frowning. Surely the distort was not so limited as that! There was a small map on the screen, red pinpoints marking the broadcast boxes. But the gauge showed a waning of power. Hurriedly she checked further.

So that was it—they needed recharging. But that was something Uncle Offlas would have been very careful about before he left. Which might mean he had been gone longer than he intended. And even as Roane watched, one of the red points flickered—disappeared. A distort had ended its sentry duty. Roane was faced with a new decision. She could visit each of those settings, replace the charges. Or she could make speed to the cave with her warning—

To visit the distorts might be a waste of precious time, could expose her once more to Imfry and his men. No—it was best to go to the cave. Once they all returned here and shut off the outlying distorts, they could turn on a central energy beam which would fortify the whole clearing until lift-off.

Back in her cubicle Roane once more pulled on the native clothing and then checked her belt, adding a freshly charged beamer, a new charge in the stunner, a detect, and a counter beam which would free her from those emanations.

It was morning when she left the camp. And it was going to be a fair day; there were no clouds overhead. She reached the cliff of the cave without picking up any trace of Imfry's party. But as she approached the narrow entrance to the underground ways, she dodged quickly into cover, her heart pounding. Not Imfry's men —but there was someone there in ambush. Only the detect she carried had warned her in time.

Roane studied the terrain. There was no way of reaching the hidden stranger. She could get a small, blurred reading on him, enough to pinpoint his position. Drawing her stunner, she made hastily calculated changes in its setting. She doubted if she could knock him out at this distance, but she could render him helpless long enough for her to reach the door of the cave. She sighted on the bush which hid him, and pressed the button.

He made no move, and she could not prove the effectiveness of her attack without exposing herself. With a shrug, she got up and walked forward, though that stretch of earth and rock seemed the longest she had ever traveled—on any world.

There came no attack, no challenge from the bush. She ran past the cover, loose stones and gravel rolling under her feet, and reached the cave mouth. There she dared to look around. A booted leg protruded from the brush. It moved feebly, gouging up the sandy soil, but that was all. She used the beam again to make sure her victim was well under.

She went on into the passage. Where before that way had been silent, now there was a continuous murmur of sound. Straining her ears, Roane tried to make out the rise and fall of voices. But this was rather a mechanical clicking. And it grew louder as she advanced. There was a glimmer of light as she came to the transparent plate. Only the panel was now gone, to leave a doorway from which issued the sounds. Roane stepped into the chamber beyond.

She stood at one end of a double line of tall columns. Each was fitted with a fore panel, lighted, on which were maplike outlines. And cresting each was something else, alien in form to the plain solidity of the pillars.

For each was literally crowned. On a small stalk on top of each pillar rested a miniature diadem, beautifully wrought, sparking with gems.

Two of the pillars in the double line were dark. On the nearer the crown was lifeless, dulled. But the rest glittered as if the metal and jewels from which they had been fashioned now coursed with energy. There were also rows of small lights above and around the map plates, and these flashed on and off with brilliant sparks of ever-changing colors.

Roane was sure now that these were no Forerunner remains. They must be connected with the experiment of Clio's settlement. But she had only a minute or two to watch before her uncle moved out into the aisle between the pillars.

She had not come unprepared for such an encounter, fearing that she might even be rayed down by a stunner before she could protest. So her weapon was ready. Nor had she been wrong in her wariness, for Offlas also had his stunner aimed.

"Roane!" He did not speak loudly, yet his voice vibrated through the chamber, filling it, just above the muttering of the machines. He moved closer. Warned by his speech, she kept her voice even lower:

"The distorts are failing." She gave him what she felt to be a needful warning.

"They don't run forever." His whispering voice was harsh, just as Basic sounded curt and hard after the softer inflections of the Clio tongue. "You—where did you come from?"

"I escaped from a keep back in the hills. But that is not important now. They are coming here to search for the Crown—"

"How many?" he demanded. "Sandar is—"

"There are two parties, one with the Princess, one of her men alone. I don't know how many. She is a prisoner; her kinsman wants her to take the Crown so he can get it." She spilled out what she had to say in a torrent of words. "The Princess says only one of the Blood Royal can handle a crown—it kills anyone else—"

Her uncle had turned to face one of the machines and now Roane, moving closer, was able to trace on its pillar the outline of a map she knew—Reveny! The crown set above that was a vision of ice. She could not have named the metal of its forming—it might even be pure crystal. It was a circlet composed of a series of points which inclined toward the center, where four of them united at the apex. Those in turn supported a star set with flashing white gems. If the miniature was so impressive, what a glory the real crown must be!

"Sandar went to hunt it," her uncle said. "He has not returned."

He hurried to the end of the aisle, returned with a portable tri-dee recorder in his hands. "Bring that—" He indicated another instrument, set to one side.

Roane scooped it up. But just as they reached the door there came the unmistakable sound of feet in the passage. More than one person walked there. It could not be Sandar.

Should they take cover behind the pillars? But her uncle did not move, seemed so sure of himself that Roane stayed where she was. Could it be Imfry—or the Princess and her captors?

Then the Colonel stood framed in the doorway where the panel had been, clearly lighted by a torch he carried. In his right hand was one of those awkwardly heavy projectile-firing weapons. Roane felt very naked as she waited for him to turn and look at her. But his attention never wavered from the way ahead. Behind him moved his men, seemingly alert for trouble, yet none of them glanced at the doorway or the room beyond it.

"Conditioned," she heard her uncle mutter. "An excellent example of top conditioning—additional proof, if any were needed."

They went on. What if they met Sandar up ahead? He would have his stunner. But the Princess and Reddick—what if they were already there? Her uncle was listening, and she ventured a question:

"What if they meet Sandar?"

He glared as if her whisper had been a shout, making no answer, a tactic which formerly would have silenced her. But Uncle Offlas was just a man, not some superpower. He might be able to force a dark future on her, but she could also fight back. And she was inwardly amazed at her own surge of confidence now.

Seemingly he was undecided. They could follow the Colonel's party, use their own stunners to clear the way. Roane wondered why her uncle did not take that course. But he was prevented from doing whatever he might have done by a change in the chamber of the pillars.

A sharp crackling drew her attention back to the machines—to the column supporting the Ice Crown. There was a wild flurry of the lights on its front—while the glitter of the miniature crown flared into a flame she could not look at. There was another loud note and the pattern of small lights steadied.

Her uncle was staring at the display and now he aimed the tri-dee recorder at it. But even the flare of the crown had speedily subsided.

Roane knew what had happened as well as if she had viewed the act. The Ice Crown had been found. But had it been claimed by the Princess? Or had Sandar taken it—or Imfry?

More sounds, loud and echoing, but not from any one of the pillars—these came from the passage. She thought she heard a shout or two also. A fight between Reddick's party and Imfry's men?

"What—" She appealed to her uncle.

But he was totally absorbed in taking a recording of the pillar.

"Changes." He was talking to himself. "At least five major pattern changes! A totally new course of events!"

A new pattern! The Princess, or Reddick? But Roane was not going to be involved again—she was not!

Telling herself that, Roane went to the door. As she stepped into the passage, she dropped the equipment her uncle had ordered her to take and began to run. One half of her mind, the sane half which was Roane Hume, was in open battle with that buried part which she thought she had had under control. She did not want to go, but that inner compulsion made her.

Roane reached the end of the passage. Now she smelled an acrid odor. With her stunner at the ready she squeezed through the rough passageway, listening for any sound. She heard a muffled clamor of voices and then saw the glow of torchlight. She crept to a point from which she could view the cave of the skeleton.

There was a raw hole where earth and rock had been dug away to make an opening to the outside. Some daylight showed there, but the torches were being used to light a second tear in the wall where the crushed skeleton had laid.

In that second opening stood Ludorica. She had her hands out before her, the fingers outspread to their furthest extent, as if she would protect with her flesh what she held. It was a copy of the Ice Crown on the pillar, save that it was of a size to fit a human head.

By the torchlight it blazed fire. And the expression on the Princess's face as she gazed upon it, entranced, was one Roane had never seen before. Greed—no—but some emotion which was alien to the Ludorica she had known—an expression which repelled, not drew as the Princess had been able to draw her into an alliance even against her own desires.

It seemed that Ludorica was aware only of what she held, not of those around her. She was flanked by a man in black who eyed her with almost as deep a fascination as she used for the Crown. On her other side was Reddick. He held one of those massive hand weapons and from its barrel still rose a thread of smoke fume.

Two of Imfry's followers lay still against the wall near where Roane crouched. And the Colonel himself—Roane's hand went to her mouth—his back was to the rock as if he needed a support. One arm hung limp and there was a dark stain spreading on his shoulder. But he was being roughly bound by two of Reddick's men, while two more stood with hand weapons trained on Imfry's remaining men.

"The King is dead—long live the Queen," Reddick intoned. Then he added, touching Ludorica's arm, "My Queen, what would you have us do with these who came to seek the great treasure of Reveny?"

She did not raise her head or look away from what she held. When she answered her voice was thin and lacking in warmth, as if she spoke from a far distance of things which mattered little.

"Since I am Queen, as all can see, let them be served as traitors, for they reached for the Crown!"

Reddick smiled. But on the faces of the Colonel and of his remaining men there was shock, as if they could not believe what they had heard.

"The King being dead, our Queen has spoken," Reddick said. There was a solemnity to his words, as if he were some official of a court of justice relaying a lawful verdict. "Let them be dealt with as traitors. My Queen"—he turned again to Ludorica—"this is no fit place for you. Let us ride to show your people that you are truly their crowned one."

There was a hint of another emotion on Ludorica's face as that mask which so repelled Roane changed a little. "Yes"—now her voice was more human, eager—"let me do so! This is the Ice Crown; I hold it, I wear it, for Reveny!"

Looking neither right nor left, and certainly not at the men she had so summarily condemned, she went to the newly cut opening, the man in black beside her putting out a steadying hand now and then. For she paid no attention to her footing, only to what she held. But Reddick lingered, watching his men bind the rest of Imfry's force. When that was finished he spoke directly to the Colonel.

"The Crown has spoken, as it always does, my brave Colonel. I think that there is certainly a new day dawning for Reveny, but I do not believe it will be greatly to your taste. So perhaps it is best that you will leave us soon. Her Majesty will give the final word as to the hour and manner of your going. But do not, I beg you, place any hope in old friendships. It is well known that the crowns always change those who wear them. It will be most interesting to see what changes will ensue once our liege lady is firmly on her throne."

"Mind-globe cannot hold her forever." Some of the stupefaction had gone from the Colonel now.

"Mind-globe? Ah, we might have used such a key to bring her here—since she alone can handle the Crown. But I assure you, my brave and interfering Colonel, what has passed since then is born of the Crown alone. To rule and reign is very different from living as an heiress to such glories. I think we shall find the Princess is no longer as you have always known her, but now a Queen! We must be riding. Bring these along—

but intact," he ordered his men. "It will doubtless please Her Majesty to make an excellent example of them."

Roane had been so startled by the abrupt reversal of Ludorica's attitude toward the Colonel that she had watched the scene without any thought of taking a hand in the action. But now, as Reddick's men prepared to drag their prisoners away, she readied her stunner. She might not be any longer a part of Imfry's efforts on behalf of one who had so strangely repudiated him, but neither could she see Reddick take him to his death.

But as she raised her weapon she was seized from behind, held in a viselike grip which did not allow her the slightest movement. And she heard the softest of whispers close to her ear:

"Not this time, you fool! This is no game for our playing."

Sandar! How he had got there—or why— Roane writhed but was unable to move any more than he allowed her. Using his superior strength, he forced her backward, so she could no longer see the cave of the Crown.

She continued to fight his hold until they reached a wider stretch of passage. There he slammed her against the wall, holding her pinned by his weight against her. There was no light, but she could hear the cold menace in his voice.

"Do you want to be stun-rayed and dragged back? I will do it if necessary. You've played the fool and worse. But you're through now with such tricks. What happens to these puppets is no concern of yours. They *are* puppets, we've seen enough to know that. They are programed just like Adrianian androids to do exactly what the machines back in that chamber tell them to do. What does it matter what games puppets play? We've learned a lot from those installations—"

"They are not puppets!" Roane denied in a burst of real rage. "Any more than we are when we are Cram-briefed. If they did not have the crowns—if those machines weren't running—they would be free— They are human!"

"But they are not." He continued to hold her in that bruising grip which hurt her. "They are acting out the lives the machines decide for them. And it is none of our concern. If the Service decides later to interfere, when they have our report, that is another matter. But it is not for us to worry about. Now—are you going to walk—or do I stun and drag you?"

12

There was no struggling with Sandar. She knew he would do exactly as he threatened.

"I will come," she said dully.

He did not release his hold on her right shoulder, and so linked, they returned to the wider passage, where they were caught in the ray of a beamer. She heard her uncle give a sigh of relief.

"Hurry!" He did not ask where Sandar had been, nor what Roane had done. The beamer swung around, pointed their way to the entrance. Her cousin gave her a savage push.

As they emerged into the open a haze of mist lay in clots of shadow beneath the trees, seeping out over the country. Neither of the men hesitated, but struck a direct path back to camp, passing without note the man Roane had stunned, Sandar still holding her as if he expected her to break for freedom.

"Distorts out—all except one." Sandar had taken a reading on his belt instrument.

"To be expected. They have not been recharged,"

her uncle replied tersely. "The sooner we get off-world the better. I don't know how much of an impression your stupid actions have made here." He favored Roane with one of those icy stares which he had used to subdue her for so long. "We can only hope that we can lift without fully blowing cover—"

"What about the installation?" For the first time since she could remember, Roane dared to ask a question in the face of his quelling. "Are we going to—will the Service—just leave it running? Sandar says that all the people here are tied to it, that it makes them puppets. That's against the Prime Four ruling—"

"Closed planets, as you well know, do not come under the Prime Rules. What the Service chooses to do once our report is in is none of our concern."

He spoke as if that was the final word on the subject, and Roane knew the folly of further argument. But her cold fear of the installation stayed with her.

The Psychocrats had once forced men on unknown worlds into experiments. And when their horrible rein had been finally broken, their mind-slaves freed, the results of both the meddling and the liberation had been, for two generations now, a dire warning to all human-kind. Even if she had not known Ludorica or the Colonel, had not been herself sucked into the web which enmeshed Clio, Roane would still have been aroused to anger by this discovery. Just as the people of Clio were conditioned to obey the machines their enslavers had set up generations ago, so was she armed to fight such influences. Sandar might name them puppets, which perhaps technically they were, but Roane had lived with them. And they were real people, far warmer of nature than the two now hustling her along.

Leave all major decisions to the Service—the safe, sane cry. But if this was left to the deliberation of men half the galaxy away, how soon would they interfere, if at all? Certainly not in time to save the Colonel! She had no doubts that Reddick would do exactly as he promised and make very sure Nelis Imfry was removed.

And the Princess with the Crown—she had been a changed person, almost evil. Ludorica deserved better than such slavery. Roane's thoughts circled round and round the same cheerless path as she trotted along. She did not believe that she was now under that curious influence the Princess had exerted on her. But neither could she turn aside from the probable dark future of Reveny and the new Queen.

Sandar pushed her into the shelter on his father's heels and then went to gather up the distorts. Uncle Offlas paid no attention to her, but went straight to the com to look for any messages recorded during their absence. He put out a finger to flick across the top of the machine, as if that gesture could summon an answer. Roane guessed that nothing had been received.

Uncle Offlas sat down and drew out the recorder. He was about to plunge in the button when he had a clear view of the reading. Then, for the first time since they had left the cave, he turned to look at her.

"There has been a recording made." Though that was a statement rather than a question, she answered him:

"I made it, when I returned here." And Roane knew a very small flash of triumph. He could not erase what she had done, for that tape was locked with the sequence of others.

But he was not frowning. In fact there was a trace of interest in his expression, almost as if she had as much value as some small find.

"And what did you record—your meddling?" Still no coldness in his tone. It was as if he honestly wanted to know. Her spirits rose a little. It could well be that what she had fed into the records might have some influence on the momentous future decision. Though that could not possibly help what was passing now. She moved restlessly—the thought of Imfry as she had last seen him, wounded, bound, very much in the power of his enemy, was a constant prod to action. But how, when, and where?

"What happened to me," she replied. Then she gathered what courage she had recently gained—to stand against a lifetime of domination—and made her plea a second time:

"They—the Duke Reddick—is going to have the Colonel killed. The Princess is under controls. It is all like the tales of the story tapes, the ones about evil spells. The Colonel is her friend, but she ordered him executed. Only she could not mean it—it was that machine! We can't let her do it—"

She expected him to dismiss her summarily. Instead he continued to watch her with deepening interest. But what had been at first encouraging no longer seemed so. It was as if *she* were a part of the installation and he was fascinated by her reactions. And at that moment she was convinced that if anything could be done to break the black pattern now being woven, she alone must do it.

"You like these people, feel a certain kinship to them?"

"Yes."

"Well, you *had* recently come from intensive briefing. That might explain why you would be more susceptible to the influence of a strong conditioning broadcast, even if it were alien. There is good evidence that the installation here maintains Basic as well as special directional broadcasts. I think, Roane, that perhaps once you are de-briefed, you will find the Service will accept such an explanation for your extraordinary conduct. In fact"—he was warming to this disagreeable train of thought—"you could well provide them with an additional check here. But as for any more interference on our part—you must understand that that is completely out of the question.

"In the first place, to stop—if we could find a method of doing so—any of those machines would disrupt the patterns they have been weaving for a couple of centuries, and the people of Clio may be so tied to their influence that failure of control would be fatal. Have you thought of that?"

Roane blinked. That the control could be so far-reaching, no, she had not thought of that. On the other hand, it was a dire possibility. They knew something of what the Psychocrats had done to manipulate their human material, but they did not know all. Patient reprograming was one thing; sudden and complete cut-off was another. Clio might be brought out of her fog by degrees, but the cutoff—Roane remembered Ludorica's tale of the country whose crown had been destroyed.

"Arothner—"

"What?"

"There was a seacoast country—" She outlined the story as the Princess had told it.

Uncle Offlas nodded. "You see, the crowns control the rulers directly, and perhaps indirectly most of the ruled. Destroy the crown and the people are as Sorfalan puppets when their motive power fails. This 'Ice Crown' had been lost for a couple of generations—but it was still in existence. The patterns broadcast by the machines had been interrupted. It could be that when the Princess found the Crown there was a sharp change to compensate and bring the country back into a determined future. This abrupt about-face could be the result of some such need—"

"Need!" Roane interrupted him. "To let *Reddick* dictate—and she was changed—evil— You may not believe me, but she was! And as for pattern—wasn't it true that the closed worlds were supposed to be given a basic background and then allowed to work out their destinies from that? that the whole purpose of these experiments was to watch such maturing?"

"That was our conception, up until we made the discovery here. But it would seem that we were wrong. We came here for Forerunner relics, but we may have found something of equal value. There is every reason to believe that this is not a basic control but a self-continuing experiment."

He returned to the recorder. "I must tape what we have learned. Remember, no more interference. If it is necessary"—his voice was once more cold—"we can put you in stass until we are back on the ship. No more action apart from what is necessary for the carrying out of our mission. Leave your belt here—" He pointed to the table before him.

So he would take from her the means of any independent action. Roane pressed open the catch. As she laid it before him he added:

"You had better break out provisions. Double rations."

Sluggishly she went to obey. The lift which the session in the fresher had given her was wearing off. Even if she managed by some now unforeseen chance to get away from the camp, she would not have the strength to reach Hitherhow. And without even a stunner, what good would revolt do her?

Roane brought out tubes and containers. Double rations? For a moment her thoughts lifted from the narrow rut of her troubles. She heard Sandar come in. And having loaded a tray with her choices, she returned to the com.

"I do not understand their silence. No reply to our urgent signal. Surely they cannot have broken orbit! Or if some such crisis arose, they would have beamed a warning." Uncle Offlas was again tapping the com.

"One distort with about a quarter power left." Sandar was piling boxes on the floor. "The rest are gone. There is a drain, there must be! To need full recharging so soon—"

"We have no idea about that installation. It may well be that it can pull from any power source in the neighborhood."

"But if that is so," Sandar said eagerly, "such an effect might be reversed. We could tap from it, maybe build up a real force wall to hold until the retire signal comes."

"Too risky." His father shook his head. "But your thought leads •to something else. We cannot recharge the distorts now without endangering our com broadcast. And to remain in this unprotected camp—I don't like the thought of that."

"Strike this shelter—move into better hiding?" Sandar suggested.

"It might be well. Unless we get an answer soon."

"So far the forest seems clear around here," Sandar reported. "We could go back to the cave, set up a repeller at the mouth. They have their crown now. I don't think they'll come back."

Roane divided the food containers, took her share. With a tube and two small boxes she went to her own quarters. Sleep was so heavy upon her that she had to force her eyelids open, keep doggedly chewing and swallowing. But before she had finished she lost the battle and was asleep.

Dreams were not uncommon. One often dreamed. Roane had wandered so in many strange places, some of them far stranger than the alien worlds she had seen with waking eyes. But this was the most vivid and "real" dream she had ever known, though in it she was only a spectator.

It was as if she had walked through the curtain of sleep into such a room as she had seen in the ambassador's mansion in Gastonhow. There were chairs with tall, much-carved backs, portions of that carving touched with insets of metal, or with time-dulled paint, to make fantastic scenes. Behind them much of the wall was covered with a stretch of tapestry on which men mounted on duocorns hunted some quarry lost from sight in thread-formed trees. This, too, had the look of something faded by many years' passing.

Yet it was as sharply clear to Roane's eyes as if she stood there in body. Before her was a long table of rich red stone which bore on its surface a mottling of twisting green lines. And set out on this was a plate of gold. By that lay a set of knive, two-tined fork, and spoon, all fashioned of crystal ringed and banded with gold in which small green gems were set.

At a good, almost awkward distance away from this setting was a second. But here the plate was of silver, the eating implements of the same material, with handles of red. All had a richness of color which warmed Roane as had her surroundings in Gastonhow—though it was far removed from the more sophisticated trappings of her own civilization.

The room lacked occupants, but there was a kind of expectancy. Roane was keenly aware that she waited with rising excitement for some action of importance.

A man wearing a richly embroidered tabard backed in, bowing low at every step to the person he ushered through the portal. He had a staff in one hand and he brought the butt of that sharply down on the floor at intervals. If his action was some signal Roane heard no sound, nor, she was suddenly aware had she heard any since her eyes had opened on this.

She whom the usher had so heralded entered, her full skirts skimming in graceful folds which she adjusted now and then with small movements of one hand. In the other she carried a flat fan of purple feathers mounted on a jeweled handle.

The skirts, with tight bodice, cut low enough to reveal much of her shoulders, were of a deep purple shade, the lacings of the bodice black interwoven with silver. And the wide necklace of many drops, the earrings her elaborately dressed hair allowed to show, were of shining black stones. There was even a small circlet of them in her hair. There was no mistaking who walked thus—the Queen Ludorica.

Two ladies followed her, their dresses of a like cut, but of gray with laces of unrelieved black. They had ribbons of the same hue tied around their throats, and their heads were covered with lacy black veils. The whole effect was one of calculated somberness.

One stationed herself at the table to face the Queen, while the other remained by the door—though not so as to obstruct the entrance of the fifth member of the party—Duke Reddick.

His clothing was also purple, a duller shade than worn by the Queen. He passed around the table, drew out her chair and seated her with ceremony before he took that place at some distance from her.

A tray was handed in from beyond the door to the waiting lady, who brought it to her companion at the table. From it the latter took two fantastic cups wrought in the form of those grotesque animals Roane had first seen being set up in the garden at Hitherhow. Having filled them from a flagon, she set them on the table with care, touched each lightly on the side. Straightway the metal feet moved and the cups started on a stately march, one to Ludorica, one to the Duke.

A second tray with food was brought in and the Queen and then Reddick were served with great ceremony. They ate and drank. Roane saw their lips move and knew that they talked, but for her the scene was played out in utter silence. Twice their walking cups were sent back to be refilled.

Then the plates were cleared and the Queen and he whom she had considered her greatest enemy sat in apparent amity. From the front of his tunic Reddick brought forth a scroll which he spread flat on the table before him. While Roane could not read the words written there, she could see the black lettering, and ribbons of scarlet and black at the foot of the sheet, affixed by an irregular blob of purple of the hue of Ludorica's gown.

The Queen leaned back in her chair, fanned herself with slow motions of the purple feathers. All the vivacity, those quick changes of expression which Roane had seen on her face in the past, had vanished. Her face was a mask under the piles and rolls of her hair. Even her eyes were half closed as if the lids and the long lashes acted to conceal what she thought or felt.

Reddick's lips moved. He must be reading aloud what was written on the scroll. He glanced up at last, looking straight at Ludorica. And it seemed to Roane that he did so searchingly, as if he expected some protest, or at least some comment from her.

But if he did so, he was disappointed. She gestured with the fan, and the usher who had led her in came out of the shadows, took the scroll from the Duke, brought it to place before the Queen.

She let it remain rolled. To all appearances she was not interested in what it contained, nor in what Reddick wanted from her. Perhaps he grew impatient, for Roane saw his lips move again.

For the first time Ludorica answered him. No show of emotion troubled her mask. Instead a faint flush arose on the Duke's cheeks. If that was caused by anger he suppressed all other signs of resentment valiantly.

But, having perhaps rebuked her kinsman, the Queen laid down her fan, spread out the scroll with both hands. Perhaps she reread what was written there. At least she sat so for several long moments.

Then she spoke again. One of the waiting ladies brought forward a small tray on which was a box which she opened before presenting it. The contents seemed a solid black block. Ludorica raised her right hand, pressed her thumb firmly against the block, and then to the paper, leaving a clear print. She then dipped her hand in a small basin the lady was quick to offer and washed her thumb clean.

She still held the scroll in her left hand, but allowed it to reroll as Reddick moved to draw back her chair. As she arose she left it lying.

Passing her kinsman as if he had become invisible, Ludorica left the room. The Duke caught up the scroll and tucked it once more within the security of his tunic before he followed her.

Roane stirred, or tried to stir. She had watched a very real scene which carried with it the conviction that by some weird chance she had been projected into Ludorica's palace and there been witness to some dire action. But why—and how—

The room was gone suddenly. Instead she faced, for perhaps the length of one breath out of a lifetime, a single face. And that was going to haunt her—

"Roane!"

She was being shaken with increasing roughness, roused out of that state which did not seem wholly akin to normal sleep.

"Nelis!" Did she call that aloud? There was danger—

Roane opened her eyes. She was being drawn out of her bed roll by Sandar, and he was doing that shaking. But Sandar was not a part of—

"Roane! Wake up, can't you? Wake *up!*" His last shake was hard enough to make her head roll on her shoulders. And she at last accepted that she was back from that strange far place. She lay in her cubicle at camp, and her cousin was using impatiently harsh means to acquaint her of that fact.

"Haabacca jet us to the Cloud!" he exclaimed. "Sniff this so you can see straight!" With one hand he pushed her head forward, with the other made a balled fist and then opened it under her nose, where the capsule he had so crushed could spend its fumes directly into her lungs. Sniffing those fumes cleared her head.

"What is the matter?" she asked sulkily. For all the ominous shadows which clung about that dream, she wanted to hold it—especially the very last—for a dream once gone is something gone forever.

"We're moving out." He stood up. "Father let you sleep as long as he could. But we're ready to collapse shelter now. Store your gear and do it fast!"

She crawled out of the sleeping bag, rolled it with the ease of long practice into a packet which fitted into a pocket in the wall. For the rest there had been a clean sweep here. All the possessions allowed her in this Spartan life had vanished. They must have been hard at work while she slept, slept and dreamed.

And out of that dream she carried the conviction that she had witnessed a true happening. Nelis Imfry—that was who it had concerned the most. The scroll that Reddick had produced and that the Queen had signed—and that last glimpse of a lean brown face before Sandar had shaken her awake—they were strung together as might be a necklace of view-pearls.

View-pearls? Roane paused in her sealing of the pocket. She had not the slightest esper rating. Had not Uncle Offlas had her tested long ago? An esper was invaluable, to an archaeologist. Retrogressive hypnotherapy could be used by a sensitive to locate digging sites. There were those who could hold a circlet of view-pearls in their hands and read the authentic past. But she was not one of them. Then how did she *know* that she had done so now? And how had she been so empowered? Was it part of the same subtle influence which had drawn her to the Princess at their first meeting, forced her to serve Ludorica? But why should that influence now switch her concern to another?

Roane's hand went to shield her eyes. She tried to think normally, to argue against this new compulsion. No—she was not going to— She was *not!* The installation was not going to use her, too. But it could not be that! The installation moved the Queen now and what she was doing was directly against her former will.

Could she herself now be a puppet—but whose?

"Roane, come on!" Sandar stood there. "What's the matter, do you need another waking inhalation?"

"No!" She needed nothing except some quiet, a calm mind, and a chance to think. But when she would get all three she was not sure.

13

The shelter had been collapsed around the packed core of equipment. Unless someone stumbled upon it bodily, it was so well concealed that the camp could not be sighted by any forest traveler. With packs of emergency supplies the three withdrew to the cave passage.

There the elder Keil set a repell beamer working at the entrance, locked it on his thumb set so that no one else might turn it off. As long as he had Roane's belt she would be a prisoner here, as safely captive as if she were chained by a collar, since without its force she could not go out as others could not enter.

Saying that there was no reason to waste time during their enforced stay in hiding, he and Sandar went back to the installation chamber. They had left a call beam at the dismantled camp to provide direction for their off-world rescuers.

Roane trailed the two men, but to watch those crowned pillars disturbed her. Was it true that the destruction of those inhuman controls might devastate Clio, bring back planet-wide chaos and death to peoples conditioned for generations as puppets? Or—but one could not be sure without careful study made by those trained to deal with such cases. And such study could take planet years.

In the meantime, Roane leaned her head against the wall and closed her eyes. She discovered she could pull from memory every vivid detail of that dream, if dream it was—from the gleam of the colors, the metals, the gowns, the high ceremony of the meal, to the expressions or lack of expression on the faces of those who had played out the scene.

Time. Her scratched hands balled into small fists which she wished she could use to batter her way out of here. Time was going to defeat her. She need only glance down that aisle of pillars to Uncle Offlas, wearing her belt draped over one shoulder. She had no plan—

Her head ached and the constant mutter of the machines seemed to match it throb for throb, until she could stand it no longer. The men were both intent upon what they were doing, studying the play of lights across those pillar surfaces. She gave a sigh and returned to the cave entrance where they had stacked their survivor kits.

There was that other entrance to the cave passages, where Reddick's men had broken through. But Uncle Offlas had set a double broadcast to operate a second barrier a little beyond the installation chamber. No—Roane knew it was hopeless. Yet she found herself pulling at the pack seals, lying out on the floor, in the light of a small beamer, their contents.

Food—plenty of E rations—a well-stocked medic kit, spare charges for beamers and stunners— Nothing of service to her.

She piled all she had taken from Uncle Offlas's kit back into it. And she already knew all that was in hers. There remained Sandar's and she turned it out, without any real hope.

Another beamer—or— Roane turned the tube around in her hands, brought it closer to the light with a small thrill of excitement. Not a regulation beamer, and not the forbidden blaster, but an archaeologist's hand tool which had some limited properties of both. She studied the setting dial on the butt and then unsealed the charge-holding stem. If—oh, if only—

Roane hastily emptied out again all three kits, dumping their contents on the stone. In a short time she had three sets of charges lined up—those for stunners, those for two sizes of beamers. And—three of the latter fitted! One of those would not give her the highest force this tool could use, but perhaps enough. Only it would be slow in working—and she could not face either man were he armed.

She sat back on her heels. There was the repeller. Roane swung up the beamer to touch the ceiling of the cave at the point above where the machine sat. What she tried was such a gamble that the promise of failure far out-weighed that of success, but she could see nothing else. And it would take time—

Holding the beamer on the spot she had selected, Roane thumbed on the tool, aiming its energy broadcast at that section, moving it with precision to cut the outline of a circle in the rock.

It did slice—but so slowly! And she could tell from the vibration of the tube in her hand that the operation was using far too much power. The charge might well be exhausted long before her purpose was accomplished. But she kept at it.

A rain of small bits of stone, gnawed away by the ray, fell toward the repeller. Heartened, Roane grew reckless, bearing down on the button to send the highest intensity of beam into that cracking surface.

Back and forth she swept, weaving a maze of cracks and cuts. The powdery fall was thicker, and larger bits of rock came. The repeller had its own protective casing. She might not be able to bring down a piece large enough to crack that, but she was forcing the broadcast to use some of its energy to protect itself. And Uncle Offlas had already set it on high. He had had to, to produce the two force walls, here and down the passage.

Sweep, sweep. Pebbles fell now. Roane used the beamer to read the dial on the repeller. What she saw there was heartening. The needle was a fraction into the red-zone warning of overload. Then a larger fragment, perhaps the size of her own doubled fist, came clanging down.

A flash from the repeller, an acrid breath of odor. Shorted! She had shorted the shield!

Until that moment she had been moved only by hope. Hope, and the desperate need to be on the move which had come from that dream. Roane unscrewed the tube, recharged the tool.

That done, she stowed it in the front of her tunic and set about making up a small pack—food, a medic kit, the third charge for her weapon-tool, a beamer, a pair of night lenses. She knotted all together in a plasta sack before she allowed herself to think seriously of what she would do.

Roane stood a moment in the dark of the cave, listening. To her alert ears the murmur of sound from the installation was steady. She picked up no hint that either of the others might be returning. But—if she left here now she was making a final choice. All because of a dream? She did not know. Perhaps it was that influence which hung here on Clio, warping her reasoning powers. She could even see clearly what she should have considered good sense, the only right pattern of living for an off-worlder. Only— Roane shook her head. She could not put name to the emotions which had shaken her out of the life she had always known, just as she could not withstand their present pull.

Taking up the sack, putting on the night lenses, Roane stepped over the repeller and walked out of the cave into a new life which she felt had been chosen for her, whether or not she consciously willed it.

Only, now that she was free, where should she go? Hitherhow was her lone point of reference. Wearing these native clothes (she had lacked another change of clothing in camp), she might be able to get into the village, learn something. That was Reddick's holding. Surely he would send his prisoners there. Though would they still be in the keep now?

Half the night later, as she had days earlier, Roane

crouched on the hilltop to watch keep and village. There were one or two lighted lanterns along the street leading from the keep's massive gate to the highway. But the houses were all dark. She hesitated, certain of the folly of her vague plans, but just as sure she must do something.

As she lingered, she heard a sound that was not one of the night noises, a pounding in regular beat, growing louder—until two duocorns, ridden at a steady, ground-covering pace, came into view from the west, the clatter of their passing awakening louder echoes as they reached the cobbled pavement of the short village street. They were brought to a stop before the gate of the keep.

A horn sounded, one of the riders holding it to his lips, blowing a series of notes with certainly no respect for the slumbers of any in village or keep, for the harsh peal shattered the peace of the night. Men spilled into the courtyard, two of them tugging at the gate bar. Then the riders were in, one coming out of his saddle to head at a hasty trot for the near tower.

The men in the courtyard scattered, leading away the puffing, foam-bespattered duocorns. Roane rolled over on her back, pulled off the night lenses to stare up at the sky. There was a paling there. It must be later than she had first thought. And she had accomplished nothing as yet. Better get down to the village. When she looked there again there were lights in some of the house windows. The horn had done its duty to awaken the inhabitants.

Then—lights in the keep—more stirring there. From the main tower came a blast of sound greater than that other horn, one that echoed from the cluster of heights ringing Hitherhow. Men formed lines on the courtyard pavement. More and more lights appeared in the village houses.

Roane pulled the Revenian hood up over her head, drawing it about her face as best she could. It was the only anonymity she had as she went down into the village. A second blast of sound which was a summoning spurred her on.

By the time she reached the short street the people were already coming out of the houses, many of them carrying lanterns, moving toward the keep. There the courtyard doors had been flung open, a line of guardsmen on either side. And from the snatches of conversation Roane overheard as she edged into the crowd, she learned that the peal from the tower was a summons which had not been sounded in years; the reason for it none about her could guess.

"War! Those Vordainians—they have always looked jealously in our direction—"

"No, we have most danger at the west—Leichstan, they have never been friendly since their king re-wed."

"It may only be some proclamation from the Queen. She is only new come to the throne and—"

"A proclamation would be delivered at a decent hour, not when a body is jerked out of a warm bed in the night. This must be something more weighty—"

Roane fastened the bag of supplies to her belt. The night lenses she had tucked into the front of her tunic. And now her fingers sweated on the smooth tube of the tool, her only weapon. If she had to use that, it would require skill.

The crowd tightened more about her as they pushed through the gate, between the ranks of the guardsmen, to stand facing the main door of the keep. Then the horn sounded for the third time and the murmur of questioning voices died away. Three men appeared so suddenly they might have materialized out of space. They wore uniforms such as Reddick's men had, with the addition of those badges and lacings which denoted officers. Two were colonels if she read those signs aright, but the man in the center must be of even higher rank.

A riding cloak hung from his shoulders and he tossed it back impatiently as he unrolled a strip of writing. Roane bit hard upon her lower lip. As well as if she stood at his hand to see it, she knew what that was. She had seen it last in her dream.

"Know you all who swear allegiance to the Ice Crown of Reveny"—the officer had a carrying voice and read slowly and clearly as if there was need that not a single word of this escape those listening to him—"on this day of Martle passed, in the three hundred and fiftieth year of the Guardians, in the reign of Queen Ludorica of the High House of Setcher, Regnant Lady of Reveny in her own right by Blood and Crown, it is decreed that one Nelis Imfry, of the House of Imfry-Manholm, be stripped of his rank as Colonel in the Command of Reveny, of his place in the House of Manholm, and of all privileges granted him by our late gracious lord, King Niklas, whom the Guardians have seen fit to take into their everlasting Peace.

"The said Nelis Imfry, being no longer of the Court, of any House, or of those who stand to arms for Reveny, shall suffer in addition the death accorded to traitors to the Crown, since diverse acts of foul treason have been proved on him.

"And this sentence is to be carried out forthwith at the keep of Hitherhow where the said Nelis Imfry lies in the keeping of our well-beloved cousin and gracious lord, Duke Reddick. Given by seal and hand, under the wish of the Crown, by Blood Right of rule, ours alone on this day— Ludorica, Queen Regnant of Reveny."

The officer allowed the scroll to snap shut again, handed it to one of his companions. He then raised his hand to touch fingers to the badge so prominently displayed on the breast of his tunic.

"So says the Queen! Let it be thus done!"

There was a somewhat ragged assent from those about Roane, repeating the officer's words, but slowly, as if those who gave lip service to the sentiment he expressed were either astounded or not pleased. And Roane heard again questioning, though this time in the most subdued whispering, a faint hissing. She was working her way to the left and the edge of the gathering, striving to do so in the least noticeable manner.

What she could do to alter the future, she did not know. But the feeling that she must hold the key to the situation had been growing stronger by the moment. She was at the fringe of the crowd now, close to the line of sentries. They might have been set there to discourage any sympathy for the condemned, but Roane saw nothing to suggest a demonstration in the Colonel's favor. The people were very sober, and even the whispers had died. Once before Roane had felt such an aura of fear—on another planet when a crowd of cowed worshipers had watched a ritual killing. This was contagious; she knew the same chill.

They were bringing out the prisoner. His arm hung in a sling, and in the lantern light his face was worn, older seeming, the bones showing more clearly beneath the drawn skin, as if in the few hours since she had seen him last a number of years has passed. But he walked firmly, looking neither right nor left, until they brought him to the wall. There were guards moving along the parapet above, towing a bulky contraption which rasped and jangled, until they pushed it over, to be lowered on chains until it thudded to the pavement.

By lantern light it could be seen clearly, a cylinder of metal hoops and netting, not as tall as the man they were shoving to it, so when they forced him inside, he was able neither to stand erect nor to move in relief from a torturous cramping. Once they slammed the opening shut, the bolts were made fast.

Then came the scrape of metal against stone as it was raised to the top of the wall, turned about so its occupant faced out to the dawn sky, there wedged fast. Those on the parapet drew back, almost as if they wanted no bodily contact with the cage.

But they left a guard on duty not too far away as the rest tramped off. There was a sigh from the villagers as they filed out through the gate toward their own homes. And none of them, Roane noted, raised their eyes to the cage. It was as if they did not want to think of its occupant.

Roane hesitated. Should she leave with the villagers? She had no idea if more was planned for Nelis, or if he was simply to be so exposed until he died of hunger and thirst. Her briefing in the customs of Reveny had not gone into the details of local punishments. It was plain that he was now considered safely pent, so that a single guard was all that was necessary. In those few seconds she made her choice.

Drawing the tool, she aimed at the one target which might cause a diversion. The officers who were in the doorway of the tower had not yet moved and over their heads a plaque of metal in the form of one of the royal symbols was bolted to the stone. Recklessly she used the cutting ray full force.

A glow appeared along the upper edge of the plaque. Her luck was better than she had reason to hope, for it swung down as if held now by a weaker fastening. She shouted, pointed to the shuddering metal. The plaque fell. There were cries, a crash. It had beaten down the man who had read the scroll. Guards ran toward him.

Roane sped along the wall, into the dark well of the stair leading to the parapet. She expected any second to be brought down by a projectile fired from one of those archaic weapons. But her luck continued to hold. She did not waste time looking back at the melee in the courtyard, where cries of help rang from the heart of the confusion, but took the steps at the best speed she could.

The sentry faced inward, leaning forward to watch what was going on below. Roane ran forward, slashing out at his neck in one of the unarmed-defense blows she had learned from Sandar. He made no sound, nor did he fall, for she steadied him against the wall, only hoping he would lean there until she was done. Then she used the tool at the lanterns blazing on either side of the cage. Their sides melted.

As she raced forward the explosive sounds of shooting came at last. Roane threw herself low, reached the foot of the cage, pressing the end of the tube to the fastenings of its door.

Metal glowed. She had to be careful in that cutting so that the raw energy would not reach the prisoner. And she could so control it only by direct contact. Now she must expose herself, clawing up the length of the bars. It seemed to Roane that those moments when she clung there, pressing the tool to the iron, were the longest she had ever known.

"Can you get out?"

He had made no sound during her work. She was not even sure he was conscious. Perhaps the rough handling they had used to push him into that small space had worsened his wound. If that were so she did not know what she could do. It all depended on his mobility.

She pressed the tube to the last fastening. But this time there was no response. She had exhausted the charge, never meant for such demand. But to take time to reload—

"I cannot cut this!" She gave him the truth. To fail—

He spoke for the first time. "Pull—now!" His order was so incisive that she obeyed, jerking the opening toward her, aware he was pushing in turn with what strength he could summon.

"It will not give!" She raised the tool, brought it down hammerwise on the reluctant fastening. Perhaps their efforts had loosened it, for a second blow made it yield. He crumpled forward and for a second she was afraid that one of the projectiles being fired at them from the courtyard had struck home. A form lunged at them, missed Imfry, but sent the girl hard against the outer wall of the parapet, driving most of the breath out of her lungs as arms encircled her. Then her assailant reeled back, was drawn tight against

Nelis's body, for the Colonel's arm was about his throat. The guardsman twisted and tore at the bar of flesh holding him so. Roane staggered forward, used the tool to strike the head held against the Colonel's good shoulder.

Imfry crouched over the body he had lowered to the stone. He straightened up holding one of the hand weapons.

"Loose that—" He motioned to the wedging about the base of the cage. Roane saw what he meant and began to fight at it bare-handed. "I will cover."

He stayed behind the parapet, watching the head of the stair up which she had come. She was able to loose the wedges at last. Imfry glanced over his shoulder.

"Can you push it over—that way—here—" He joined her, set his good shoulder against the bulk of the cage and shoved, she lending her weight to his.

The heavy mass of metal swayed, inclined forward, toppled to slam against the outer parapet, and then overbalanced, to fall. There was a clanging crash. The wall under them vibrated as it caught at the end of the chain length. Roane divined his purpose. They had now a way down outside, if, one-handed, he could take it. And it seemed he would try. For he edged his arm well free of the sling.

"Down!" he ordered.

She fingered the chain nearest her, drawn taut by the weight of the cage, though it swayed. The links were large. She thought she could fit fingers into them. But could it be descended one-handed?

"Can you—"

"Get down!" he repeated.

There was movement at the head of the stair. He had brought out the weapon, shot at that shadow, to be answered by a cry.

Roane waited no longer. She started down that improvised ladder, and later her feet struck the cage, so that she must climb over it. When there were no more holds, she dropped, using her space training for the best landing she could make.

It was not a light one. She would bear away more than one bruise. She turned. Surely some one of the garrison would be waiting here. But while there was a milling about, shouts and shots around the angle of the wall (the gate being hidden from sight here), as yet there were no soldiers.

" 'Ware—I am going to drop—" She heard Imfry overhead, saw him holding to the cage, his feet moving as if he were trying to kick away the wall. Then he let go.

She ran toward him as he made no move. Stunned? Broken bones? The ordeal of that descent with a wound might have been enough to— She pulled at his body, trying to roll him over, knowing they must get away.

Men were coming—out of the village. That weapon— did Imfry still have it? She tore at the front of his tunic, trying to find it. But there was nothing and the strangers were upon them.

She aimed a blow, had her hand caught in a tight grip.

"Friends!"

The man who had her arm pulled her up and away from the Colonel. Two others were at the side of the fallen man, lifting him between them. Then Roane's guide drew her along at a half-running pace, while the two carrying Imfry matched that as well as they could. They were past the houses, into a clot of shadowed shrubbery before she fairly caught her breath. She heard the stamp of duocorn hoofs against the turf and they came into a clearing where four men were mounted, holding on checking reins animals manifestly fresh and ready for the trail.

"Ride!" ordered the man with Roane.

The duocorns wheeled under spurring, pounded off to the south. But the men in her party pushed back into the shadows.

"Haffner knows these trails. He will lead them a

good chase," commented one of Imfry's bearers with satisfaction.

"He had better," said his fellow. "We shall need all the time we can win. Help with the Colonel, he's bleeding bad. Needs looking to as soon as we can get him hid."

14

The medic kit! There was the slim chance that its drugs might not aid one born on Clio. But if they could—

"Please." Roane moved in the grip of the man who had pulled her into this temporary safety. "I have that which will aid him. Let me—"

"Well enough. But we cannot remain here. There is a chance they may not be misled by that false trail. To the hound hut, Mattine."

Dawn was well upon them, but it appeared that these men knew what they were about. Even burdened with the Colonel they melted into the brush with fluid ease, while Roane's guide drew her through openings she herself could not distinguish.

This was not quite one of those hidden brush-and-tree-walled roads, rather a slot in the earth along which they trotted. Roane could hear the heavy breathing of the two carrying Imfry as she followed on their heels and the other man served as a rear guard.

That journey seemed very long, though it could not have been so in either time or distance. Then the bearers halted, and the man behind Roane wriggled through what again appeared a thick wall of brush. Roane tried to get a good look at Imfry.

His head lay against one of his bearers, and his eyes were closed. There was a sticky patch on his shirt.

"Let me—I can help him—" She tried to edge closer, but the man who supported Imfry hunched his shoulder as a barrier.

"Not yet!" His whisper was fierce. "Quiet!"

She huddled, listening. There were sounds. Noises which came, she thought, more from animal than human throats. Then she did catch a voice.

"Ha, Brighttooth, Rampage, Roarer—down—sit! And you, Shrew, Surenose—quiet! Eat, drink, and be quiet!"

The brush screen trembled as their guide returned. All three men wore their hoods pulled well about their faces, so Roane saw little of them save the thrust of their chins. But there was an air of authority in this man.

"Take these." He had some strips of material in his hands.

From them—Roane's nose wrinkled in disgust— steamed a nauseating stench. The last thing she wanted to do was touch those rags. But she was given no choice. One of the men supporting Imfry accepted three of the strips, hung one about his own neck and draped one on his fellow and one over the Colonel, while the fourth was thrown in her direction. Reluctantly, her hand shrinking from contamination as she took it, she picked it up.

"Our key to the kennels. I do not think we shall be disturbed there. At least not for a while. Now—before they cast in this direction, let us move!"

They pushed out into a cleared space. There stood a tall fence made of stakes set firmly in the ground, tops sharpened into points. Tall as those were, Roane caught sight of a roof pitch beyond. There was a gate not too far away and their guide went directly to it, drawing a bar which was weighty enough to lock a keep.

Those carrying Imfry crossed the open at a shambling run, as if they were putting forth their best effort to get their burden quickly into hiding, and Roane trailed them. The gate slammed behind her and she heard the bar thud into place, so fastened by the man who had led them. But her eyes were for what lay within.

Direhounds! Like the duocorns, they were not native to Clio but had been imported. And she did not know any planet, save perhaps one of the inner worlds supporting an exotic zoo, which allowed the import of Loki direhounds. Deceptively they were not large, nor ferocious to look at, though the odor given off by their spotted hides could choke one. Their maned heads were down as they tore at chunks of meat.

As the human party moved toward the hut in the center of the pen, two swung around, making no sound, their black lips wrinkling back to bare the double rows of green-scummed fangs. And there was a hot and terrible hate in their eyes.

One took a step and then a second, moving to intercept the men, who had halted, visibly bracing themselves. Then those fringed ears, which had been flattened to narrow skulls as the creatures sniffed the air, went up as if they had caught a familiar sound or their noses some usual scent. Roane held closer to her that rag she had so disdained. It was indeed a key here.

The leading direhound gave a last sniff, turned away to a clay-smeared chunk of meat, its companion copying its action. The men moved on, though it was very hard for Roane not to turn and walk backwards as they passed among the gorging animals, the sensation that they would be attacked from the rear so weighed on her.

"The door—open the door—" one of Imfry's supporters ordered.

She edged past the men, still watching the direhounds with small, distrustful side glances, to push. The door opened readily and they entered into darkness and the stench of the animals, even worse in these confined quarters. Involuntarily she snapped on the beamer.

Along one side of the small room hung joints of meat,

blackened and evil-smelling. Above those was a series of narrow shelves on which crowded stoppered containers. From spikes driven into the other walls dangled whips, leashes, collars, and muzzles massive enough to imprison a direhound's fangs.

To their right stood bales of straw trussed with rope. One had been cut open and half its contents taken. Roane laid down the beamer to attack that, spreading out the rest for a rough bed on the floor as fast as she could.

As they laid Imfry on that she brought out the medic kit. No time to test her remedies. The more she saw the gray-white of that face, the less she liked it. Now it was her turn to give orders.

"Room!" Her hands—she looked at her dirty, scratched fingers. "Here—" She picked up a spray tube. "You—" She held it out to the nearest man. "Press this down, carefully now—it must not be wasted."

Roane bathed her hands in the antiseptic vapor. "Enough!" She held them away from any touch which would infect them again. "Ease his shirt away from that wound. No—use the spray first—on this—" She pointed to another tube to be prepared.

Then, taking it, she carefully dribbled a few drops of its contents over that stain. With the tips of her fingers she urged the fabric gently away from the flesh to which it had been glued.

"Now—tear it!"

As the contaminated cloth came away from an angry-looking wound, where blood still oozed sluggishly, Roane went to work with all the skill she had, spraying—twice with antibiotics, and then with Swiftheal—before applying a final sealing of plasta-flesh with double care, since it might be put to unusual tests before this journey was finished.

She sat back then to consider the remaining contents of her kit. Examination had assured her that the fall had not brought broken bones. It was the extra strain upon his wound which had sent him into the present state of unconsciousness. Certainly the longer he could rest, the better chance the plasta-flesh had for a firm closing. She thought it best not to try to arouse him.

The air of the hut was thick with the stench of the direhounds and the decaying meat. Roane was so hot she pulled off her hood, loosened the lacing on her tunic. For the first time she had a chance to inspect her comrades in hiding. Both men had now relaxed against the bales of straw.

One was familiar—the other strange. But she put name to the one who had supported Imfry's head during that escape.

"You are Sergeant Wuldon. You went with us to Gastonhow."

He was older than the Colonel, it seemed to her, though it was difficult to judge ages on alien worlds. But his brown hair had a wide strip of silver over each ear. His face was as weathered as Imfry's had been before the sickly gray tint had overlaid that healthier hue. And there was a small puckered dot in the flesh of his chin, slightly to one side, like a misplaced cleft.

"Ysor Wuldon, yes, m'lady."

"You came to save him." She made that a statement rather than a question. Wuldon nodded.

"We had hopes. There were a few in Hitherhow ready to give us some aid. The Duke is not greatly loved. But they would not promise too much—and we would have failed, m'lady, without you."

Roane leaned back against one of the bales, raised her hands to brush straying hair out of her eyes. The smell, the heat made her feel ill, and again she wondered at her actions, as if that part of her which was the old Roane now stirred from captivity to view with dismay what had happened. This odd sense of being two persons added to her growing state of misery. She gulped, trying to subdue nausea, and feared that soon she would lose control.

The other man stirred restlessly. "This stink—" he muttered.

"No garden of turl lilies," agreed Wuldon. "But out there—" he jerked a thumb to indicate the enclosure of the direhounds—"we have about the best sentries we could wish for."

Roane swallowed again. "How long—" She found she could not complete that, but Wuldon had no trouble in understanding. Only he could not be reassuring with his answer.

"Who knows? Until nightfall, if we are lucky and they follow that false trail. If they can be drawn into the hunting preserve our men can lead them astray and lose them. Then we can move out. But with the Colonel as he is—" He shook his head.

"How is he, Lady?" the other man asked. "You have him fixed good enough to ride if we can move out? We cannot go far if we have to lug him."

There was a dissenting growl from the Sergeant, but the other man faced him squarely. "That is the truth and you know it. Me, I am liege man to m'lord. My own mother's sister fostered him when his lady mother died. Do you think I would say no to getting him free? Did I when you and Haus came asking? But we cannot carry him. He has to be able to ride. It is a long way to the hills."

"They will outlaw-horn him," the Sergeant said slowly. "Then how much help can he claim anywhere in Reveny? Best over the border. He would not be the first good man driven to that, and he has a sword worth selling—if not in Leichstan, the Isles of Marduk welcome mercenaries—"

"Thank you for the testimony, Wuldon." The voice was low, strained, and it startled them.

The Colonel's eyes were open. There was even a little color in his sunken cheeks.

"What a smell!" He sniffed. "Direhound! But where in Reveny—" He moved as if to rise but the Sergeant had clamped a big, gentle hand down on his uninjured shoulder, holding him where he was.

"Haus's idea, sir. We are in the hound hut at Hitherhow."

"The hound hut!" Imfry repeated. "Out of one cage, into another. But I must say that for all the smells, I find this one easier than the last. But—how did you plan—this—"

"Well, we did not—not together, sir. I saw them bring you out of that hole in the ground and Spetik and I split up and went to where we thought we could get help. He came to Hitherhow and talked to Mattine and Haus. There were some men in the village who were willing to risk a little. Though they were not going too far, being a bit mindful of their necks."

"For which you cannot blame them, Wuldon. Treason is not a crime one wants to aid. Spetik, and Mattine here—Haus, and you— Then what else did you do?"

"Well, I went back to the post. There were four or five of the men ready to see what we could do. So—we left—"

The Colonel frowned. "Deserted?" he demanded.

Sergeant Wuldon grinned. "Better say 'detached duty' —serving with our commanding officer. No man had named you different then. Nor have we been personally told so since."

Imfry's frown disappeared. "You heard it loud and clear in Hitherhow."

"No, sir. Ever since I was caught in that rock fall last year, sir—when you dropped down on a rope and pulled me free—well, I have not heard too clear at times. I did not hear anything about your not being my commanding officer."

"Impaired hearing can take you out of the service, Sergeant."

"It has, Colonel. If anything is said to Reddick—it has."

Imfry laughed, but sobered quickly. "If we are taken, no such flimsy arguments will get you out of a hanging —or worse."

"Then we shall take care we are not caught, sir.

But we did come here, me, Haffner, Spetik, Rinwald, Fleech. They got duocorns, best mounts in the stables, and stood ready to either ride or set a false trail. But we did not know just how we could get to you. She did that in the end." He nodded at Roane.

"You were a part of this?" Imfry asked.

"Of their plans, no. I came—I came because I had to. It was my interference which began everything. I could not let it end so because of my meddling. But we could not have made it without your men."

"It is very strange." The Colonel's eyes rested steadily upon her. "From the first I knew that you held some fate in your hands, though that it was mine, I did not guess. I thought it was the Princess's."

He stirred again. "Odd, all the pain is gone" He looked at his wound, where the plasta-flesh had taken on the hue of the skin around it.

"What did you do to me, anyway?" he asked Wuldon.

"The lady did it, from her own supplies."

"She seems good at a great many things," commented the Colonel. "Wuldon, you would not have such a thing as a saddle bottle of water about you?"

"Sorry—"

"That is all right."

Roane forced herself to move. The fetid air and heat made her weak. But she found one of the E ration tubes, turned the twist cap and held it out to him.

"Suck this," she said. "It is about half moisture, so it ought to help." She brought out two more, offered them to the men. They examined them curiously.

"How about you, m'lady?" the Sergeant asked.

Roane made a hard business of swallowing. "I cannot—it makes me sick. If you will— Please, Sergeant"—her voice became more urgent—"the kit—push it to me."

She thought that she would not be able to make it in time, but she hunted with one hand among the containers, came up with a capsule she broke between her palms, bending her head to sniff and sniff again of the reviving fumes. But she had too few of those to waste them. If they were here long, how could she stand it? Conditioned she might be to withstand alien worlds, alien odors, alien foods—there were some strains which her body could not take and it seemed she was meeting them now in this prison-like hut.

"I will have to go soon." She raised her head when the vertigo subsided a little and she was temporarily the mistress of her body. "They do not know me here— I ought to go safely."

"Do not believe that, m'lady," Wuldon returned. "With the Colonel free they will look thrice at any stranger. You leave this place and the first one to see you will call for the guard. Every man, woman, and child in Hitherhow will be glad to help run down a stranger—if only to turn the Duke's men away from sniffing at their own doors."

"Exactly right." The Colonel's voice was stronger, had back that sure note which had once troubled her with its assumption that his way was the only right one. "And where would you go? Or will your people come looking for you?"

She shook her head, and then wished that she had not made that gesture, for it left her dizzy. "That is the last thing they would do. I broke orders to come here. They will believe anything that happens to me is richly deserved."

"What kind of talk is that?" the Sergeant asked. "No one would turn his back on a lady who had come to help—"

"There must be a good reason," Imfry cut in. "Some time, Lady Roane, I would like to hear it. Now—I will admit that to stay here any longer than is absolutely necessary is something we all cannot do. Have you any plans, Sergeant?"

"Haus may have. He brought us here to wait. And he knows Hitherhow. Also—they know *him*, well enough not to go throwing any trouble in his way. It is good to be the only man who can really handle direhounds;

keeps everyone on his toes seeing as how Haus stays happy and in good health. Of course, they could shoot them all to get to us. Maybe the Duke might do just that if he knew we were here. But the belief would be that those devil animals would not let us inside the gate, which would be the truth if Haus had not given us a key through their power of scent."

"Listen!" Imfry ordered.

Once more Roane could hear the loud grunting of the hounds.

"Someone's coming!" Sergeant Wuldon, weapon in hand, crossed with a silent tread Roane would have believed impossible for such a powerful man, to stand at the door of the hut. He hunched a little, apparently finding a crack through which he could see something of the outside.

"Haus!" The name was a hiss of whisper and then Wuldon added, "alone." But he did not reholster his weapon and Mattine moved, if not as noiselessly, to the other side of the door frame. Roane watched from the apathy of her discomfort.

"Sooooooo." The voice of the man outside rang on a crooning note. "Good boy—brave—brave— Easy, girl, there is enough for all—mind your manners."

If she had not known what sort of beasts did roam without, Roane would have believed them the gentlest and most agreeable of pets. People did have odd tastes, as who should know better than she, who had been exposed to a variety of worlds and customs—but to find a man who dealt unreservedly with direhounds!

"It takes many kinds of men, m'lady, to make a nation." The Colonel might have read her thoughts, if not her expression. "There is"—his voice dropped to a whisper she could barely hear—"much to be said between the two of us. I know not why you came—but to you my—"

"Wait until you are free. Ill luck can come from too early thanksgiving." She had never been superstitious before, but now, uneasy as she was inwardly, she could understand primitive natives who feared to invoke wrong powers, tempt retaliation from ill luck.

"Until another time, then. But, believe me, we shall have you forth as soon as we can—"

She looked at him steadily, a dull wonder in her. He spoke now as if she were the one to be concerned about, when *he* was the hunted man.

The door opened and the man who had led them here entered, dropping a heavy sack, which added another sickening odor of dog meat, on the floor with a thud.

"How is he—" he was beginning, when the Colonel spoke up.

"Come see for yourself, man! Your pets have played guard well."

"M'lord." Haus crossed the small room in a couple of strides, knelt, and laid his hand palm down on the one the Colonel held out to him, bowing his head for a moment as if the gesture was a small but solemn ceremony.

"It has been a long time, Haus."

"One can forget the toll of years, m'lord, when there is good reason. Now"—he sat back on his haunches so that his face was more or less on a level with that of the man he spoke to—"there is a plan, desperate, but the best which can be done for now. They have sent to Urkermark for *his* orders. Luck has so far served us in two ways. First, when the badge of Hitherhow fell in the courtyard, it brought down the Marshal of the West. He still lies unconscious and they do not know when, or if, he will come to his senses. Colonel Scharn got a broken collar bone and a bad scrape on the head, so he's not been much use in leading any hunt.

"While this other—this Colonel Onglas—has been fluttering around without much more wits than the least of my pack out there. He put most of the guard to searching the village, routing folks out of their homes to ask questions and seek for traitors.

"Two hours ago he demanded the direhounds. Some of the patrolmen found the tracks and he wanted to set the hounds to those."

Roane heard the men around her exclaim over that. "Yes." Haus nodded. "I told you he had the wits of a peckfowl! I told him how a coursing such as that would end. Even I could not hold them to any set trail which was not that of a spaybuck or a roffer. So—he ordered me to make identification scent."

"He is plain mad!" burst out the Sergeant. "Using what?"

"He has straw out of the cell they kept you in, m'lord, and some of the rags they used on your arm when they brought you in. It would be enough, and he will see that I do it. He is sending down guards to watch."

"Here? Then what—" Wuldon began.

"They will not come in, never fear. But I told him the truth, that even direhounds cannot pick up a hunted man's trail if he is mounted. So he is having a duocorn killed and the carcass brought here, too."

"A duocorn! Let your pets sniff that and they will turn on any like beast—even those of the hunters," Imfry observed. "He is truly insane."

"He is fear-mad, I think, m'lord. He does not dare face the Duke with no better news than he has now. But I told him straight facts, and others listened, if he did not. Never mind about the straw and rags. I can doctor those. But it goes against my liking to make a duocorn into bait. The hounds could head straight for the stables. And why should innocent beasts suffer? Only there are those with him, lesser officers, who have their heads screwed on. One of them is going to Colonel Scharn right now, sure he can get that order countermanded. But—this is what I rightfully want to say, Colonel—that dead duocorn they are bringing down—I think that will get you out of here."

"Keep talking, Haus. This is beginning to interest me."

Haus nodded. "Like the old days along the border

when the Nimps were raiding. Yes, m'lord, I thought
you would remember. They deliver this duocorn, but
none of them is going to risk his neck to push the
cart inside that gate. So I fetch it in, with Sergeant
Wuldon here—"

"Me!" The Sergeant jerked back a fraction of an inch.
"But everybody knows that you are the only one who
dares come inside—"

"I already told them I have a forester to help with
the bait and the coursing—said you were wearing a
treated coat to keep the hounds off, but it was mine
and I only had the one. I also told them that you had
helped on other hound hunts. The Duke did turn up
some men he wanted trained, but none of them lasted
long." He laughed. "All right, we drag the duocorn
carcass into this hut to work on. In spite of all Onglas's
raving, none of them is going to get up nerve enough
to push in to watch. Then—we take out the Colonel, only
he'll be wrapped up in the skin. We put him in the
cart. Down comes Scharn's officer to say there has been
enough of such foolishness. I say we have to get the
bait out and bury it before the hounds go wild. I tell
you, these men know nothing of the nature of the
beasts. They are ready to believe anything one bab-
bles about them. We take the cart back into the woods
and I have a little show ready waiting to cover us out
there."

"And what about m'lady here and Mattine?"

"They go out now, to lay low in my place. I make a
big to-do later about needing help with the cart, and
bring them along. That's the best I can offer, Colonel."

"It is clever, Haus. But I do not want m'lady and
Mattine to run a risk."

Roane found her voice. "I run a greater staying here.
I tell you, it will sicken me and I have no remedies
which will help."

He looked at her, searching, but she knew she spoke
the truth.

"They will have protection, m'lord. I am taking the

she hound Surenose up to my house. She is near whelping and I always take such to snugger quarters. With her loose in the inner yard, no one is going to stick nose through the gate."

"A lot of things can go wrong," Sergeant Wuldon observed. "What if this Scharn does not speak up in time and Onglas makes you take the bait to the hounds?"

"I can spend a long time making it. I tell you he knows nothing about direhounds, and he is not one to come and see what goes on here. I will get the guards to protest, and, if necessary, he will find he cannot force a hunting party into the chase. Sure it is risky, but so is any game you are going to play to get the Colonel out. And I cannot promise better."

"He is right," Imfry said. "There is no way I am going to get out of here without taking more risk than I care to think about. And this game sounds as if it does have possibilities."

15

Roane, her hood once more well over her face, slouched along in the wake of a bobbing cart. She was no actress and now was the time when the slightest error might arouse the suspicions of those following them on this faintest of tracks away from the village and into the forest. At least Haus had been able to prolong his bait preparations until midafternoon, and it was close to evening when they had been ordered by Scharn, come to his senses enough to take charge, to do away with the carcass. She gave silent thanks that at least there had been no further message from Duke Reddick.

The cart creaked and bumped. She would hate to lie therein, wrapped in a bloody skin which already attracted a trail of insects, as Imfry had to do. The Sergeant and Mattine pulled the shaft of that crude transport. No duocorn could be brought near the smelly cargo. Which was why the rear guard went dismounted. And now Haus, who walked by her side, proposed to get rid of those guards she could not imagine.

Thus far his plan had worked, and Roane could not quarrel with anything which brought them into the clean air, farther and farther from Hitherhow. At least she had slept away some of that period she and Mattine had been in Haus's house, so she felt more alert. Though as long as she knew of that installation, the machines clicking away to regulate the lives of those who could not imagine they were so governed, she would be ill at ease.

Roane plodded along, trying to act the sullen role of one pressed into unwilling service. She hoped to be ready for Haus's move, or one from Imfry.

"You—Haus!" A voice rang out from the rear. "How far do you expect to travel before you bury that carrion? We are not going to tramp all over this forest—"

"Neither do I want to worry about the hounds taking to our trail and getting a taste for duocorn the first time they are uncoupled in chase," Haus replied. "I do not fancy having to explain something like dead mounts to the Duke."

She heard grumbling, but no open protests. A moment later Haus's shoulder brushed hers and he said harshly:

"Can you not even walk straight, boy? By the Arms of the Guardians, what help are you? Get up ahead there and lend a hand to pulling or we are going to be half the night going a quarter league!"

Roane pushed between the cart and encroaching brush and saplings, reaching the Sergeant, to lay hand to the shaft beside him.

"Not long now, m'lady," he whispered. "Be ready to jump to the right when I give the word."

Jump right— She glanced in that direction. There was a tumbling pile of stones, a trail of them, as if a wall had once stood there. But in that were frequent gaps which were filled with rank grass and matted vines. Also there were brush and trees. It was a gray day, without sun, and there was a damp feeling of coming rain in the air. Jump right—she ran her tongue over very dry lips.

The track they followed, if track it really was, took a sharp angle left. And they had the cart half around the bend when out of the brush fronting them arose a grunting which could only be a direhound! The Sergeant shouted, gave a swift jerk to the pull, and the cart trembled. Mattine pushed as if in panic and the small transport began to tip toward Roane.

"Now!"

Once more the direhound sounded. Behind men yelled warnings while Haus bellowed confused orders. Roane took the chance that Wuldon knew exactly what he was doing. She leaped for the cover of the tumbled stones, plunging on away from the track. As she went she heard the crash of the cart hitting on its side.

"Run, you lack-witted fools!" That was Haus. "They must have broken out the gate, are circling for a kill. Get away or face them!"

Roane slammed against a tree, held to it, her heart pounding. It could not be as the hound master said because Wuldon had been expecting something. But this was her chance to be free of the whole action.

She gave a sob, would have stumbled blindly on, when she heard a crashing behind her. So she backed around, the tree against her spine, half fearing to face death on four feet. What came was the Sergeant supporting a bloodstained, half-clothed man—Imfry! He must have been able to claw out of his reeking cover as soon as the cart overturned.

"Come on!" The Sergeant and his superior officer passed, Roane followed.

Though she could see no guide through this wilderness, the men before her went with as much confidence as if they were following one of those off-world homing devices. But they had not gone too far before Mattine came into view also. He was laughing.

"That Haus! He has stampeded the whole squad! They are hearing twice as many hound calls as he sends, and they are racing back to the keep, doubtless to report we have all been eaten alive. M'lord, he is better than half a regiment by himself."

"He had better be! Were Reddick to suspect him—"

"Would not do the Duke any good. With those pets of his Haus has a better bodyguard than any king." Mattine lost none of his cheer.

"They are mortal; a few well-placed bullets— I hope he has a tight tale for Reddick when he comes."

"You think the Duke will come, sir?" asked the Sergeant.

"I do not flatter myself, Wuldon, that I am any great prize for myself alone. As you suggested, he will undoubtedly have me horned as an outlaw. After that"— Imfry shrugged—"I shall be meat for the shooting with a reward to top the fun of the chase. But Reddick knows that as long as I live I shall not rest until I know what spell he has set on the Queen!" There was such cold determination in that, Roane shivered.

"He had her under mind-globe back there in the cave—but this goes deeper than anything Shambry can devise, holds longer and tighter. You heard the proclamation, the earlier one, that she is going to wed Reddick. It will follow that she will raise him to Prince Consort, and, then—how long will it be before he rules Reveny? If she wakes from that spell with his creatures around her, what chance will she have? I tell you, she is as much a prisoner now as I was at Hitherhow. Though she may not yet realize it."

"Sir." Mattine was serious now. "I always heard it

told that mind-globe spells cannot make anyone do what is against his inner nature."

"I will not believe," Imfry said slowly, looking at Mattine, a set, hard line to his jaw, his eyes cold, "that the Princess—the Queen—would have signed my death warrant of her own free will. Nor can anyone who knows her well. Ask you the Lady Roane. She had been much with her."

They looked to her now. And she gave them the truth. "She is under a spell."

Mattine and the Sergeant looked disturbed, but Imfry nodded, and some of that hardness left his face.

"You see? The Queen needs our aid. Can we deny her aught we can do?"

"Sir, we can raise no army. If we hide out in the Reserve and send the word about we can muster men, yes, that much I grant you. But an army large enough to go up against those Reddick can easily put in the field, no. And if the Soothspeaker Shambry is so powerful that he can hold the Queen in thrall against her nature, then it may be possible he can do likewise with even us, if he can find a way. Sir—if you will only go over the border—to Leichstan or—"

"And would any neighbor give me refuge? The Queen went to Leichstan and was met by treachery. Could we hope to fare better? We cannot let Reddick drive us out now or there will be no return at all."

"Well, we need not set off today, sir. We had better think about saving our hides or Reddick will have them skinned off our aching backs," returned the Sergeant.

"Right you are," Imfry answered. "This lay-up Haus told you of, is it far?"

"Far enough to keep us moving well for awhile, sir. You feeling it now?" Mattine cut in.

"Less than I thought that I would, thanks to the Lady Roane and those miracles she carries in her jars and tubes. And you, m'lady, do you go with us now?"

He was giving her a choice. But as he spoke she

discovered she had already made it—long ago. He wanted an answer to the change in Ludorica, she was sure she had it. Facing Reddick bravely would do no good, not so long as those installations kept clicking away. They would control all—maybe they did even now. And the Service would not move in time to aid, even if Uncle Offlas managed to bring down the LB and return to the mother ship out in orbit.

"Yes," Roane answered simply.

If she expected any encouraging comment from him, she did not get it. Mattine fell into step with her.

"It is still a far piece, m'lady. But at least we can lay up there snug and tight, and watch our back trail without worry. It is one of the old war camps of the Karoff rebellion. The enemy did not take it by storm when it fell, but by treachery. Since we have no traitors we do not have to fear that, now do we?"

Moonrise came, had the moon been able to penetrate thoroughly the drifting clouds, before they reached their destination. Roane never discovered what guides the Sergeant and Mattine used to bring them through the forest to a stony rise and up that by a very wandering and narrow way to a plateau.

There were walls here, crumbling. But, while they had not been built with mortar, they were still intact enough to afford shelter. And that Roane was glad to have. She was breathing hard as she sank down in a corner niche and sat, her feet stretched out before her. They had not pressed on as hard during that journey as she had imagined they might, probably because her companions had wanted to spare Imfry. But the Colonel had regained some of his old endurance, for which she thanked her medical supplies. His shoulder seemed to give him much less trouble. Even during their last climb he had not favored it much.

Where they were in reference to the off-world camp or the hidden installation, Roane did not know, but that Imfry might be able to find his way to the latter she hoped. The question remained as to whether he

would do it if he knew of the danger Uncle Offlas
had prophesied. On the other hand, she was as sure
as if she had definite knowledge that there was no hope
of freeing Ludorica except via the defeat of the machines.

"Now, sir." Wuldon had made a circuit of the ancient
fortifications, returned to stand before his officer as if
on duty and making a formal report. "We got you here
safe and sound. Our boys who laid that false trail
should have been free long ago and ought now to be
waiting at the Twisted Sword. We will all breathe easier when we get together. So, with your permission,
I will jog on to pick them up. And Mattine—he has to
reach Pin Crossing to see about fresh mounts—"

"Sounds as if you have made a lot of plans, Wuldon." Was there a hint of surprise in Imfry's voice?

"Best we could, sir. Not knowing that you would be
more yourself—as you are. If you want to change
them—"

"Why? I can be sure that they are the best under
the circumstances. Good luck—Guardian's Fortune—to
you both."

"We will whistle the old call, sir, when we come
back. There is a good deadfall over the high path in,
one of those traps we used to set in the Nimp times.
Pull the lock rock and it will close off the path—take a
full company a day to clear it. Guardian's Fortune to
you, too, sir, and to m'lady!"

He gave a salute which Mattine echoed, and they
were gone, lost in shadows before Roane could blink.
In this dark she could only be sure she still had a
companion when he moved. Fingers touched her arm,
slid down until they closed, warm, alive about her wrist,
where her own hand lay limp on her knee.

"Why did you come?"

Enmeshed as she was in a tangle of thoughts she
was too tired to bring into order, she answered with
real truth:

"Because of the dream—"

"Dream?"

Somehow it was easier to talk when there was only that quiet question out of the dark, that loose clasp about her wrist. And there was relief in speech, as if she were ridding herself of a long-carried burden. Whether he would believe it or not, Roane did not at that moment care. It was enough to put it all into words.

She began with the dream, trying to make it live for him as it had for her, bringing every detail to mind—the room, the dishes on the table, Ludorica's ceremonial entrance behind the usher, her ladies-in-waiting, the presence of Reddick—

"I could not hear what they said, I only saw their lips move. It was like watching a defective tri-dee in which the sound track had been cut away. But it was alive—it was!" She lost herself in remembering. There was a need to make him understand how she had seen it all. "I have dreamed before, who does not? But never like this."

"A true sending." His words reached her out of the dark. Now she realized also that his grasp on her wrist had tightened until it hurt by its pressure, and she pulled, trying to free herself.

"A sending?" She made of that a question.

"You have far sight—"

"No," she objected. "I was tested—I have no esper power. It was a dream."

"Of the small chamber in Urkermark High Keep, of the Queen wearing Court mourning, of the signing of the warrant which may mean my death. When were you last in Urkermark High Keep, Lady Roane?"

"I was never there."

"The time has come"—his words were even, measured—"for us to speak frankly. If truth does not lie between us now, it never will—and we must have truth! Do you understand that?"

The last choice of all. And she saw in the dark, as well as if she did indeed face it, that row of clicking machines, each with its crown, its slaves. And she saw the Ludorica she did not know, the stranger she feared, who held a crown in her hands:

"Who are you," he continued, "or what?"

Roane drew a deep breath. "I am—a woman," she said, answering his last question first. "Also I am Roane Hume. But I am not of this world—"

Having taken the plunge, she dared not think, but struck out into the current of truth, which not only might sweep her away but could end everything she had been schooled to believe in.

She told him of the Service, of why they had come to Clio, of her chance meeting with the Princess, of the installation, and of what that meant to him and his people. When she had done she was drained, emptied, glad of that warm encirclement of her wrist which linked her to a living world.

"This is a tale beyond belief," he began and she tried to jerk away from his hold, chilled—frightened that he could not believe. Immediately his hold on her tightened. "Yet," he continued, "I know that it is true. You say you have no ability to foresee. Perhaps by the reckoning of your people, you do not. But my own House—we have that talent in part. We have also a strange tradition which had been a closely guarded secret for generations.

"It is one I would not ordinarily speak of to any, be he even close brother-kin, unless he knew it by right of birth. But because it is akin to what you have told me, I will speak of it now. The Guardians—we worship them after a fashion, and to most they are supernatural beings. But in my House there is a tale that he who founded our line was a direct servant of Guardians—who were *not* immortals as all believe, but had flesh and substance. And he did certain tasks for them in that far beginning which were connected with the ordering of Reveny life.

"When men awoke here at the Guardians' bidding and set about living, my forefather retained hazy memories of another time and place. These he kept to himself, speaking of them only to his son, and so it passed through my line. We have in addition other things. There have been soothspeakers of our name. That is how I am sure that the Queen was not what she seemed when she found the Crown and ordered my death.

"Now you make plain she was not being moved by the control of any mind-globe, but that she, the Duke, all of us, are game pieces moved about to fulfill some plan made by men long dead, ones who had no right to set our forefathers into such patterns. But you fear that to destroy these controls would be to destroy us also."

"My uncle feared that. He wants to bring in the experts of the Service. They would study the installation, make sure—if they came at all."

"If they came at all!" That was bitter. "Then they would have chosen, had you not broken *their* pattern, to let us live forever under the domination of chattering metal things! What right have they to allow such slavery? Or are they themselves slaves to other patterns? Is it so from star to star, with no one really free?"

He was now echoing one of her own recent thoughts.

"And these men of your Service, *if* they come, would take time, maybe years, to study before they moved. Is that not so?"

"Yes."

"And all that while we would continue to be secretly ruled. Ludorica, who is good, would do evil. Reddick, who wishes to bring war and worse upon Reveny, who would slay even the Queen if by her death he could take the Crown, would continue in power. I— I shall do what I can against him. But if these machines will otherwise, I am defeated before I begin!"

"The installation can be destroyed."

"There was Arothner, which lost its crown—"

"The Princess told me that story," Roane admitted.

"Then you know what chanced there. To risk that— for Reveny—for all the world!"

"The result may not be the same. A lost crown could differ in effect from a silenced machine."

"But the risk—it is too great!"

"The choice is yours." She had done what she could. If he said now that Clio must remain in slavery, let it be so.

She turned her wrist again and this time his grasp loosened and fell away. With its going she felt as alone as if he had arisen and walked from her. There was no road back. She was locked in a prison she had built herself stone by stone. Yet she was unable to regret what lay behind.

Roane settled her shoulders against the harsh stone of the wall, raised her knees, and folded her arms across them as a pillow for her head. That emptiness she had earlier welcomed now became a billowing fog of fatigue. She did not care if morning, light, or the need to take up the burden of living ever came again.

But tired as she was, sleep did not come. Instead her thoughts twisted and turned as an insomniac might twist and turn upon a bed during a wakeful night. She walked again on other worlds, relived this small fragment of the past and that. It seemed to her that she had always been part of a set pattern, also, imposed upon her by Uncle Offlas, by the life he introduced her to. Was it true as Nelis had said, that even from star to star there was no freedom? Yet the rules of the Service called for no interference, no meddling even for good in the destiny of a troubled world.

Pattern upon pattern, tie and bond upon tie and bond, no freedom. Roane stirred and then once more that hand out of the dark reached her, slipping across her shoulders to draw her to rest close to the warmth, the safe anchorage of another body, human, alive, no longer exiled alone in the dark.

"What is it, Roane? Why do you cry?" His voice was a breath warm against her cheek. And she knew then that tears did wet her face and that she wept as she could not ever remember having done since she was a small and lonesome child.

"I think it is because I am alone." She tried to put that desolation into words.

"But that you are not! Is it because you come from the stars and here find no kin? Would you return to your people? I promise I shall take you to them—"

"They will not want me now."

"Do not think that others believe in that fashion." The grasp about her shoulders was very comforting. "I have been wondering—why was it, do you think, that you saw the Queen and Reddick in this dream? You were not reaching as a Soothspeaker does to read some peril or fact needful to your life. Yet you saw that which brought you to Hitherhow, to aid in my escape. And such visions are not ordinary. From whence came this one?"

Perhaps he was kindly trying to make her think of something else. But there was certainly a strangeness to that dream.

"I do not know. But I am sure I have no esper powers. My people understand these things, they checked me. It was important that they make sure."

"Yet you have also said that you have done things on this world which were counter to all your training, to what you were taught was lawful. And I do not believe that you are one who has ever deliberately chosen to break rules and flout authority before. Is that not so?"

"I do not know why, but when I first saw the Princess, in that tower, I had to help her. Uncle Offlas said you were all conditioned. Perhaps when I had left the safeguards of our camp that also influenced me."

"Yet you could see these machines. The Princess could not. So if there was conditioning, for you it was not complete."

"What difference does it make now? I broke the Service rules, I—perhaps it was I who started the whole tangle. The Princess would not have known of the Crown had she not gone to the cave. And if she had not found the Crown—"

"Roane, Roane, do not take on yourself guilt for a whole country!"

Fingers touched her cheek gently, exploring, though that arm was still a barrier between her and dark loneliness.

"You are crying once more! I tell you, this is not of your doing! You have brought good, not evil. Had you not taken the Princess from Reddick's men then, you might have left her to her death. And had you not come to Hitherhow—I might have died, too, and been a long time in doing it."

"There was the Sergeant, Mattine, the others—"

"Who could well have thrown *their* lives away and to no avail. Nor would we ever have known of these machines. For had you not taken the Princess there for shelter, would you ever have found them?"

"Perhaps."

"And perhaps not. Nor without the knowledge you have gained from us would you have known what they were. No—there is a meaning to be read in all you have done, if we can see it."

"I do not understand."

"Neither do I. I can only sense it is there, a reason to move you to aid the Princess, and later to do all else. You say that those we know as the Guardians are long dead, have been judged evil by those beyond the stars. They used men as tools and it did not last. Now your people fear to upset what they have done. But— why have you told this story to the one man in Reveny who could believe it, because his far-off ancestor escaped the full blight sent on Clio?"

"Chance—fortune— I do not know—"

"Neither do I. Save that it is making me think. Roane, can you find this cave again?"

"Do you mean you wish to free the Crown?"

"I do not know. I think that I shall not be sure until I stand there and know what such slavery means. But that I must do; I know it now. Can you take me there?"

"If we dare go back. It lies near Hitherhow."

"Dare we not now?" he countered.

"The LB may have come. If not, they—Uncle Offlas, Sandar—they will try to keep us away and they have weapons—"

"Did you not use one such on me? Yes, I have tasted the power of those strange arms of yours. But that we must chance also. And I think time is fast running out."

"You mean we go now? Before the Sergeant and Mattine return?"

"I think for what we may have to do we should have as little company as possible. But let us wait for dawn before we take the trail. Sleep if you can, Roane."

He did not release her, so that Roane's head slipped down to rest against him as indeed she found now she could sleep.

16

Roane awoke as if summoned by some imperative call, though there was silence as she roused. The light of dawn lay outside their small corner of refuge. Imfry's arm was still about her. They had huddled together in the night. Turning her head with care, she saw he still slept, or at least his eyes were closed.

There was a stubble of dark beard on his jaw, yet in sleep he looked much younger, unguarded, that rigidity of feature which usually masked him gone. There were lines perhaps born of pain, or the burden of decisions, but now they were faint. Studying him so, Roane thought of the one part of her dream she had not told him—the face she had seen at its ending.

For that had not been Ludorica's, nor Reddick's, and yet it had stung her into action.

Had Nelis been right in his theory that some force had moved her to play the part she had since she had landed on Clio? Superstition, common on a backward world, Uncle Offlas would term that, note it as a native trait on his tapes put aside for the anthropologists to study.

Many worlds had their strong faiths in powers greater than human, clung to beliefs in purposes beyond the comprehension of man. She had watched worshipers in temples, been moved once or twice by ceremonies which seemed to give those who took part an inner security and peace. But there were many gods, goddesses, nameless spirits and powers—unless each and every one was a small splinter of something greater toward which her species yearned and groped blindly. A something they must *have* to believe in, or be vanquished.

All her training balanced against the thought that she was moved now by any such influence! But if she could so think— Roane envied those with the faith, even those who looked upon Guardians here as beings to whom they could appeal in times of stress.

If they destroyed the installation would they in a way also be destroying the spirit which was Clio? What might enter in thereafter to fill the void?

Roane shook her head—fancies. She had been too often in the past ordered to restrain such imaginings. And if she had ever betrayed such irresponsible speculation before the Service she might even have been considered a suitable candidate for mental reschooling.

She shuddered at that thought, gazed out over the tumbled walls of the fort. There was already a tinge of red-gold in the sky—sunrise.

"Nelis—" She spoke his name softly, moved out of the hold he had kept on her during the dark hours, though his arm tightened even as she put it aside. Then his eyes opened, squinted in the light.

"Dawn," Roane told him, thinking he might still be in the lingering backwash of a dream.

"Dawn—" he repeated as if the word had little meaning. Then the lines of his face tightened once more, alert intelligence and awareness flooded back. He straightened up with a grunt, as if stiff and sore, and stretched.

"Your medicines do well by one." He flexed his arms again and then gently touched the plasta-skin covering over his wound before he picked up the jacket the Sergeant had left behind. "Have you any more of that strange food?"

"Enough." She knelt to open her bag. The night lenses —how had she come to forget that she had those? They could have started last night with their aid. And there was the tool—she could put the last charge in that now.

"Another of your strange weapons?"

"Not quite so. But it was what freed you from that cage. It can be used as a cutter or a digger—breaking stone, melting metal. But I have not the proper energy charges for it, only one of these left, and they are meant to power a beamer." She screwed the butt back on and laid it to one side. He picked it up.

"This is not what you used on me in the forest—"

"No. That was taken from me."

"But that is your best weapon?"

"It merely stuns. There are others more forceful, but we are forbidden to carry them on sealed worlds. There is a blaster which slays with fire, other devices. But those are employed only in the last resort."

He held the projectile thrower he termed a "gun" in one hand, the tool in the other, comparing them. "You people work in metal in a way we cannot begin to equal. Just as we ride duocorns, you visit stars. What is it like to stride from world to world, m'lady?"

"It is like being always before a constantly changing

picture. Sometimes it is good, sometimes"—she remembered and shivered—"it can be very bad."

"As this world has been for you?"

"No! That is not so! Here—" She had found the ration tubes, twisted the cap of the first and handed it to him, taking up another for herself, using all, as they needed the strength. The warm semiliquid did not seem to taste as it always had, but even flatter, less appetizing.

She finished it quickly, squeezed the tube flat, put it under a stone before she reclosed her pack. The sky was now afire with sunrise. Had Imfry changed his mind during the night, or did he still want to go to the installation? She glanced up to where he stood, his head half turned from her, looking toward the blue-shadowed roll of the heights beyond.

"We head west." He pointed. "There are Thunderbolt and Lhang's Beard—"

So he was picking out landmarks. But once they were down in the forest cover, how could those guide them? She asked as much.

"We are not so helpless as you would believe, m'lady." He pressed the wide buckle on his belt, showed her a small dial within. "This is a device which works as effectively for path finding for us as your off-world trappings do for you. Now—" He surveyed the ground closely, knelt at a smooth stretch of earth, and there began to set up a tight circle of bits of rock, the center left bare while he flattened and smoothed it. With his fingertip he gouged a series of lines and dashes there, digging them in as deeply as he could.

"For Wuldon and the others," he told her. "This will let them know the direction in which we have gone and that we appoint a meeting place for later."

The warmth of the sun was on the rocks as they started on the down trail. Roane, looking about her, and then hastily averting her eyes from anything but the path, thought it had been well she had come up in the dark. It would have been difficult for her to make that climb otherwise. The zigzag of the trail brought them to the bottom, where Imfry consulted his belt disk and struck out briskly.

There was no straight trail, of course. They detoured, lost time, came back. But if any hunt for them was in progress, it had not spread so far. There were birds and once or twice short glimpses of animals, but no sign men had ever walked this way.

They traveled in silence for the most part, and Imfry moved with an energy which suggested his wound no longer gave him any trouble. Roane refused to think of what lay ahead. It was enough to savor this one day which lay as a safe haven between the past and the future. She made no complaint at the steady pace her companion set, though now and again he did pause, suggest they rest. It was then he talked, though nothing of what they did, or had done, or would do—almost as if to speak of what concerned them most was to summon ill fortune.

Rather he painted for her the Reveny, the Clio, that he knew. And Roane listened as to a tale told in the Markets of Thoth, where, as all know, the most skillful of story spinners compete. He spread before her his home stead of Imfry-Manholm, which lay in mountain country where they raised the long-fleeced corbs, and grew, on small terraces bitten out of the steep slopes, vines which bore those berries from which the sharp-tanged winter wines were pressed.

"My brother is lord there, being the younger son. Though his mother ruled in his name during his childhood—she being my father's second lady. He came to take liege oath at Urkermark last year. He is a good lad, steady. And he is already ring-promised to the daughter of Hormford Stead across the valley."

Imfry dug his boot heel into the soft earth as they sat side by side on the moss-cushioned trunk of a fallen tree.

"The younger son inherits? On most worlds it is the eldest."

"But this is the sensible way. A man's older sons are usually well grown, settled in lives of their own, at his death hour. But the youngest may still be unable to make his way in the world. Therefore it is only just that he be so provided for. I was a court fosterling, because of my mother—" He paused for a long moment and stared down at the hole he was excavating. "My father had good reason to believe my rise in the world would be favored. My sister was ringed young to the son of his best friend—Ward Marshal Ereck. But what of your life, m'lady?"

"There is little to tell. I am without parents, raised in a Service crèche where my Uncle sought me out. I tested well for memory work and in certain learning arts, so he knew I could be a useful member of a team. So has it been."

"And you are perhaps ringed to this cousin of yours?"

"Sandar?" For a moment the speaking of his name evoked a sharp picture of him in her mind. Perhaps once, in the very beginning, she had nursed a few small colorless dreams. But those had been quickly quenched by working with Sandar—with whom her role had been that of a kind of dull-witted servant—and Roane found the memory of them embarrassing now.

"Certainly not Sandar!" she repeated firmly.

"But some other—on one of your star worlds?" he persisted.

"There is no time in the Service, or at least as Uncle Offlas plans one's life, for such things. He does not even think of me as a woman. I am another pair of hands, often clumsy ones, to his mind. He takes me with him because, as I am his kin, he is allowed to use me on sealed worlds, where a stranger might cause trouble." Suddenly Roane laughed. "But this time he was not fortunate—I have done just as he has always feared someone would do. And do you know, Nelis—I think—I hope—I no longer care!"

For that was true! Last night when she had told him her story a burden *had* rolled away. Uncle Offlas—she did not *have* to be his puppet. Let him blacken her to the Service—she had a world before her here. They could not hunt her down, or at least she thought they would not dare.

"Strange ways—" Imfry's comment did not seem to be exactly an apt answer, but he did not enlarge upon it, only got to his feet as a signal to push on.

That odd lightheartedness with which she had begun this march, that feeling of being apart from the past and the future, being in the safe present, faded as they went. She had thought, for a few moments, that she did not have to fear Uncle Offlas. Perhaps she did not, if she kept away from where he was to be found. But she was heading right back there. Why?

"Please." She slipped around a bush to match pace with Imfry. "We must take care. You cannot guess what they can do. If the LB has come there will be more—"

"But you have said that the crown machine is the control—that we must destroy it. Was that not what you urged on me?"

"Yes. But I forgot—" To her vast surprise and self-disgust, she felt tears rising again. What *was* the matter with her? She had never done this in her life. She was no longer herself. Desperately she fought for control. "Yes. I am sorry—it is the only thing to be done." She fell behind, intent on restraining her troubling emotions. "I only urge caution. They have instruments which can detect us at a distance."

He shrugged. "We can only do our best and hope for the continuing favor of fortune. We are"—he consulted his guide disk—"not too far from the cave. And we shall approach it from the side where Reddick's men broke in."

Now she was able to watch a master woodsman at work. It seemed to Roane he melted into the brush, able to become invisible at will, while she sweated over her own efforts, which now appeared infinitely clumsy, to follow his example. But she applauded the caution he brought to the advance. If there were no repellers or detects—

They looked out on a slope of raw earth eroded by rain, flanking the hole Reddick's men had made. Imfry spoke so low Roane had almost to read the words from his lips as he shaped them:

"Is there any warning set here?"

"I do not think so. Unless they have a new one. I burned out the repeller."

His body was as tense as a runner's waiting at the mark. "Get in, as quick as you can!" And he was off in a dash to cover the stretch of open ground, disappear between mounds of earth and rock. Roane followed, to stand where Ludorica had held the crown in her hands.

"Wait!" She held up her hand in swift warning. From her former experience with the distort Roane knew she could feel that were it present. As Imfry's skill had been their guide in the woods, maybe she could serve equally well here.

Roane slipped into the rough passage, heard him move in her wake. So far, there was no trace of the protective measures she feared. But she could hear, every time she paused to listen, the faint pulsation of the installation.

They came to the smoothed portion of corridor. There was a faint glow from the machine chamber. Roane touched his arm, put her lips close to his ear.

"What do you see—right there?" She indicated the faint light.

"Nothing."

"You hear?" she persisted.

"Nothing. It may be that I cannot. The Princess could not, you said."

If that were true—had she failed before they had begun? Would he take on faith what she might describe to him? She slipped her hand down to lace his fingers with hers.

"Come!" Hand in hand, linked as children on their

way to some day of play, they crept along, edging
warily toward the open panel.

Sandar? Uncle Offlas? If they were still within— Roane
had no way of making sure. However, if she and Imfry
were not spotted at the door, then there were places
of concealment inside. Even the crowned pillars were
tall enough to provide temporary cover.

At the panel Roane loosed her hold, pushed a step
across the threshold. The mutter of noise, those lights
which seemed so bright since she had been moving in
the dark. But she could see no one there.

"Now!"

Roane could not see the expression on his face, but
he caught her hand, held it in bruising pressure.

"You—went—into—the—wall!" He spaced his words as
if he were struggling for some control.

"Through an opening. Close your eyes, do not try
to see—but come—" Roane had a sudden inspiration.
Perhaps conditioning existed only at the panel, and
once inside, he could see.

She led and he followed. "Raise your feet, there is
a step barrier—"

His eyes were closed, his hand out as if to feel the
wall his confused senses said was there. Then she
caught his fingers, drew him on until he was in.

"Look!"

He opened his eyes. A spasm crossed his face. "Dark
—blind dark!"

"Hush!" Roane searched for any stir among the pillars. But it would seem that their luck held. The chamber appeared empty.

"It is all dark." He had himself under tight control
again. "I see nothing—"

"Close your eyes once more." If he could be more
sure of touch than sight—

Roane drew him to the first of the pillars.

"There is a column here." She made the description
as simple as she could. "It has a wide plate set in the
surface facing you. Around that are rows of lights which

flash on and off constantly in patterns of color. At the top is a small crown about the size of your fist. It is in the form of—I think you might best term them flames —and these are brilliantly red, glowing as if actually afire—"

"The Flame Crown of Leichstan!" he cried.

"Now—give me your hands." She had to move very close to do this, press against his back, reach around his waist to direct his fingers to the surface of the map and the lights, making him trace across and around.

"Do you feel?" She waited anxiously for the answer on which so much depended.

"Yes! These then are the lights? And the crown?"

"It is too far above to be touched."

"And where is the crown of Reveny?" he demanded eagerly.

"Here—" She led him along to stand before the proper pillar and described it in patient detail.

"Tell me now of the others!"

Roane did, guiding him to each in turn, though he only touched a pillar now and then to reassure himself they were there. At last she came to the dead one, and since it had no light of its own she trained the beamer on it.

The diadem of fluted shells had turned an unpleasant green color which hinted of decay.

"The crown of Arothner in truth," he admitted. "You have marked each nation that I know— Are these all?"

"Yes."

"And *these* you believe can govern our thoughts, raise a kingdom high, smash it low—"

"We think so." Again after some space of time she allied herself with the Service. "Though the records of the Psychocrat hierarchy were largely destroyed in the blasting of their command station, some pieces of information have been fitted together. We ourselves have extensions of computers which are akin to these in general formation. There must be a broadcast linkage between pillar and crown."

"Which explains much," he said as if to himself. "There have been puzzles a many in the past—why some kings seemed to reverse themselves. Roane"—Imfry swung around, his eyes open, searching for her though she stood there directly before him—"you are very right. This is evil, the blackest kind of evil! And it is better to face chaos than such slavery. I have seen it work with the Queen before my eyes. She became someone else when she held the crown. The person—the *thing* this wanted her to be! There must be an end!"

His voice rose but that did not distract Roane's own warning system. A distort! Somewhere within these burrows a distort had begun to broadcast.

"Quick!" She pulled at him, forcing him around the edge of the pillar which stood farthest from the door. The sensation was growing stronger.

"There is something—I feel the need to get away," he said.

"I know. That is a distort, a protective device. If they set it here—" Perhaps she could break out, as she had before. But Roane seriously doubted Imfry could.

Movement at the panel—Sandar! He slipped through with supple agility, took cover in the dark behind the pillars. So he must suspect their presence. Roane did not doubt he was armed with a stunner. He need only use that spray at will, to render them helpless. Unless he was afraid of unguarded use of any ray around these pillars.

She pressed Imfry's arm in warning, felt him tense. Had his sight been equal to hers, they might have chanced skulking behind this row of pillars, opposite to those behind which Sandar had gone to ground. But if there was a distort at the door to bottle them in, even reaching it would do no good. For the present Roane could think of nothing but to remain in silent hiding.

Imfry had his "gun," she the tool, but neither was any defense against a stunner. Could the tool take out the distort, unseal the doorway as it had finished off the repeller? Perhaps, but Roane could not lead Imfry through hide-and-seek. And to leave him here would expose him, helpless, to Sandar.

That her cousin was on the move she had no doubt, though she could hear nothing but the click-click of the machines. And so engrossed was she in listening for some betraying sound that she was almost startled into betrayal when a voice called:

"Roane, I know you are here—" The words were in Basic and the loud tone echoed so she could not be sure of the direction from which they came.

"The LB is coming in," Sandar continued. "When it lands you know what to expect—stass. If you surrender, you'll escape that. The more you give evidence of abnormal behavior the worse it is going to be for you when the inspectors arrive."

He was trying to frighten her, and Roane had to admit he was succeeding in part. If the landing party had been warned about her, they would have no mercy at all—the quickest method of dealing with her would be used. They need only bring in a stass projector and spray, and she and Imfry would be locked in a prison as tight as the cage of Hitherhow. Her eventual fate would be no less now than complete mental re-education. Which meant that she must—*they* must escape before that happened.

"You can't get out." Sandar's voice continued to echo. But she must wait no longer. And one chance was as good as another. This duel was between them. He would be concentrating on her, not Imfry.

She took the chance of a whisper—"Stay here!"

His hand brushed her shoulder with reassuring touch, letting her know he understood. Roane slipped to the next pillar. She was more used to the echoing now and she thought that Sandar was still close to the door.

If she could create a diversion—there was the ruined crown of Arothner. Roane stood out and took aim on that discolored crest with the tool.

A flash of brilliance and the crown was gone, melted

into fiery droplets. At the same time she saw Sandar
begin a leap from one pillar to the next. In turn she
took a desperate chance, swinging the tool around,
aiming for the rock ahead of him. He cried out as footing disappeared, stumbled— But his stunner was coming
up, he had not dropped it. Roane rayed again, trying
to nick that. The edge of the beam did touch it, but
the full force she released cut across the pillar which
held Reveny's Ice Crown.

17

Roane cowered as the world split apart in incandes-
cent flame. Under her the rock floor was as unstable
as bog scum. It swayed, buckled. The pillar which had
taken part of the tool's energy was now a torch, its
brilliance blinding. And from that leaped tentacles of
yellow-white to touch its fellows, so they also blazed.

Imfry—he could not see and he was behind one of
those pillars. He might be caught in the holocaust sweeping from one column to the next. Only now she was
as blind as he—

Roane began to crawl, feeling her way. A torrent of
sound deafened her, even as the blaze sealed her eyes.
That mutter arose to a shriek, as if the pillars had life
and were now in torment. There was such a wave of
heat that she could hardly breathe.

She never knew how she reached Imfry. Only by fortune she ran against his body. She clawed her way
up to her feet, using him as a support, and then forced
him back with her until they crashed against the far
wall of the chamber. From there there was no escape,

not with them both as blind and far from the door as they were. They could only endure and hope that they would not be utterly consumed in the fury which raged, sending out sound and stifling heat.

Sandar! For the first time Roane thought of him and winced. Had he been in the direct line of that blast? If so—it was by her doing he was dead. She had not wanted that. She had not intended him any harm, only to knock out the stunner, give them a chance—

The roar was dying—or else her ears were becoming dulled. And the heat—surely that was not so great. Roane fought to see, moisture welling in her smarting eyes, trickling down her cheeks, where she impatiently smeared it away with one hand while with the other she kept her hold on Imfry. But all she could make out was a blood-scarlet curtain against the world.

There was no measurement of the time that devastation raged. It could have lasted an hour, a day—for it seemed endless. But at last Roane was certain that it was nearing the end, for the heat was gone now, the sound. They were trapped in a dark which was complete, where it was hard to breathe. Her gasps matched the ragged breaths of her companion.

"Get—out—"

Feel their way along the wall to the door? It was their only chance. She tugged at Imfry, but he was already on the move. Roane was not even sure of the direction, though she thought they must go left, their guide being one hand against the warm stone, while they linked fingers lest they lose contact. Roane's eyes continued to tear and smart. In her a new fear was born. Had her sight been blasted? Then, for the first time, Imfry spoke:

"Where—where are we?" There was an uncertainty in his voice which she had never heard before. He might have been one who had suddenly awakened from a deep sleep in a strange place.

"In the installation. No—stay with me!" For the hand she held fought against her, and he gave a sudden lunge as if to break her grip, but she held tight and pushed him on.

"Who are you?" Again that dull wonder. "What—what am I doing here? Where is this?"

"Hold—keep hold or we cannot get out!" She summoned what small authority she had to impress that need on him. "We cannot see. But if we keep to the wall we can find the door."

"Who are you?" He no longer struggled, but he stopped short so she bumped against him.

"I am Roane—Roane Hume—" What had happened to him she did not know, and her fear grew. What if— But she would not allow herself to think of that. "Come—you must go on—we must get out!" Her control wavered and her voice rose shrilly.

"Out—where?" He took another step forward as if her urgency as well as her strong push had activated him.

"Out into the open! Please, we must go. Oh, please— Move, you must, you must!"

At least she had him on his way again. And a moment later, when he halted once again, she dared to beat one fist against the shoulder touching hers.

"On!"

"There is no way. It is all solid."

For a second or two she was caught in panic and then a small measure of reason triumphed. Of course, they must have reached a corner! They had found the wall in which the door panel was set.

"Right—turn right—" Roane tugged and pulled at him. Perhaps "left," "right," had no meaning for him. Somehow she got him around, started in the new direction. And then—blessedly—cool air and an opening!

"Through here! Be careful, there is a step up—"

Somehow she got him through. The distort— But the blast must have rendered that harmless. They were safe in the passage, breathing untainted air. Roane leaned against the wall drawing that reviving coolness into her laboring lungs.

The scarlet curtain before her eyes had faded. There was one thing she might try. She fumbled at the supply bag, brought out the night lenses, was almost afraid to look as she got them on.

Her eyes still smarted, burned, felt as if hot sand had been poured into their corners, under their lids. But—she could see! Though it was as if she peered through a haze. She drew close to Imfry, surveying him searchingly. He leaned against the wall as she had done, his hands raised to his head where he pawed feebly, as if trying to rub away something clinging to his face. But she could see no sign of burn or injury.

By so much they had escaped. *They* had—but what of Sandar? She looked back. There was no radiance within the chamber now—and dead silence. Dead— She hesitated. It could well be that the shock of what had happened here could be detected by the crew of the LB. Against them she and Imfry were defenseless. Yet she could not take even the first step toward safety.

Roane caught Imfry's hands, held them tight, trying to get his unfocused eyes to meet hers as she spoke. "You must stay here until I return." She accented each word with force.

"Stay—return—" he repeated. His mouth hung slackly open. She had never seen anything as empty as his face. Horror fed her fear. She dared not think about his condition.

She fled back through the panel, making herself concentrate on Sandar. Dim as her sight was, the lenses were an aid to show what had been wrought here. Where the pillars had stood, there were now rent and blackened stubs, the crowns gone. Bitter fumes made her cough, rasped her throat.

Where had Sandar been? Without the crowns to guide her she could no longer be certain. Roane stumbled on, not sure she would even find evidence of his being, a sour bile rising in her mouth so that she had to keep swallowing to fight it. Then she saw the huddle of body and flung herself down beside it.

The horror of a fire death did not face her. But when she pulled at his shoulder, he rolled heavily limp. If he still lived she must get him out of this poisonous atmosphere. Somehow she was able to grasp him under the armpits, scramble backward, dragging him.

She bumped him across the panel barrier, letting him sprawl out into the corridor. Once more she rolled him over, her hand seeking a heartbeat. And she found that flutter just as the ground under her shook. Roane cried out—was the whole tunnel about to collapse around them?

Sandar coughed feebly, his head turned from side to side, his hands tried to dig into the rock as if he would lift himself. The tunnel—

Then Roane understood. Memories from the old life which might have been lived by another person reassured her. That had been the shock of deter rockets. The LB had landed.

A clear warning to move out. She arose. Her cousin was not dead, and he would soon be in the hands of his own people. If she and Imfry would escape, they must do it now. Nelis still stood against the wall, but now his arms were out, braced against the smoothed stone, his head strained forward as if he listened for what he could not see. As she moved, his face turned quickly to her.

"Who is there?" There was a new crispness in his demand. His voice was not dazed as it had been earlier.

"Roane. We must go now."

When she touched him his tense body was iron-hard. He raised a hand, struck out blindly, as if to ward her off.

"Go where?" he demanded.

"Out of here. And quickly. They will come seeking Sandar, to see the installation—they must not find us here."

"Who must not find us here?" He was impervious to her urging, stubborn in his rigidity of body.

"Uncle Offlas—those from the LB. We must go!"

"You mean that. You are afraid," he answered her. "I can feel your fear. Who are you?"

"Roane! I am Roane." She was close to tears. His voice was clearer, his face no longer had that slack, mindless look. But that he did not know her—there was something very wrong.

"Roane," he repeated. "And who am I?"

She was trembling. Her worst fear was being dragged into fact. "You are Colonel Nelis Imfry. Do you remember nothing—nothing at all?"

He made her no direct answer. Rather he seemed to wish to avoid that. "You are afraid for yourself?"

"For myself, yes," she answered honestly. "And for you. They will have good reason to wish us both under their hands. Please, we must go." She reached for him again, fearing that he might strike her, yet determined to start him in flight.

But when his hand came this time, it was not balled into a fist, but open, stretched to welcome hers. She seized it eagerly.

"Come!"

Again she pulled him along the passage at as swift a pace as she could urge on him. Then at last they were able to grope out into the open. She had hoped that, once free of the installation room, Imfry would regain his sight. But he still depended upon her guidance even as they walked into the night.

The wind, untainted by corrosive stench, was sweet and cold around them. Roane saw him lift his face into it. Then he said without visible emotion:

"I can see now."

She gave a cry of relief, dropping his hand. Her own sight was dimmed. Even the lenses could not give things clear-cut outlines. That that impairment might be permanent she dared not consider.

"It is very strange," Imfry continued. He might have been thinking aloud rather than speaking to her. "There is a kind of emptiness—"

Then more forcibly, as if he were uttering some necessary formula to establish a fact:

"I am Nelis Imfry, of the House of Imfry-Manholm. I am a Colonel in the service of Her Majesty, Queen Ludorica of Reveny. I am me—Nelis Imfry!"

He was quiet then, his eyes seeking the stars where the wind-tossed branches alternately revealed and hid their glitter. A waning moon was rising, its sickle of silver cutting the cloudless sky.

"I remember, but it is as if those memories have dimmed. Yet I am Nelis Imfry, and the rest of it is true."

"Yes," she told him.

Her agreement appeared to startle him out of that trancelike state. He turned swiftly as if he feared to face an enemy. Gazing full at her he stood silently, as one might study a landmark which was altered from what he thought it had been.

"Tell me," he ordered, "what has chanced. While I was in darkness."

"When I tried to stop Sandar the energy ray lanced across one of the pillars. It set off a chain reaction—all the installation was destroyed—the crowns are gone." Would he understand?

His dark brows drew together in a frown. "Crowns? Pillars?"

"The installation left by the Psychocrats to rule this world—"

His mouth set firmly. "The *Queen* rules Reveny."

"Now she does," assented Roane, wondering if that were indeed the truth, or if the destruction of the crowns had pulled down upon Reveny the fate of Arothner.

"You speak of facts you believe in, but it is not clear to me. Make me understand!" He advanced as if he intended to shake it out of her.

She was afraid again. This haggard stranger was not Nelis Imfry. Was this what the destruction of the crowns meant? For there was as noticeable a change in him as there had been in Ludorica when she held the Ice Crown.

"It is a long story," she said helplessly.

"That does not matter. Tell it!"

So once more she went over the familiar tale. Only this time she had no relief in the telling, only a cold feeling born not of the chill wind about them, but rather of a great loneliness.

He listened intently, though little change of expression was apparent on his lean face. He might have been some judge presiding over a trial where she was the accused.

Imfry did not interrupt her with any questions, but heard her through to that end which was the unplanned destruction of the installation. And when she was done Roane wavered. The pain in her eyes was worse, spreading back into her head, so that she was more aware of that than her surroundings.

"You understand the danger if those of the Service find us. They must not!" She put all the energy she had left into that last warning. Her eyes—her head—she could not stand it any longer. She remembered swaying, the sound of a cry, and then pain, a great sea of fire, engulfed her.

Coolness, blessed coolness—dark and cool. To hide in this dark, cool place and never venture forth again. Sensation rather than thought. Cool and wet—the fire going. She did not want to move, yet she was moving. Roane tried to protest, discovered she had not the energy to form words. She heard dimly a moaning sound.

"Roane—" A ripple through the cool dark. No—let her alone—just let her alone!

"Roane!"

Dimly she knew that for a summons. She would not answer. Let her be! She was moving, though not on her own two feet. And the jar set her head hurting, so she made a great effort and thought she begged to be let alone. But if they heard her they did not heed. She escaped once again into the cool dark.

But the second time she was drawn out of that refuge she could not slip back. She lay on a surface which was not soft, though there was that under her which cushioned it a little. Her face was wet, as if she had been out in a storm, but that came from a soaked cloth laid across her forehead and eyes. At least she lay still, no moving racking her body.

". . . tall as a keep, I swear to you, sir. Nothing like it I have ever seen. And I counted five men come out of it. They went in and out by ladder, taking stuff back in. But a couple more went into that cave. Seeing that thing, you have to believe the whole story. But men traveling to the *stars?* You have to have proof of a tale such as that. And with one feeling like his head was empty—well, I could say this was a dream—or some Soothspeaker trick. Are you sure, sir, it is not? I mean, if Shambry was strong enough to hold the Queen in thrall that way, maybe he could be working on us now—even at a distance."

"A man cannot make you see what he does not know exists. That star ship has no match here."

"True enough. But this queer feeling in one's head—though that is wearing off now, sir. But I tell you it was really bad when it first hit. Mattine ran around in a circle for a space, actually yelling he was a Nimp scout or some such nonsense. At least I thought I heard him say that. Hunlow had to lay him out when he drew steel. And the rest of us, we did not even know our own names for a while. If it was like that for us here, just think of what might have happened in a town with all the people going dazed or crazy. Some seem to take longer to get over it. Fleech did. We had to lug him along for quite a march and tell him over and over who he was and where we were. Nasty experience. Worse than facing a Nimp charge."

Wuldon. Roane's sluggish mind matched a name to that voice. Who else was with him? They—or Wuldon

—must have seen the LB. But what if its crew was now hunting them? She must warn—

It required such an effort to force her hand up to her face, to tug at the fold of wet cloth blindfolding her.

"Nelis—" Hers was a ghost voice, a thread of whisper.

But it brought quick response. "Roane!" And her hand was stayed in its effort to sweep aside the cloth, put down to lie once more at her side. So he knew—understood again?

"Let that be for a while yet. Your eyes are badly inflamed. Do you know who I am?"

Did he think *she* was the one who had been out of her head? "Nelis Imfry," she answered with a spurt of indignation. "And Wuldon is here, too. But—" She remembered that other urgency. "Nelis—the ship—they must not find us!"

"I assure you they shall not. We have a range of hills between us, and scouts out. I have all the respect for their powers you wish me to show. We take no chances. And at the first sign of any hunt we shall be on the trail again. Now"—a strong arm was slipped under her head, she was raised a little—"drink this!"

Cool metal against her lips. She sipped and then choked and coughed, for the liquid had a spicy warmth.

"No—" She found his hold was such she could not avoid what he offered. "More—it is what you need now."

After the first mouthful or two she discovered it was not bad. So she obediently drank until the cup was taken away.

"My bag—the medicines—"

"Here, m'lady!" That was Wuldon.

"Look for a white tube." With the spicy drink downed, Roane was regaining both strength and the ability to think for herself again. "It holds a green liquid—drops for the eyes."

"Got it!" Then Imfry added, "How many?"

"Two each—for now."

He settled her back on the thin bedding pad and the wet cloth was pulled away. Light dazzled and hurt, but she forced herself to lie still as the moisture dripped in. That burned, but with none of the pain she had known earlier. She held her lids tightly closed. If there would be any relief it would come quickly.

Slowly she counted to a hundred, but not aloud, hearing small sounds as if they were repacking her bag. Then she opened her eyes. The light hurt, but she could see—and more clearly than she had since the chain reaction.

Nelis, the stubble beard longer and darker, a tousled lock of hair sticking to his forehead as if plastered there—the Sergeant at an angle.

"I can see," Roane said, more to assure herself then to inform them. "Let me look—please, let me look." For suddenly she must reassure herself of this recovery.

Once more Nelis raised her before she could struggle up on her own. They were in a clearing and she thought it must be midmorning. Men moved or sat some distance away. Behind them a rope was strung between two trees, a tie place for the reins of saddled duocorns, who stamped or wrinkled their hides to drive off insects.

Some of the men were in uniform. Others wore civilian clothes or the green of foresters. Their small band of fugitives had doubled many times.

"Could you eat, m'lady? We have nothing but field rations—or there is one of those tubes of your own food left."

"Get that," Nelis ordered and the Sergeant moved out of her line of sight.

"How are your eyes?"

"I can see!" And she knew by her very joy how deep-reaching had been her fear.

"Do the others know what has happened?" she asked.

"Not the whole of it. It is not the kind of story to be widely told. To know one has lived in slavery to a machine—" There was a hot undercurrent in his voice. "And how far that domination has gone—"

"Ludorica and the crown." Her thought followed his. "If it has so affected all of you who had no direct contact with it, what will it do to those who hold the crowns?"

He was looking beyond her, as if he did not want her to see what lay in his eyes.

"That we must learn. The destruction seems to have affected people in various ways. So far all these men have come out of it. But with some the daze was longer, deeper. And they are all relatively far removed from influence. As you say—what has happened close to the crowns—"

"Here, m'lady." The Sergeant was back with the E ration. Roane sucked at the semiliquid avidly, for she discovered that her hunger had awakened.

Her recovery seemed to be the signal for which they had been waiting. Sergeant Wuldon went to the picket line, and men began to ride out, in twos and threes, each saluting Imfry as he passed. In the end only Wuldon, Mattine, and two others were left.

"We had best be on the move," Nelis said. "I know you are not strong enough to ride alone, but we have a mount that will carry double, and that we can share."

So it was that after Imfry had mounted, Wuldon lifted her as if she had no weight at all, passing her up to his superior.

"Where do we go?" Roane asked as the trees arched over them, shutting out the sun.

"Skulking. Until we know more of what chances. We shall follow the river road. The men are scouting in a wide sweep to see what they can pick up. If there is an open path we shall head for Urkermark."

"The Queen?"

"The Queen—if she is still Queen." His voice was remote, cool. "We do not know what we shall find, we can only ride to find it."

"You had no part in this." She tried to guess his line

of thought. "It was my hand—and chance—which did it."

"I told you, I do not believe that chance alone ruled this," was his reply. And he did not add to that as they jogged ahead.

18

The room was warm in spite of its size, almost too warm. But the light from the two lamps on the table and the fire on the hearth did not reach the corners, where shadows crouched. Roane looked about her with an interest fatigue did not quite dull. This was the first time she had been in any house on Clio save a forester's and the border keeps, with their rough frontier interiors, and the magnificent mansion in Gastonhow.

This was an upper private room of the Inn of the Three Wayfarers, within a half day's ride of Urkermark. Their steaming cloaks lay across a bench pulled close to the fire, for outside came the steady beat of rain. And it was under that cover they had ridden so far into the land.

Three days—Roane counted them off. The first had been much of a blur for her. They had spent that night in the forester's cabin. And there the first reports had come.

Reveny was in a state of chaos. And the dislocation had been the greater in the upper reaches of authority. The yoeman farmers, the "little" men and women, made better recoveries from the initial state of bewilderment. But in turn they had been alarmed by the erratic actions of their leaders.

Some appeared to go insane, either sinking into a state of idiocy to give no coherent orders at all, or mouthing such irresponsible ones that their own servants and followers refused to obey. Fighting had broken out, stopped as the men engaged suddenly asked themselves what they were fighting for. There were bands of raiders taking advantage of the misfortunes of others.

The closer their own party came to Urkermark—and now they traveled openly, having little to fear during this confusion—the wilder became the stories of what chanced there. Imfry grew bleak of expression, curt of tongue, with every succeeding report from his scouts. That there was dire trouble was certain. Three times they had met parties of refugees spurring away from the city. And each time those riders, men guarding women, some of whom had children in their arms, had refused any contact, twice shooting to warn off Imfry's men. There had been wounded among them. And seeing those bandaged bodies, Roane was deeply unhappy. Chance or not, she felt that each of those hurts had come from her hand.

Imfry's company had grown. The scouts who had spread to gain news brought, or directed, back to him more and more guardsmen, foresters, even stragglers from the private guards of stead nobles. He interviewed each newcomer himself, trying to sift from their stories a clearer picture. He was doing so now, sitting at the table, listening to the rambling story of a man in uniform.

There were few officers among these so far, and the one or two who did appear were all of lower rank, though some of them still held together a nucleus of their former commands.

". . . the incall came," the newcomer was saying. "And Major Emmick talked to this other officer in the guard-room. We heard a shot. When we broke down the door the Major was dead—took it right though the head. This strange Colonel—he started to say that the Major was a traitor, which we did not believe, then he grabbed at his head and ran straight at the wall and smashed aginst it, knocked himself right out. Well, we did not know what to do. The Captain, he was still dazed like, lay on his bed and just laughed when the Sergeant asked for orders. So Sergeant Quantil, he said up with the gates and not to let anyone else in, not until we got some news that made sense. And he sent three of us out—Mangron, he was to ride to the Westergate, Afran up to Balsay, and me, I was to try to reach our own Colonel in Urkermark. Only the gates were up there, too. They will not let anyone in. And I think there is a fight going on inside—there are fires blazing, anyway. Then I met up with your man, sir, and what he told me made a lot more sense than anything I heard since Major Emmick was killed, so I came here."

"And this man who brought the incall, this Colonel—you did not know him?"

"Never saw him before, sir. He had a new royal badge, too—a black forfal head, with the mouth open and a forked tongue out, nasty-looking thing. The Sergeant searched him for papers afterward. Nothing but the warrant on the table. It was all written up like a real one but it did not have the Queen's name. It just said 'in the King's name'—and King Niklas has been dead for days now! It was just some more craziness!"

"'In the King's name,'" repeated Imfry. And then he shot another question. "What king?"

The man stared at Imfry and then hurriedly pushed away from the table, glancing from side to side as if seeking some escape. Roane guessed his supicions. He must think that Imfry was mad now.

"No, guardsman, I am not crazy. But there is good reason to believe that there is one near the Queen who might try to seize power in a time of trouble. If he has done so—"

The man swallowed. "Oh," he said eagerly, "that could explain— I cannot remember any name signed. There was the thumb seal on the warrant proper enough

—but no name! Maybe that was what made Sergeant Quantil think it so queer. It was a warrant telling the Major to hand over command, but no proper name signed. But, sir, where—where is the Queen?"

"In Urkermark, or should be!" Imfry said with the emphasis of one taking an oath. "You say the city is closed?"

"Every gate sealed up as tight, sir, as it was the time the Nimps got down within siege distance in the old days. It would take the biggest siege guns to force those."

"The outer gates, yes, but there are other ways. Guardsman, how long will it take to get a message back to your post?"

"If I have a fresh mount, I can make it by midnight, sir."

"Well enough. You know what you have seen. Report it to your Sergeant. And take him this message from me." Imfry drew toward him a writing sheet, the small ink holder, and the pen. As he had before at the conclusion of such interviews, he wrote a few lines, dipped his fingertip in ink to impress beneath his signature.

"Mattine!" he called and as the forester appeared in the doorway, "a fresh mount for this guardsman."

"To be sure, m'lord."

When the man was gone, Imfry stared into the fire. Roane stirred, unable any longer to bear the silence in the room, the circling of her own thoughts.

"You say there is a way into Urkermark besides the gates?"

"It was meant to be a bolt hole out. Our history has never been without its wars and alarms, dynastic struggles. The games in which we were the pieces have often been bloody ones. I wonder who took satisfaction from that? The machines could not. But were the results somehow known to those devils who fostered them upon us?" He looked at her as if he wanted an answer.

"At first they must have been. There would be no

other reason for experimenting. But the Psychocrats have been dead a long time."

"The machines have only been dead for days and look what is upon us now. I wish I knew why it seems to affect some more than others. At any rate, the Queen is our first concern. It could well be that Reddick has set himself up as king. Which leaves two possible fates for Ludorica—either she died with the destruction of the crown, or else she is held captive to back Reddick's intrigues. In either case he must not be allowed to—" Imfry fell silent again, his face repelling Roane. That there was a strong bond between him and the Queen, Roane had known from the first. And if the Queen was dead—

She gave a sigh, wondering if she herself would ever be free of her burden of guilt. It seemed that as soft as that sound was, it was enough to arouse him from his dire thoughts, and when he turned to her there was a faint relaxation about his mouth.

"Rest, m'lady, while you can." He nodded at a door to an inner chamber. "We may have precious little time in which to do so."

Yet it was morning when the inn maid drew aside the curtains to let in a pale sunshine.

"M'lady." She curtsied when she saw Roane watching her sleepily. "The Colonel says you must be on your way soon. But there is hot water for washing, and these also." She pointed to folded clothing on a chair. "They are not what a fine lady wears, being of my own seaming, but the Colonel says they will do."

"But I cannot take your clothes," Roane objected, even though she shrank from drawing on again the stained and sweated garments in which she had lived for days.

"Oh, m'lady, the Colonel has given me that which will buy me twice what he selected from those I showed him. And much finer! But these are new, and there is a rain cloak to wear."

Roane bathed, thankful for the water and the soap, which smelled of sweet herbs. She put on one of the divided riding skirts and the tight bodice jacket, both of green-blue, but lacking the bright braid and embroidery she had seen before. There was a gray cloak, lined in green-blue, with an attached hood. Roane tried to order her hair. It had grown from the close crop and had now reached a length difficult to keep in order, straying about her face. She was still tugging at it as she went out into the other room, where the maid was putting a platter of food on the table.

"Please, m'lady, the Colonel asks that you make what speed you can."

"Surely." Roane found that for the first time in days she was really hungry. Though she ate as fast as she could, she left a well-cleaned plate behind her.

The maid ushered Roane down the stairs. There were many men in the common room, most of them eating in a hurried fashion, calling for refills of tankards. Most of their faces were strange but Mattine waved to her from the doorway and they quickly made room for her to pass.

Imfry stood by a duocorn, critically surveying a second mount. As Roane came up he gave her a quick greeting and then indicated that animal.

"She is warranted sound and steady-going, and we shall not have to use her for long, but she is a sorry-looking beast."

The mare was, Roane had to admit, a scrawny being, with a very ragged, rough mane at the root of her stubbed horns and only a wisp of a tail. Also she bawled a protest as the Colonel swung Roane into the saddle on her bony back, where she held on with a grim determination to last out the trip.

They rode out at the head of a troop which had been even further augmented during the night hours.

"We make for Urkermark?" Roane asked.

"Yes, but by the hidden way."

So they turned aside from the highway onto the

second lane feeding into it. And a little farther on they leaped their mounts over the way hedges, and crossed open fields, where hoofs cut into crop planting, trampling half-ripened grain. It seemed that Imfry was taking the straightest line possible to his goal.

They veered to the west, seeming to Roane's mind to be heading directly away from their goal. But that brought them at about noon to the bank of a river and along that they angled back east, following the course of the flow as a guide. Not far along they came to one of those bridges with a small triangular tower as a part of its structure.

There they dismounted. Imfry and the Sergeant, plus two guardsmen, went to the tower. The men produced iron bars and set to work pounding in and breaking loose the blocks below the offering slit.

A block of masonry crumbled only too readily under that assault and they dragged the stones out of the way. With the same bars they swept the floor within. Coins spun into the air, fell into the grass, but the workers paid no attention.

Now the sun shone on the dusty floor, making plain a groove in the stone. Sergeant Wuldon worked the tip of a lever into the depression, under a small bar of stone set across it. He put his full strength on the lever, the men and the Colonel joining in his effort. There was a harsh grating, and the stone moved complainingly. Once it was up the two blocks on either side were released and drawn out in turn.

A short time later Roane found herself descending a steep ladder of stone, lit by the glow of lanterns held by those who went before. Then she faced a long passage walled and buttressed with stone slabs.

The way was dark and there was an unpleasant smell of damp. But also there was now and then a very welcome whiff of fresher air, as if a ventilating system existed. There was only room for two to walk abreast, so their company was strung out, Imfry and Mattine at the head, Roane with the Sergeant, and the remainder of the troop behind.

For the most part their path was level and Roane thought that the making of such a way had been a formidable task. She was beginning to wonder if it did run for leagues clear to Urkermark when they were faced by a new series of steep steps, down which they went to a yet deeper level. Here there were no signs of man's building, but rather a series of cuts and caves, opening one into another, some large beyond the reach of lantern light.

Imfry went boldly on as if he knew the way well, though by all indications it must have been a long time since any had passed on this hidden road. He paused at last to consult his direction disk.

"Turn right here—" He signaled with the lantern. They were in one of the wider caves and the men were bunching up behind them.

Imfry went more slowly now, he and Mattine holding higher the lanterns they carried. And at length these revealed another stair, down which moisture dripped from where it gathered in great beads on the stone.

Roane climbed warily, fearing the slipperiness of the stone and the steepness of the steps. They ended in a stone passage fronting a fourth flight of stairs. The steps were enclosed on one side with wooden paneling, hung with thick spider webs heavy with the dust of years. Up and up, though Imfry went slowly, and apparently counting as he went, as if some tally of the steps was a key he needed.

He signaled by hand wave and the Sergeant edged around Roane, touching her shoulder lightly as he went.

"Pass that back, m'lady."

She did, the signal halting the line of men.

Now, handing his lantern to Mattine, who held both lights closer to the wall, the Colonel felt across the wooden surface. His shoulders hunched as if he were exerting pressure on some stubborn fastening. Then a portion of the paneling swung open to make a door.

When it came Roane's turn to step through she found herself in a room as richly furnished as had been that dining hall of her dream. The same kind of massive, heavily carved furniture stood about; the same colorful, if time-faded, tapestries ringed the walls.

She stepped to one side as the men following her fanned out. Imfry was at another door of the room, the Sergeant flanking him, both with those guns in their hands. The Colonel edged open that barrier, looked beyond, and then waved them on.

So they came into the heart of Urkermark High Keep. And it was through its rooms Imfry led them. Twice Roane waited with a beating heart, listening to the sound of shots loud in these echoing rooms. And once she hurried by a body lying face down, from under which runneled a thin red stream.

But there was no unified resistance to their passage and they went swiftly. Here and there small squads of the company broke off under low-voiced orders. So that when they reached another door, before which the Colonel again paused, there were only ten of them, counting Roane left.

Imfry tried the latch carefully before he gave a quick, sharp pull, at the same time moving to face whoever might be within, gun ready.

"Drop it!"

There was a queer sound like broken laughter. The Colonel was already inside, the rest crowding behind him, so Roane was the last to enter. She did not find a battle about to begin, but rather a strange scene, as if the actors had been frozen in place by their entrance.

On a couch lay Ludorica, her eyes closed, her dress disordered, even torn, with draggled trails of black lace hanging from the bodice. Her hair was loose, matted in tangles.

Beyond her was a chair in which sat Shambry. He

held both hands breast-high before him, and on them rested a glowing ball of rippling light. His mouth was slackly open, a thread of spittle drooling from one corner. But as he looked at Imfry his lips wrinkled in a hideous grin.

"Quiet, sir, the Queen sleeps. She sleeps, she dreams, dreams of us, and if she wakes, why, we shall all cease to be. Because we are her dream creatures. Only I, Shambry, can keep her dreaming so, and us alive!"

The men moved uneasily, edged a little away. Only Imfry continued to front the Soothspeaker. Then he went into action before Shambry could dodge, plucked the ball from the other's hold.

With a cry of pure terror, Shambry flung himself at Imfry, his crooked fingers reaching for the ball, or perhaps the Colonel's throat. But Wuldon interposed, hurling the man, now mouthing curses, back into his chair with such force that it went over, spilling Shambry to the floor.

Roane was already at the Princess's side. Ludorica's face was very pale, worn, but it had lost that shadow of evil the crown had laid upon it. Her skin was hot and dry as if she burned with fever, her lips cracked and peeling. But she still lived, and her breathing was the even rise and fall of one who slept.

Wuldon had his hands hooked in the collar of the Soothspeaker's black cloak, was pulling the groveling Shambry to his feet. He shook the man, who now hung limply in his grasp, and looked to Imfry.

Imfry moved to the couch, took one of Ludorica's hands between his.

"She is under mind-globe, I think. If so, there is one drastic remedy for that." He turned and caught up the ball, which had spun away to the floor. Raising it high he deliberately smashed it. Shambry gave a wild beast's cry, fought with such a frenzy that Wuldon could not hold him alone. Two of the men came to his aid.

Ludorica's head turned on the pillow. Then her eyes opened. But there was no recognition in them.

"See to her," Imfry told Roane. "There is one lacking from this company who must be found."

He strode across the chamber to the second door, setting his shoulder to burst it open by force. Beyond, Roane saw part of a pillared hall, most of which swept beyond her range of vision. But what the door framed was undoubtedly a throne on a dais, yet set low enough for her to see that it was occupied. He who sat there wore a crown which was a glitter of icy splendor. And he did not turn his head to view Imfry's abrupt entrance.

Neither was he alone. But those who companied him were not standing to attention in their king's presence, but rather sprawled on the floor before him, so that when the Colonel, gun still at ready, went to confront the usurper, he had to step over and around their bodies.

"Reddick!"

There was no sign that the Duke either heard or saw Imfry. He sat so still he might have been frozen by the ice of the Crown. The Colonel studied him, and then went swiftly up to the throne and laid a hand on his enemy's shoulder.

He started back with a quickly suppressed cry, for his touch broke the dream in the form of a man. There was a chime of sound; the Crown shattered, fell in a rain of splinters about the head and shoulders of him who wore it. Then Reddick shriveled, blackened, turned into something Roane could not bear to look upon. She cried out and hid her face in her hands.

Lamplight showed the richness of the heavily embroidered cover on the daised bed. Though that radiance was far less than what Roane had been used to, it was enough to fully illume Ludorica's face. They had propped her up on a backing of pillows and Roane fed her bite by bite, giving her many sips of watered wine.

The Queen did not lift her hands, seemed unable to help herself. She smiled now and then, once murmured

Imfry's name when he came to look upon her. And in that much they were assured she had some measure of consciousness. Only she was very weak.

Roane tried with caution two of the remedies from her kit. But neither seemed to give any strengthening to this slender girl who was now a helpless child in her care.

Perhaps they would never know what had happened in the High Keep before their coming. It could be that Reddick had already taken the Ice Crown to wear before that fateful moment when the distant controls had blazed into nothingness. That could well explain his gruesome death on the throne, the ending of those committed to his rule—for all in that chamber were dead. Shambry was insane, retreating into a catatonic state they could not break.

Roane watched the Queen. She was now afraid that Ludorica might be beyond the aid of untrained help, though they could cling to the hope that she would gradually awaken fully. But Roane had told Imfry the truth, that it would be well to seek the aid they needed elsewhere. And his messengers had already ridden to ask it.

Meanwhile the keep was coming to life. That town which had been in the iron grip of Reddick's traitors was freed. Some of the lawful councilors had been killed, one or two had disappeared, but four had been found, brought back. The servants were returning, other help had been recruited from the city, and the guards were all Imfry's men and so trustworthy. Roane knew this was in progress, but her own field of battle remained this bedroom.

She had two of the Princess's maids with her. They had been discovered locked in their chambers and freed by Imfry's searchers. They had at first been jealous of Roane, but then were worried enough about the state of their mistress to welcome the stranger's aid. At night Roane herself rested on a divan at the other end of the room, ready for any summons.

Imfry had not returned since she had begged him to send a messenger to contact her own people. If the LB was still there, and the off-worlders were willing, now that the installation was gone and Clio was no longer slave to the past, they could have better help than any she thought native to Clio. But it could be they were too late in seeking it.

The Queen opened her eyes. She fell asleep during these hours in the blink of an eyelid and roused as quickly. Roane took those two inert hands into hers.

"Ludorica!" she called softly as a summons.

It seemed that this time those blue eyes did indeed focus on her and hold steady—as if she were a recognized person and not a part of the room. The cracked lips Roane had soothed with salve parted and the faintest ghost of a whisper reached her:

"Roane?"

"Yes, oh, yes!" The off-world girl tightened her grip eagerly. "I am Roane!" That the other knew her was a great leap forward out of that shadow land.

"Stay—"

Roane understood that as a question.

"Yes, I shall stay." But she could not be sure she had replied in time for the other to understand, for the heavy lids had fallen again and once more the Queen slept—though this time Roane watched with a lighter heart. She thought Ludorica's sleep more natural, not just a giving way to a blanking unconsciousness. At last she laid down the hands she held and at that moment one of the maids came into the circle of lamplight and beckoned, slipping into Roane's place as she arose.

The chamber door was ajar and she went to it. Imfry was in the room beyond. He was wearing full uniform, and his thin face was shaven. He had been, she was aware, on his self-imposed duties to bring order out of chaos.

"Your ship was gone." He broke it to her abruptly.

For a moment all she thought of was the lost opportunity to aid the Queen. Then the true meaning struck home. They had gone, leaving her behind, marooned it might well be for life if the Service decided against any further contact. Roane put out her hand for support, suddenly feeling a little dizzy, reaching for a chair back. But her hand was caught as he came to her, steadied her.

"I am sorry," he said and that crispness of command, much in his voice these past few days, was softened. "I should not have told you so."

"No, it does not matter." She shook her head. "I could not have expected otherwise. They knew we had been discovered, and they would not wait to find me. They may never come again. But Nelis, listen—the Queen —Ludorica—a short time ago she knew me! Perhaps we can hope she will come back to us. We might not need their help after all."

"You are sure—she is on the mend?" Something in his eagerness, the way he turned his head to look at the door into the bedchamber made Roane want to move away. She tried to pull her hand from his, but he would not loose it.

"I have a duty." He spoke slowly, almost as if what he said now was painful. "You have heard her call me 'kinsman'—"

Because, thought Roane with a wry inner hurt, Ludorica wished perhaps an even closer relationship with her Colonel.

"You see, there is in truth a bond between us—"

This she did not want to hear. If the bleak truth was not put into words, if she did not have to hear it just yet— And to have *him* say it! But she was not able to protest, and he was continuing:

"I took an oath long ago at my father's wishes—and it has ruled my life. Our rulers marry for reasons of state, the well-being of their countries. But often such unions are no more than formal alliances, though they are required for the begetting of true heirs.

"Our King Niklas accepted the royal bride from Vordain, as his advisers made plain was his duty. But his heart had already been given elsewhere. And such affairs can lead not only to pain but to cankers like Reddick's ambition—which was in part my father's fear after my birth.

"My mother was the King's daughter, but no princess. She wanted nothing from her father; in fact she refused all he would have gladly given her. And when she wed with my father she was pleased to leave the court.

"By her wish I was to claim nothing from the King, and this was my father's desire also. I was not to be 'kinsman' though I could easily have been so. To me Ludorica will always be the Queen whom I serve and honor. Beyond the service I owe her thus, I go my way, and she that which destiny points for her. Do you understand what I would have you believe?"

Roane could not answer save with a nod. She was unable to sort out her emotions. For that she needed time and quiet and a chance to face a new self, a very new self which she must learn to know.

"What of you? Your people have left you—"

"Yes."

"But that is only as you think; the truth is otherwise!" There was hot emotion in his voice which she was too bewildered even to try to read. "*Those* have gone, your people are here! You are of Reveny, as much as if you were born among her hills, schooled in some stead hall. Believe that, Roane, believe it! For it is true!"

She was not just imagining what he said—it was the truth now. And with the tone of one wholeheartedly swearing allegiance she found voice enough to answer:

"I do—Nelis, I do!"

Andre Norton

- ☐ 12314   Crossroads Of Time $1.95
- ☐ 16664   Dragon Magic   1.95
- ☐ 33704   High Sorcery   1.95
- ☐ 37291   Iron Cage   1.95
- ☐ 45001   Knave Of Dreams   1.95
- ☐ 47441   Lavender Green Magic   1.95
- ☐ 67556   Postmarked The Stars   1.25
- ☐ 71100   Red Hart Magic   1.95
- ☐ 78015   Star Born   1.75

Available wherever paperbacks are sold or use this coupon.

ACE SCIENCE FICTION
P.O. Box 400, Kirkwood, N.Y. 13795

Please send me the titles checked above. I enclose _____.
Include 75¢ for postage and handling if one book is ordered; 50¢ per
book for two to five. If six or more are ordered, postage is free. California, Illinois, New York and Tennessee residents please add sales tax.

NAME_____

ADDRESS_____

CITY_____STATE_____ZIP_____

ANDRE NORTON

WITCH WORLD SERIES

89705	**Witch World**	$1.95
87875	**Web of the Witch World**	$1.95
80805	**Three Against the Witch World**	$1.95
87323	**Warlock of the Witch World**	$1.95
77555	**Sorceress of the Witch World**	$1.95
94254	**Year of the Unicorn**	$1.95
82356	**Trey of Swords**	$1.95
95490	**Zarsthor's Bane** (Illustrated)	$1.95

Available wherever paperbacks are sold or use this coupon

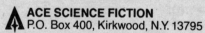 **ACE SCIENCE FICTION**
P.O. Box 400, Kirkwood, N.Y. 13795

Please send me the titles checked above. I enclose _____.
Include 75¢ for postage and handling if one book is ordered; 50¢ per
book for two to five. If six or more are ordered, postage is free. California,
Illinois, New York and Tennessee residents please add sales tax.

NAME_____

ADDRESS_____

CITY_____STATE_____ZIP_____

Ursula K. Le Guin

POUL ANDERSON

78657	**A Stone in Heaven**	$2.50
20724	**Ensign Flandry**	$1.95
48923	**The Long Way Home**	$1.95
51904	**The Man Who Counts**	$1.95
57451	**The Night Face**	$1.95
65954	**The Peregrine**	$1.95
91706	**World Without Stars**	$1.50

Available wherever paperbacks are sold or use this coupon